CAHAS MOUNTAIN

"A riveting first novel with revolving first-person narratives by deceptively simple rural folk in the first half of the 20th century in southwest Virginia, "Cahas Mountain" is as rich with memorable stories of love and loss as are the seasonal apple orchards that climb the mountainsides and offer nurture, shade, and the fruit for moonshine. Innocence is corrupted, ambition derailed, and families splintered as one "bad apple" rolls selfishly through the lives of his kin. Familiar quotations from the Bible and famous writers head up many chapters, adding depth. A true "slice of life" because of Simmons' careful research and historical details of the region, World War II, and the underworld, this Appalachian novel is a satisfying medley of wisdom, struggle, and resolution."

Elizabeth "Ibby" T. Greer, author of "Moonshine Corner, Keys to Rocky Mount" and widow of T. Keister Greer, Esq., author of "The Great Moonshine Conspiracy Trial of 1935."

"The story unfolds along the winding roads of a family saga that begins on the sunlit peaks of Cahas Mountain and travels along the rocky streams that course through the crevices of the hills that hid moonshine stills, infidelity, betrayal and a deep and forbidden love. Simmons' paint brush follows the curves of the valley, painting the city of Roanoke in the light and dark colors of a world coming alive in the aftermath of the Great Depression. Throughout her story, Simmons allows her own love of the Appalachians to echo through the voice of the mountain people, inviting and drawing her reader forward. This is a book that will stay with me. A really good read."

Ginny Brock, author of "By Morning's Light."

CAHAS MOUNTAIN

LINDA KAY SIMMONS

Linda Kay Simmons

To my dear loving caring Jane,
What would any of us do
without you? I can't imagine.
Thank you, Thank you, Thank you!
All My Love, Linda Kay —

DEDICATION

TO MY BEAUTIFUL DAUGHTER NOELLE,
TO TIM FOR READING MANY VERSIONS OF MY STORY,
TO EVELENA AND JANE FOR YOUR SUPPORT,
AND TO MY SPIDERS, YOU KNOW WHO YOU ARE.

CAHAS (KUH-HAZE) - ORIGINALLY PRONOUNCED FOR THE SOUND A CROW MAKES

"THE CAPTAIN OF ALL
THESE MEN OF DEATH
THAT CAME AGAINST HIM
TO TAKE HIM AWAY,
WAS THE CONSUMPTION,
FOR IT WAS THAT
THAT BROUGHT HIM
DOWN TO THE GRAVE."

JOHN BUNYAN

I was but a young girl, when the world around me began whirling with the dizziness of fear and dread. I didn't know it then, for I climbed so high up on Cahas Mountain it was difficult for my family to find me. I walked and daydreamed through this mountainous forest of wonder, eating apples I picked from orchards on the lower mountain spurs next to my home. How I loved my mountain and the wildflowers that grew there. I was forever reaching for the soft white haze of clouds I could almost touch. During the haunting nights, the moonstone hung over the mountain so bright and lovely, I'd not come down all night but lay my head on soft moss and dreamed the night visitations that came and played within my soul, calling my name in the whistling wind, "Rhodessa Rose, Rhodessa Rose."

I didn't know what I looked like then, nor cared 'cause Mama would not allow mirrors in our home. She thought them bad luck. "If you look in one long enough, you could be sucked in and never be heard from again," she always said. All I could know was my reflection in Maggodee Creek. I knew my hair was long and black as it hung loose down to my waist. My eyes were big in my face and cheekbones high. I looked like Mama, I was told.

My sister Ruby was two years older and took after Papa with red hair and a fiery temper. Papa was a tall, thin man who worked ten hours a day at the apple packing plant where he also got apples to make his 'shine. My oldest sister Hattie looked like none of us. Mama said Hattie took after Papa's people, and we didn't know much about them.

Mama taught us reading and writing. She wanted us to learn everything she knew and more, but who wanted schooling at the top of Cahas Mountain?

I knew my way up the mountain by heart having often followed the rocky path by moonlight. I sat silent for hours, learning the language of the night. Papa called me his Indian princess for the way I could become part of the woods and never be seen.

Indians had lived on our very land. I found pieces of filed flint and a broken pottery bowl which I hid with my other treasures in the roots of the evergreens. Proud Indian blood ran in me. Mama's roots were from the Saponi tribe in West

Virginia. I grew up dreaming what life was like then.

All the years of my childhood I gathered white rocks for Papa. When I was small, he dug a hole so deep I thought it went to the other side of the world. Papa made walls within the well with the rocks I gathered. He made a little house to sit upon it. Papa wanted only the purest water for making his apple shine. People came to us and paid for this elixir made from our special water, and we would never have to leave Cahas Mountain in search of work for this was our forever home.

We had pigs, a mule and chickens. Mama had a vegetable garden. She taught us to grow and can our food. Come early spring, Mama's favorite flowers, daffodils, grew everywhere. In the summer, rose vines climbed up the walls of our house and the smell of lavender blew softly in the wind.

Mama said we were blessed by God as our wells were always full, and our water had been kissed by angels; you could tell by the shiny silver sparkles. Papa called it mica, but I believed what Mama said to be true.

Always there was a dipper of water for the wayfaring stranger to cool his thirst and for the wives and children who came with their men to collect their 'shine.

Most often, the men talked among themselves, chewing and spitting, their sputum drying in the dust. The women gathered by the front yard well and gossiped as their children played and sang, "Ring around the rosy, pocket full of posies, ashes, ashes…"

But dizziness began to speak into the whistling winds. It seemed the words of folks that heard it soon started to spin around and round and some fell down and nothing was ever the same again.

RHODESSA ROSE

I was deep asleep when I heard Mama ringing the dinner bell on the back porch. I didn't like it when she did that. The dinner bell should have been used for meals only but Mama said it beat any alarm clock to get us up and going. I knew Mama was agitated and would have a pile of chores for us from the many times she rang the bell. That old metal bell could wake the dead and have them coming for breakfast it was so loud! My sisters and I came down the stairs rubbing our eyes from sleep. We knew better than to keep Mama waiting.

"I want you girls dressed in ten minutes. It's going to be a busy day," Mama stated.

Hattie and I raced up the steps. We knew better than to be late. Mama was in one of her moods and couldn't nothing get in her way.

"If we lived in the city, we wouldn't have to be up this early," Hattie complained loud enough for Mama to hear all the way downstairs.

I knew one of Mama's lectures was coming on and sure fire it came. "You girls live under my roof. When you are married women with homes of your own, you can do things your way," she scolded us when we were back in the kitchen.

"I'll get the water Mama," Hattie offered trying to get into Mama's good graces.

"Don't be slamming the screen door when you go out and make sure it shuts so no flies get in," Mama warned.

Within minutes, the door slammed and Hattie was back with a pail of water.

"Help me sweet Jesus," I heard Mama say under her breath.

"Ruby, go get wood; this stove isn't going to cook anything without it," Mama ordered.

"Make Rhodessa do it. I don't want to get any scratches or bug bites. Rhodessa doesn't care how she looks, and she doesn't like boys," Ruby said eyeing me.

"I care about how I look and I do like boys a little." Tears stung my eyes as Ruby stormed out of the kitchen.

"We are going to the barn dance tonight aren't we Mama?" Ruby nagged when she came back with an armload of firewood. "Papa likes to play his fiddle at the dance."

"This isn't the time to be asking with chores to be done. Rhodessa, you make the breakfast. Your sisters get in too much of a hurry and are forever burning things," Mama instructed.

"Mama, are we going to the dance? You do remember don't you Mama?" Ruby continued.

"Have the eggs been collected? I bet nobody has done the milking neither," Mama scolded.

"Mama, we want to have fun and not do chores all day," Hattie complained.

"I'll make up my mind after you three have helped your father pick the apples off the ground when the plant closes. I'll be looking at what you get. No rotten apples and no worms! Don't get lazy and pull apples off the trees or Mr. Killgore will stop selling us ground apples for cheap."

"We won't have time to look presentable if we have to pick up stinking apples before the dance!" Hattie complained.

"Well, it won't matter none if you don't get your chores done, now will it? Before I get back this afternoon, I want all the ash cleaned out of the woodstove. And I don't want to hear another word about the dance or the answer is No!"

Willard

I got up when the rooster crowed. I wanted to be out of the house before Pa saw I was leavin' and be full of questions. He would have plenty of farm chores for me to do. I hoped it wouldn't be long before I had money and could move into my own place where nobody knew my business.

I wanted to spend the better part of the day at Shootin' Creek sampling 'shine and buyin' what I could. I needed to conduct a little business in Roanoke first. It was fifty miles from Roanoke to Shootin' Creek and a mountain to climb to boot. Luckily, Endicott wasn't a far piece from Shootin' Creek so I could probably get everythin' done. I only had a few customers and I wanted more, lots more. Trouble was the still operators at Shootin' Creek were small time and couldn't sell me the amount I needed and it wasn't high quality 'shine neither. I was particular as to what I bought as I didn't want to buy bad batches and ruin my name before I got started. I wanted my reputation to be of a quality bootlegger.

It was early afternoon when I met up with a couple fellas in Shootin' Creek. I was hopin' through them I could make connections to some bigger 'shine operations. The problem was I didn't have much cash and people are always suspicious with somebody they don't know. The meetin' went well enough, but I left empty handed. They would have to check me out before I could be trusted. I bought enough 'shine in Endicott to sell to my main customer in Rocky Mount, so that was somethin'.

I had sunk all the money I had into my Packard automobile. I bought it cheap from a fellow who had gamblin' debts. Not a speck of dirt on it if I could help it. I had to look the part of a successful operator.

It was early evenin' before I made my delivery to Maybelline Johnson who ran one of the bawdy houses in Rocky Mount. You never would have known what kind of house it was as it looked like any other white framed farm house, except for the painted red door and shutters. I had first visited Maybelline's establishment some years back for another kind of transaction. Maybelline got ten jars of 'shine from me on a monthly basis and sometimes more if I could get it. She claimed it was for her customers. I expect right much of it was for herself. Maybelline must ha' been in her fifties but I'd be guessin'. It was hard to tell what with her man's haircut and wrinkled face. I never saw her wearin' nothin' but trousers and she always had a plug of tobacco in her mouth. I knew I never wanted to cross her 'cause I'd heard tales, some true, some probably not. I knew she kept a shotgun behind the front door.

"Willard, how about us making a trade? Your 'shine for some time with one of my girls," Maybelle offered me while we stood in the doorway.

"I can't be doing that. I need hard cash to get my business goin' but thanks for the offer."

"You can't blame me for trying. Business is business. I appreciate your delivering my 'shine. I had a fellow buying shine for me but he was skimming the pot. He was always saying the cost had gone up or a bottle got broke. I never got the full amount I paid for. Are you sure you won't stay a while and let me offer you some services for a good discount?"

"I got to get goin' now," I said. I knew better than to enter through the red door and into the parlor with the velvet walls where several mostly naked women waited. It was all too tempting with the dim lights, sofas and mirrors everywhere.

"Since you are driving through Boones Mill you ought to stop at the barn dance. Old Man Hartman plays and he makes some good, clean 'shine. Tell him Maybelline said you were ok. He is real particular who he sells to."

I thanked Maybelline. It wasn't no time before I was in Boones Mill. The little town was bustling with people. I found a place to park not far from the general store. I took a few nips of product and followed the music to a large barn where there were all kinds of pretty girls with picnic baskets and young bucks standin' back takin' it all in. The fiddlin' had already started. It wasn't long before someone got to callin' and the square dancin' began. I hung around askin' when Old Man Hartman was goin' to play and was directed to his daughters. There were three of them. This was goin' to be fun. Two of them looked old enough to have a good time with. The young one was a little squirt but prettier by far than her sisters. I was feelin' chipper with Maybelline's cold hard cash in my pocket. I moseyed over to the girls askin' when their daddy was goin' to play.

"Papa should be up next," one of the daughters said.

I could tell she was lookin' me over and I tried not to chuckle. Ruby was her name. The other was Hattie. The youngest was Rhodessa who didn't say much. The older girls were full of questions like where was I from and did I like to dance. I wasn't there for meetin' no women, no sir; it was their daddy I wanted to meet. The older girls told me what I needed to know and before the evenin' was over I met Old Man Hartman and we had us a fine conversation.

"And in the land were no women found so fair as the daughters of Job; and their father gave them inheritance among their brethren."
Psalms 42:15

RHODESSA ROSE

I remember the first time Willard came calling on Papa to buy 'shine. He was all spiffy in a brown striped suit and driving a Deluxe Black Packard, with silver chrome, like he was putting on the Ritz or something. I had never seen an automobile as nice as that. I heard Willard tell Papa he needed the car for the big boys to notice him. Usually all I'd see coming to the house was old Model T's or people walking in on foot or horse to buy Papa's 'shine.

Willard had the bluest eyes I ever saw. They reminded me of coneflowers and they sort of sucked me in, like the mirrors Mama talked about. Were his eyes mirrors that saw into my soul? Should I have been afraid of him? I was pretty brave at thirteen. Papa and Willard had a long conversation, and Papa gave Willard some jars. After that day, Willard started coming by pretty often to talk to Papa and to make some transactions.

Before long Willard was calling me his cute little tomato and saying he would come back and claim me when I was ripe. "Leave the baby alone!" Papa yelled at him. Willard liked to tease Papa like that, getting him all riled up. Willard didn't pay Papa no mind, 'cause by the time Willard left Papa was near ready to upchuck or pass out from everything he'd been drinking with his customers. The cost of doing business, Papa used to say.

One day I came upon Willard, Papa and a couple of Papa's other 'shine customers in the barn playing cards. I had seen Papa play poker before but this was different. Willard had something in his hand he was shaking.

"Go into the house, honey. Don't pay no mind to what we are doing out here," Papa told me.

Willard winked at me. I wanted to know what those little boxes with the black dots were for. I hung around outside the barn where nobody could see me. Papa's friends were complaining about losing all their money to Willard. It wasn't long before the men cleared out and Willard headed for his car.

"Willard, can I see those white boxes with the dots?" I bounded over to him.

"Sure Rhodessa, but not here. Your Papa wouldn't be happy. Walk over to the side of your house and I'll meet you there in five minutes."

That is where Willard taught me to roll dice. He told me to call out a number and roll the dice down the dirt path. I rolled a seven. "You won. Roll again," Willard told me.

"What do I win, Willard?" I asked.

"We didn't place a bet. But we will, after you get a little practice," Willard answered.

We continued to play until I got the hang of it. I didn't like it when I rolled a three 'cause Willard said I shot craps and that sounded plain vulgar.

"Rhodessa, I think you are a natural at this," Willard laughed.

"It is kind of fun, except that craps part. But we better stop now, before Papa catches us. Can I keep the dice, Willard, to remind me of today?"

"Sure thing, baby girl, but next time we play we bet."

"On what?"

"A kiss, Rhodessa, what else?"

RHODESSA ROSE

It was plain to see my sisters had crushes on Willard. Ruby and Hattie were always asking Willard to take them to the speakeasies they heard about in the big city of Roanoke. Willard said no 'cause how would it look when he came back for Baby Girl when she'd grown up, if he'd been taking her sisters out first? How Willard liked to tease me!

"It's not fair, Rhodessa! Roanoke has everything to offer and it's only thirty minutes from here. It might as well be a hundred miles with no way to get there," Ruby scolded me.

"I know it's not your fault Rhodessa, but talk to Willard and see if you can convince him to take us," Hattie said softly, hoping to butter me up.

Willard filled his car with jars of Papa's 'shine. Sometimes I helped him. Willard never got real drunk like the other men when they came over or like Papa. Willard was a real businessman. He talked about the repeal of Prohibition that had just happened. Willard said even if it was 1933, nobody had the money to pay the heavy taxes on liquor and them that could pay didn't have a mind to. He expected business to stay as good as ever, if not better.

Pa's customers liked to argue back and forth about Prohibition but if someone happened by the men would clam up and not say spit. Our house sat just off a country road right next to the apple packing plant. People heard rumors about Pa's shine and would find their way to our house. It took Papa a while to trust somebody new that dropped by asking to buy 'shine. He would do a lot of jawing at the rock well in the front yard until he trusted someone enough to become a customer. Papa said you never could be too careful about some folks.

Only the most trusted of Papa's customers were taken to the moonshine still in the woods.

Ever since I was a little girl it had been my job to see that the little still house stayed hidden out of sight with growing vines, evergreen branches and a babbling creek nearby. I pretended it was my little play house even if it held the copper still, wooden barrels, bushels of apples, sugar and such. The house was Papa's and my special secret. Hattie and Ruby did not know where it was, but I suspect Mama did. Sometimes if Papa had to be gone he would let me show a trusted customer the crooked path that led to the still so they could collect their jars. Papa also let me collect the money. Papa and his customers knew they could count on me. Sometimes he would give me a nickel. Papa told me it was our secret I was his favorite. He knew I loved the mountain as much as he did and that I would never leave it or him. Papa said the first chance Hattie and Ruby had they would leave the mountain and move to Roanoke. He said he could never begin to understand their foolish ways.

Willard made a proposition to Papa to become his principal driver and delivery man. Papa laughed and said he didn't think he needed no principal driver, as he never had a driver before. All Papa's customers came directly to him. Willard said he could help expand Papa's business and his own. After a lot of Willard's smooth talking and Papa's drinking, Papa said he would give it a try and see how things worked out. That's how Papa and Willard started doing business together.

Willard took supper with us every Sunday. He was respectful calling my parents Mr. and Mrs. Hartman. Most people around here called Papa Old Man Hartman. Papa and Willard usually got to talking about 'shine at the table. After a while Mama would hush them down. "You both stop talking about the business over the supper table. You know I don't like it. I might not have my way about us attending church or having Preacher Shiflett over for dinner, but I put my foot down on talking about 'shine when we come together as a family."

Mama didn't like it that Papa wouldn't take us to church. Papa said we could talk to God on the mountain instead of in a building made of wood and stone with a bunch of people acting good only on Sunday.

After supper, we listened to the radio together while Hattie, Ruby and I cleared away the dishes. Sometimes we cranked up the Victrola. Mama had lots of records she had ordered from the Victor Record Catalog over the years. The catalog came every month and we spent hours looking at it. Mama had records with opera while Papa had records by John Philip Sousa. When I was little I marched around the house pretending I was playing in the band.

I think Mama liked to have fainted the night Willard took her in his arms and tried to dance the waltz with her to Bessie Smith's song, "Down Hearted Blues." Halfway through the dance, Mama got so tickled she couldn't dance anymore and had to sit down at the kitchen table, she was laughing so hard. That got us girls giggling until we were in full belly laughs. No one ever got to Mama that way!

After that every time Willard came to supper, there would be dancing. Willard was happy to oblige my sisters but made sure I got a turn to dance with him too. Papa would join us for a while, usually while drinking some of his apple 'shine. "This ain't my kinda of music. I like the kind of pickin' I do with the boys." Papa would say when he excused himself.

Mama claimed to stay in the kitchen to make sure Hattie and Ruby behaved. But I could tell Mama was having a good time and chaperoning was only a part of it.

Willard had all kinds of moves and was big on dipping. Sometimes I thought my head was going to hit the floor. Dancing with Willard was more fun than that stiff dancing from the waist up, with only your feet moving fast, like the folks around here did. Being held by Willard was nice, and I liked being whirled around. Poor Willard, by the end of the night his feet must have been plumb worn out.

RHODESSA ROSE

I was up in a tree picking apples for Mama early on a Saturday morning when I saw Willard's car coming up the road. Mama had plans to bake an apple cake to take to a friend who just had a baby. By the time I got to the house Willard was leaning back on his freshly waxed Packard. "Rhodessa, you little bearcat, when are you gonna go ridin' with me in my car or am I just beatin' my gums, girl?" Willard said grinning at me like he was some movie star.

"Baloney Willard, stop your teasing! You got hundreds of girlfriends probably. Besides you like Hattie and Ruby. Which one, Willard, which one do you like best? I want to know," I teased him.

"I have just been waitin' for you to grow up. I'm not interested in those silly sisters of yours. I never have been. I thought you could tell that!"

I was the baby! I wanted to go with Willard but Hattie and Ruby would be furious and I wouldn't know how to act on a real date with Willard.

"Rhodessa, you done turned into a real Sheba, and I want to take you out and not bring you home till the owls go to bed. How about it Sheba, I mean Rhodessa Rose? You are sixteen now. I have already talked to your Mama. It took a lot of convincin'. She said I had to wait till now before I could come courtin' you."

"Are you on the level, Willard? You and me for real? You know I won't be no pushover if that's what's on your mind!"

"Just put on some glad rags, and I'll get us a little hooch or should I say giggle water for you. Come on now, let's go for a ride."

"Says you," I laughed.

I turned away from Willard and ran up the path, through the woods, heading to the top of my mountain. Willard had chased me before, always giving up. But this time was different; Willard stayed after me. I ran faster, hiding behind trees, peeking out so he could get a glimpse of me and start the chase again. Willard chased me until we were breathless and could run no more.

We sat for a while, near Papa's still, just looking at one another. There weren't no words for what I was feeling. After a spell I took Willard's hand and led him to my private hiding place. I had never shown anyone my Indian treasures before. I could tell by the way Willard looked at me that he understood what I showed him. Then Willard took me in his arms and kissed me, my first grown up kiss. I didn't know what to think other than my heart was beating fast. Willard pulled me down on the soft mossy ground. I liked the kiss and wanted another.

Willard

Try as I might I couldn't get Rhodessa out of my head. I didn't have no business thinkin' of her the way I was. Better I thought of Hattie or Ruby, they were older, and I knew they liked me. They didn't interest me 'cause of their silly ways, always fightin' between themselves and talkin' back to their mama. Both girls needed to go to the wood shed if you asked me. But not Rhodessa, she was something special: respectful, hardworkin', and a beauty to look it. Smart too. She knew as much about her daddy's business as he did.

Business was growin' thanks to Mr. Hartman's fine 'shine. He followed his recipe exactly and never took short cuts. Runs never come out exactly the same but with Rhodessa's daddy it was always damn close.

I was going to Shootin' Creek and Endicott more often. My customer base had taken off so much that I had heavy duty springs put in my car 'cause of the weight of the added 'shine and the dirt roads I traveled. I was thinkin' of puttin' an extra fuel tank in as well. Sometimes when I made a delivery to Maybelline I stayed for a nap before headin' back to Windy Gap Mountain. The ride wasn't long but there weren't no privacy at home. Pa couldn't understand why I needed to sleep durin' the day when I should be out workin' in the fields with him. It wouldn't do, Pa knowin' my real business. Occasionally Maybelline would send me a girl "on the house." I always left Maybelline extra jars for the consideration, but it was Rhodessa I thought of when I laid with those girls. I wanted Rhodessa's pretty face on the pillow next to me and Rhodessa's soft words and easy laughter.

I couldn't think of anything else but meeting Willard's family the following Saturday. I was real nervous about it. What would I wear? Ruby and Hattie were of no help since they found out Willard had designs on me and not them. Mama offered suggestions but her ideas were too old-fashioned. I was at a loss. I finally decided to wear my blue flowered dress that had a sash around the waist. It made me look a little more womanly than my other dresses. Willard liked this dress; he had commented on it before.

Willard showed up at ten in his fancy automobile. "Mrs. Hartman, I have a special day planned for Rhodessa. After dinner with my folks, some of us are goin' to Lakeside Amusement Park. With your permission, can I keep Rhodessa out until eight?" Willard asked.

"Yes, since you asked so polite and all. I'd like to meet your parents sometime as well," Mama said.

"Yes ma'am, that would sure be fine. I'm sure my folks would like that too."

It wasn't long before Willard and I were heading out of Boones Mill. "Come here my little Rosebud, scoot a little closer to me," Willard said and I did.

Willard put his arm around me. I could hear Mama's voice ringing in my ears about a man's physical desires being more intense than a woman's. I knew it was going to be me to set limits if Willard tried any funny business.

"In just a little while you are goin' to see another mountain. It's a sight Rhodessa, just wait and see."

It took just under an hour to get to Willard's home place in Hardy. We had to go over Windy Gap Mountain and it had plenty of sharp turns. The mountain seemed to go higher and higher, and I thought it might never end. I tried closing my eyes but my whole body felt the curves, and I started to feel sick. I begged Willard to slow down, as I was afraid we were going to run off the road and fall to our deaths.

"It's alright Rhodessa. I know what I'm doin'. I can drive this mountain blindfolded. We are through the worst of it now."

The trees were so tall and there was vines climbing up the mountain walls. When I dared look over the edge of the mountain, I saw views and depths I never imagined. Cahas Mountain didn't have the danger I felt on Windy Gap. My mountain felt gentler and safer - probably because it was home.

"Only ten minutes more, Baby Girl, and we will be on Eton Road," Willard announced.

"What if your family doesn't like me?"

"Not a chance," Willard replied while squeezing my knee.

I was nervous. I never had a beau before, much less met one's parents. I was wishing I hadn't come when Willard turned down a dirt road, off Eton, leading to a two story white farm house with a picket fence all around it. There were rocking chairs and a swing on the porch. Next thing I knew Willard was helping me out the car door.

"This is Rhodessa Rose," Willard said to those who had gathered in the front yard to meet us.

"We could hear you come down the road," spoke a young woman.

"Rhodessa, this is my sister Myrtle. She's two years younger than I am but she thinks she's the boss of me," Willard teased.

Myrtle looked me over head to toe. I felt like a farm animal being inspected, and I didn't like the feeling, not one little bit.

"Good to meet you gal, I'm Willard's Pa. Mrs. Grimes is in the kitchen. Everything is about ready I expect. It isn't everyday Willard brings a pretty girl home for dinner," Mr. Grimes laughed while extending his hand in greeting.

"He never has Pa," a young boy said, and everyone laughed.

"I'm Jonah and I'm 12. My little brother Michael is in the kitchen with Ma."

"We better get to the table now. Mrs. Grimes will skin us if dinner gets cold," Mr. Grimes said taking my arm and leading me into the house. Inside the kitchen Mr. Grimes offering me a chair between Willard and Myrtle. Mrs. Grimes' chair was where she could get up and get to the stove easy. Mr. Grimes' place was at the head of the long table, which had four chairs on each side and a chair at each end. It was covered with a pretty flowered cloth of red, white and yellow. Michael sat by Mrs. Grimes and Jonah was by Mr. Grimes. I suspect it was that way so they could control the boys if they got to acting like rascals during meal time. They must have had company real often 'cause of the extra chairs.

The table was covered with fried chicken, cornbread, green beans, turnips and sliced tomatoes. There were lots of sweet cucumber pickles as well. Most of Willard's family drank buttermilk. I am not partial to it, so I had black coffee which had already been made. Usually I drank it with milk but I didn't want to ask.

"Now that everybody's round the table, let's bow our heads," began Mr. Grimes.

"For food that stays our hunger,
For rest that brings us ease,
For homes where memories linger
We give our thanks for these,
From thy bounty,
Through Christ our Lord. Amen"

"That was a nice prayer, Mr. Grimes. Thank you for saying it on my account," I said trying to make conversation.

"Rhodessa, that wasn't just for you, it was for all of us. We say a prayer at every meal. Doesn't your family?" asked Mr. Grimes.

"Papa don't much like praying or preaching. He and Mama have an agreement that we say meal prayers only on Easter and Christmas."

Nobody said anything for a few minutes. It was like they were all thinking hard. Then the talk started up again.

Willard's people were like mine in some ways. At dinner, I learned they had a big garden with beef and milk cows, pigs, and chickens. There were two mules for plowing, Jack and Rowdy. Jack, they said, was a mean mule and plowed better than

Rowdy. Rowdy liked to pull a wagon but went too fast. We had some good laughs at the table as everyone told stories about their misbehaving mules. Willard's people were real farmers. In this they were not like my folks whose real business was running the still.

Willard's people went regular to the Church of the Brethren. *Mama would like that about them*, I thought. *Maybe sometime Willard will bring me back to visit so I can go to church with them.* When the meal was done, I offered to help with clearing the table.

"I wouldn't hear of it young lady; you are our guest. Have Willard walk you around and show you the creek and the garden. They are real pretty right now after the rain," offered Mrs. Grimes.

I looked around for Willard but he was gone. "Where is Willard?"

"He's in the back yard. Jonah wanted Willard to see the new puppies," said Mr. Grimes.

I stayed in the kitchen trying to make conversation with Myrtle as she cleared the table. But she didn't seem to have anything to say to me. After a few minutes, I wandered outside to find Willard. Jonah was rolling around on the ground with three brown and white beagles which were pouncing on him and pulling at his clothes with their teeth.

"They sure are cute pups," I said as Jonah sat up.

"Pa says they will make good hunting dogs. One day real soon Willard is going to take me hunting with him."

"Do you know where Willard is now?"

"I think he went around to the back of the house. He was looking for Michael," Jonah said.

I went to the back looking for Willard and peered in through the back door. It took my eyes a minute to adjust to what I was seeing. Willard was on his knees rolling dice down the hallway! Michael was standing beside him. "Willard Grimes are you teaching your little brother to shoot craps?"

"Michael's gotta learn somethin' about the world, Rhodessa. He's gotta know how to handle himself like a man when he gets off this farm."

"He's only eight-years-old! Isn't that a bit young?"

"Come on Willard; let's play some more," Michael said giving me a hard look.

"Sure thing little brother, let's play," encouraged Willard.

Michael was still staring at me. "She won't tell on us will she Willard?"

"No, she won't tell." Willard winked at me. "Rhodessa, go sit on the porch swing and wait for me. I won't be but a minute. Lester Boyton will be getting here soon. He's goin' to Lakeside with us. He's sweet on Myrtle. Lord knows why."

I did as Willard said and waited on the porch. I was glad for a moment to myself to take in this farm where Willard grew up. I could picture him here as a small boy much like Jonah and Michael. I didn't have to wait long before Willard joined me.

Willard walked me around his home place. I couldn't believe he was holding my hand where anybody could see!

"Pa cut down the trees and cleared the farm, doin' most of the work himself. He built the back part of the house first. Later, Pa added the front with extra bedrooms," Willard said.

"Why so many rooms?" I asked.

"They figured on a lot of children. Sometimes my Aunt Nancy comes and stays. She likes to think she is helpin' out. She and Uncle Henry live in town," Willard said.

Willard showed me his Pa's sawmill and the garden, which had the biggest cabbages I had ever seen.

"I think I'll start makin' 'shine with these cabbages, we sure can grow em' here," Willard said.

"I expect it would be real smelly, don't you?"

Willard laughed out loud 'cause I had taken him serious. About that time we heard a car horn tooting. "That's Lester. He always likes to make an entrance."

Myrtle made us wait while she finished getting ready. I could see Lester was smitten with Myrtle. He whistled at her when she walked out on the porch.

"You better not let Pa hear you whistle at me or he won't let me go off with you," Myrtle warned.

"Pa won't mind if you whistle at her, Lester. He would like to get Myrtle married off. She can't keep a beau around here; she's too contrary," Willard teased.

"The truth be told, Willard Grimes, it's the other way around! I have high standards. If you ever stayed at home instead of gallivanting all about you would know that," Myrtle scolded.

I felt bad for Willard. Maybe Myrtle didn't understand about Willard's business.

We left for Lakeside Amusement Park in Willard's Packard. Myrtle and Lester followed us in Lester's automobile. When I looked back at them, I could see Myrtle sitting really close to Lester. I scooted as close to Willard as I could. I wanted Myrtle to see I was just as worldly as she was!

"Let's go win these gals some stuffed animals," Willard said to Lester as soon as we walked through the gate of the amusement park.

I know my eyes must have been big as saucers. I never imagined it would be like this! There was a merry-go-round, the peanut ride, a roller coaster and many more. I could smell all kinds of food cooking and music coming from all over the place. There were plenty of booths with hawkers trying to get us to play their games. There was a man walking on stilts. I never laughed so hard as looking into the fun mirror. I looked like I had gained fifty pounds and shrunk two feet where Willard looked to be ten feet tall! Willard and Lester played a shooting game aiming at moving ducks. Lester didn't do so good but Willard didn't miss a shot. The man in the booth looked relieved when Willard stopped playing. My arms were full with a large stuffed dog and a teddy bear Willard won for me.

"Willard, I didn't know you could shoot that good. You shot all those little ducks and didn't miss one!" I squealed in delight.

"Comes from shootin' rabbits and squirrels, I guess."

"We've walked ahead of Myrtle and Lester. We better stand here and wait until they catch up. Lester doesn't look so good. Do you think Myrtle is pouting 'cause she didn't get any stuffed animals?"

"Lester hasn't had much practice shootin' a gun. He works at Mountain Trust Bank as a teller. He wants to be a bank president some day. I reckon I better go win a prize for Myrtle or she won't be fit company," Willard laughed.

"That's a good idea. These animals are so big I couldn't carry any more anyway," I said. Willard quickly won Myrtle a big stuffed bear. She looked happy as punch.

"Come walk with me, Willard. I'm hungry and want to pick out where we eat. There's lots of vendors to pick from," Myrtle said taking Willard's arm and leading the way.

I felt bad for Lester. It was like Myrtle was trying to rub Lester's nose in manure for him not winning her a prize. I didn't mind walking behind with Lester. He seemed like a swell guy and it gave me a chance to talk to him without Myrtle hearing. "I don't think Myrtle likes me. She's hardly said two words to me since we met."

"It's just her way. I know she worries about Willard since he stays out all night without telling her what he's doing. She doesn't like Willard keeping secrets from her," Lester answered.

"Why do you like her? She doesn't seem very nice to me."

"I never met anybody like her. She's unpredictable. I heard she shot a gun at her old boyfriend and missed. Just barely."

"And that don't scare you?"

"No, it's just a rumor. The hole sure is there though, broader than daylight in the side of the house by the front porch swing. I'm not her steady beau. She's got others or at least I think she does."

"You don't care about that?"

"I don't like it, but there's not much I can do. Myrtle is fun to take to dances. She and Willard can really step to the music. They must have practiced a lot together as kids, even if they weren't supposed to cause of the church. Hey, you ought to get Willard to bring you to a dance sometime!"

Before I could answer, Willard turned back to trade girls. "Let's try the roller coaster."

Afterwards, I clung to him. "Willard, I never had so much fun in my whole life. I sure was afraid of that roller coaster."

"Windy Gap Mountain doesn't seem so bad now does it?" he teased.

"You're right about that," I giggled.

"Things never are so scary after you do them once or twice. Now how about some cotton candy for my girl?" Willard said winking at me.

"Sure, I've never had it before."

"Another first for you, Baby Girl. Just one of many."

On the ride home, Willard pulled down a dirt road and parked the car. He took me in his arms and kissed me long and hard.

"Willard stop. One kiss like that is enough!" I said, pushing him away but I wasn't strong enough. He pulled me to him and kissed me even more.

"Willard Grimes, you stop this right now!" I said giving him a big shove. Willard laughed and started the car. He got me home right at eight just like he promised Mama he would.

"The north wind driveth away rain.
So doth an angry countenance
and backbiting tongue."
Proverbs 25:23

Willard

I was leavin' for Wheelin' and would be gone at least a week callin' on 'shine customers. I wanted to sit in on a game or two and go to the track. Big Jim Amos needed to like me enough to let me be one of his boys. I could make big money with Big Jim if I could get into his good graces.

I decided the best thing to do would be to write to Rhodessa tellin' her I'd be gone for a bit. I had never written to her before. She would probably like gettin' mail from me and it would drive her nosey sisters crazy tryin' to imagine what I wrote. The thought of her sisters made me laugh. It took me a while to think about what to say but I was pleased with my effort. I wasn't one for schoolin' but somehow this was different. I enjoyed writin' to Rhodessa:

My Dear Rhodessa,

I desire to see you alone a week from Sunday as there is a matter I want to discuss with you. I plan on being at your home around three in the afternoon. If the weather is good perhaps we can walk to your special place in the woods?

With all my affection,

Willard

I chuckled when I posted the letter and hit the road to Wheelin'. I had plenty of time to think about my big plans for expandin' my business with Big Jim. I was goin' to a high stakes poker game and Big Jim would be there. I'd been puttin' back money for this very night. I couldn't look like some poor country boy with nothin' to bet.

The night went well enough with me losin' all I had. I acted like it didn't matter 'cause Big Jim had to think I had more where that came from. Big Jim slapped me on the back and called me a good loser. I had gotten his attention and that was what I wanted. Before long we were talkin' business.

Big Jim kept me busy the next three days. He wanted to know how much 'shine I could supply to the coal miners, my plan of operation and details I had never thought of. I was on my toes though, and came up with answers for everythin'. I needed Big Jim to see I was man enough for the job and could be trusted.

The third night in West Virginia, Big Jim sent me off with two of his boys. I knew better than to ask any questions. I didn't know they were plannin' to break into a man's house and take him for a ride to a cabin deep in the mountains. The man was plannin' to turn state's evidence on Big Jim, and the boys were there to teach him a lesson. I didn't lay a hand on the man but I watched the beatin' he took. I knew he was hurt real bad. He died a day later. I read about it in the paper. He had a wife and two kids. There wasn't nothin' I could have done about it. Big Jim was testin' me, and I had to make the grade.

When I got back I didn't get past the front door. Rhodessa about knocked me over throwin' herself in my arms. "Willard I missed you so much. Don't ever go away that long again!"

Feeling Rhodessa in my arms made me forget about the events of the past week. "Rhodessa I have somethin' I want to ask you, but I should probably talk to your parents first."

"They went to visit neighbors."

"How about Hattie and Ruby? Where are they?"

"I'm not sure."

"Then I am goin' to kiss you while I can."

"Aahhh-shoo, Aahhh shoo!" came an exploding sound from the hall closet.

Rhodessa Rose jerked open the closet door. "My own sisters spying on me!"

"We read Willard's note and had to know what he is going to ask you," Ruby squealed, hopping out of the closet with Hattie right behind her.

Within seconds a sisterly squabble was in full force.

"Rhodessa, what I wanted to speak to you of can wait," I said. I ducked out as fast as I could. There was entirely too much female goings on for me.

I was so mad at my sisters I didn't speak to them for a week. Papa thought the whole thing was funny but hid his mirth when Mama was around. After things calmed down, Mama made Ruby and Hattie apologize to me for spying from the closet. We all sat formally at the kitchen table. Mama was going to make sure they did it right.

"Rhodessa, we thought Willard was going to propose. That's why we hid in the closet when we heard his car pull up. Ruby and I wanted to know what you're doing to make Willard fall in love with you," Hattie explained.

"Are you going to marry him or not?" Ruby asked.

"I think she will have to marry him to get rid of him," Mama laughed.

"Ruby and I are much better suited for Willard. We don't want to see you make a big mistake," Hattie said.

"Willard hasn't proposed to me. I don't know if he ever shall have sisters like you two!" I busted out in tears.

Mama made them both say they were sorry, but I knew they didn't mean it.

Later that day, when Willard came over, he did not seem to have anything special to talk about, and this time my sisters were nowhere around!

"And the day came when the risk to remain tight in the bud
was more painful than the risk it took to blossom."
Anais Nin

RHODESSA ROSE

Willard seemed to love my mountain almost as much as I did. Sometimes I packed us a picnic and we took walks up the mountain trail. Willard liked to talk to me about his dreams for his business. Every now and then, Willard would tell me to get a wiggle on, and he'd take me with him to a gin joint where he would conduct a little business. His favorite joint was behind the railroad tracks in Roanoke. Willard had to knock on a green door in back of the house. Once he said the password, we were in.

One afternoon, Willard and I were sitting at a table having cocktails. I was having a gin and ginger. I needed the ginger to make the bathtub gin go down. Willard always made sure my drink came in a teacup. He wanted to make sure people thought I was a lady and not one of those women who sat around with powdered faces and red lips listening to jazz. Willard was in one of his talkative moods. I could tell he had something on his mind.

"Baby Girl, I am goin' to take you to the West Virginia State Fair. It's a long drive, probably six hours. We will have to spend the night. I wanted to ask your folks first, to sort of get them used to the idea, but I didn't get the chance with your sisters hidin' in the closet," Willard laughed.

"I have never in my life gone so far from home and another state to boot! Mama would never let me go that far without us being married!"

"Don't you worry none about your Mama. I can take care of her, and if she agrees, your Papa will go along with it."

I could hardly believe it! Willard was going to take me to the fair!

A few nights later, Willard came calling. He brought a bouquet of flowers he had picked himself.

"Willard, they are beautiful. Thank you so much!"

"Don't be thankin' me girl; they are for your Mama. I need to start butterin' her up so I can take you to the fair."

Mama wasn't about to let me go even when Willard convinced her I would be staying in a respectable rooming house for women, and it would only be for one night. I heard Mama coming up with more and more reasons why I couldn't go. "Willard, it doesn't look respectable for an unmarried girl of any age, going off with a man, boarding house or not," Mama scolded.

"Mrs. Hartman, you haven't got a thing to worry about. I'll take perfectly good care of Rhodessa and be a perfect gentleman at all times."

Willard told Mama all the wonderful things I would experience at the fair. He was so charming, I could see her weakening. For every argument Mama gave Willard for me not to go, Willard gave Mama two reasons why I should. At last Mama gave in.

"Willard, I am going to let you take her but not for the reasons you think. My mother and father came from Cold Knob Mountain, West Virginia, although it was still Virginia then. I always wanted to see where they were from but never had the chance. Life wasn't easy for my parents with her being Indian and him being white. People wouldn't sell land to them. My father had a friend who settled here on Cahas Mountain. That's how we came to be here. I am going to let you take Rhodessa to West Virginia. I want her to see where her grandparents came from. But I am warning you now, Willard Grimes, there is to be no funny business, or there will be me to answer to!

Willard picked me up on a sunshiny Saturday morning. I was standing outside waiting for him when he drove up. I had been up for hours full of anticipation about what the day had in store. Willard's automobile was all shined up special like just polished shoes. The chrome was shining bright, and the car smelled new even though it wasn't. When Willard got out of the car, he was dressed so handsome I could scarcely believe it. He was wearing a white linen suit I had never seen before. He even had a new straw hat.

"We better go into the kitchen and tell Mama and Papa we are leaving. You will probably have to answer a lot more questions," I laughed.

"I am prepared for that. Just let me get something from the backseat of my car."

In the kitchen, Willard handed Mama a box of Whitman's chocolates. "Mr. and Mrs. Hartman, I want to thank you for trustin' me to take Rhodessa with me to the fair. This is for you." Willard remembered his hat was still on his head and took it off. He stood there, turning it round and round like a steering wheel while Mama and Papa asked a million questions. Finally we were able to say goodbye after getting an earful of warnings and instructions.

After we had been riding for a couple of hours, I got the feeling Willard was up to something. "Willard how much longer is the drive?"

"It is gonna take us time Baby Girl, don't worry. We'll get there soon enough. Just enjoy the ride," he said with a crooked grin on his face.

"Willard Grimes, I can tell you are up to something. Tell me right now what it is!"

"Change of plans, Baby Girl, we aren't going to the State Fair, we are going to the Charles Town Race Track! If you're gonna be my wife some day, I want you to see how I make money. I don't want to make no bones about how I make my living. Either you can accept it or not. If you don't, you aren't the right girl for me."

"Willard Grimes, you turn this car around and take me home! You should never have told such a whopper of a tale about the fair." In truth I was scared. I couldn't believe Willard had done such a thing. What kind of man was he and what kind of girl did he think I was?

Willard pulled to the side of the road and stopped the car. He got out and reached into the backseat and pulled out a big fancy box.

"Willard, what's that?"

"Just a little somethin' for my girl. You are my girl aren't you? Say you are my girl, and I'll give you the box."

I felt myself softening to him and getting excited about the gift.

"Oh Willard, you know I am. So give it here!" The box said what was in it was from a store called Heironimus in Roanoke. It was written right on the box! I couldn't contain my excitement as I tore open my gift. "Oh, Willard! It's the most beautiful dress I have ever seen." It was taffeta and the softest blue.

"It has a pinched waist, and fitted bodice. That's what the salesgirl called it anyway. You will look like a million bucks in this dress, Rhodessa."

"Isn't it a bit daring being off the shoulder?"

"It's what all the high fashion ladies will be wearin' at the track, besides your shoulders won't be bare. You will have this on." Willard put his hand in the inside pocket of his suit jacket and pulled out a string of pearls. "These are the real things, Baby Girl, you can bet on that. Stick with old Willard, and good things are gonna come your way."

"I couldn't possibly wear this dress or these lovely pearls. Mama would never approve, you know she wouldn't," I protested.

"Mama's not here Baby Girl. It's just you and me," Willard said gathering me in his arms.

Oh, how I loved every minute of this, feeling all grown up and away from Mama who would have said the devil was doing my thinking, tempting me to listen to Willard's smooth talk.

"There's one more present for you Princess."

Willard reached into the back seat and pulled out another box. In it was my first pair of high-heeled shoes. A perfect baby blue to match the dress! "Now you will fit in with all the high fashion ladies at the track and be by far the prettiest woman there."

I could feel my face was blushing but how could I be mad at Willard for deceiving me and Mama now?

I watched twelve races that Saturday afternoon and evening. Being at the track was so exciting especially when a race started. The horses took off running with jockeys on their backs barely able to hold on. This sure didn't look like horse riding back home! I got to yelling and jumping up and down like the rest of the folks. Willard let me bet on several races. One of the horses I placed a bet on was Lucky Lady. She didn't win, but she did come in second. My winning was twenty dollars and Willard told me to keep the money!

I had never seen so many people in my whole entire life. I met people from Maryland and Washington, not to mention West Virginia. So many places! Willard knew so many folks, and they were so kind to me, making me feel welcome. Several of the men told me I looked right spiffy and gave me big winks. Willard gave them a hard look in return.

I could tell Willard was important! Men were continually coming up to Willard, slapping him on the back and shaking his hand. I asked Willard if he had met the President. He laughed and said not yet but that Franklin D. Roosevelt had been all for the track being built. He wouldn't have been surprised if we ran into the President that very day!

One of the nicest people I met was Willard's business partner, Big Jim Amos from Wheeling. He had all sorts of friends around him. Big Jim seemed to win a lot. Every time he did he would hand out dollar bills. Between puffs on his cigar, Big Jim talked about wanting Willard to lease his slot machines because, he said, every gin joint in Roanoke should have one. Big Jim insisted on buying Willard and me a fancy dinner at a swanky steak house restaurant when we left the track. Willard and I followed Big Jim's car to the restaurant which had a concrete fountain out front with flowing water that made a pretty arc. I had never seen such a thing. Willard said it was good luck to throw coins in the fountain and gave me a few pennies to do just that. I made a wish for a wonderful night and hoped my wish would come true. We walked in the restaurant and a man, dressed in a suit called a tuxedo, showed us to our table. He pulled out a chair for me to sit in and unfolded a cloth napkin and put it in my lap. The light was so dim I could barely read the menu I was given. Willard just laughed saying he would order for me. I was glad he did. I was real confused about the little forks that came with the shrimp cocktail that was placed before me, but Big Jim laughed and helped me out. Willard ordered steak and asparagus with hollandaise sauce for us both. I wanted to eat everything on my plate it was so good, but I couldn't, I was just too full.

After dinner, Big Jim took Willard and me into a back room where people were playing cards. Big Jim showed me how to play the slot machines and gave me a handful of coins so I could play myself. I had so much fun pulling the handle, seeing all those pictures go round. When I won it was so exciting! I could see why Big Jim thought every gin joint should have a slot machine.

Big Jim kept having a girl bring Willard drinks. He also offered me something "with a little kick to it." But Willard insisted I have only Coca Cola. Willard usually let me have a drink or two in the gin joints in Roanoke so I didn't understand why I couldn't here. I sipped a little out of Willard's drinks. He didn't seem to mind.

Willard and I played the slot machines until well past midnight. One of Willard's lady friends, Belle Adler, was also playing. Willard had told me earlier Belle was in business with Big Jim and that I should be especially nice to her. Belle was a big woman with the reddest and biggest hair I had ever seen. It was all piled up on her head, a foot high it seemed. She also had on bright red lipstick. Belle was just swell to me. Belle didn't dress like the other women. She had on a cowboy shirt and big overalls.

Willard had it arranged that Belle and I would spend the night at Big Jim's house with his wife and kids. Willard said Big Jim had so much money he had houses everywhere. He owned racehorses, too. I couldn't imagine someone having that much money. Willard said it had to do with Big Jim's investments and wasn't it lucky he had a business partner such as Big Jim? Willard kissed me and left me in the care of my new friends saying he had to leave and do some late night business.

I couldn't believe the house I was taken too. It looked like the White House. Big Jim laughed at that. Belle showed me to a guest bedroom. It had a big four poster bed.

"I think you will be comfortable in here Rhodessa. The bathroom has everything you might need including a new tooth brush. Feel free to take a long soak in the claw foot tub, there's all kinds of ladies' products to use. After a while I'll have a cup of tea sent up to you," Belle offered before leaving me alone. I couldn't believe the big fluffy towels and soft bathrobe. I must have soaked in that tub for a full hour. I could barely wait to tell Willard about all my experiences!

Willard was back the next morning at nine. I was having a big breakfast of poached eggs, pancakes, fruit cups and orange juice with Belle, Big Jim, his wife and daughter. A Negro woman had brought our breakfast to us on large silver trays, sitting the food on the biggest dining room table I had ever seen. It was covered with a white tablecloth with embroidered flowers all over it. Fourteen fancy chairs fit around that table! I was eating off real china and having my coffee poured from a silver coffee pot. Willard sat down next to me. All he wanted was black coffee.

Belle was wearing the same thing she had on the night before. I reckon she hadn't brought a change of clothes. Big Jim's wife was wearing a flowing silk green gown over her night dress. Her hair and face were already made up fancy for the day. She talked about the weather and ordered the poor Negro woman about. I couldn't help but notice her huge diamond ring. I asked her if it didn't hurt her finger and everyone laughed at me, especially Big Jim. Mostly Big Jim's wife sat with her lips pursed together in a thin line. She looked sad really, in a haughty kind of way. Big Jim's daughter was thirteen. You could tell she was the apple of her daddy's eye by the way Big Jim carried on about her, talking about how well she rode, and how she was gonna take over his business someday. After a while Big Jim and Willard left the table to talk while I sat and finished my coffee with the women.

When it was time to leave, I thanked everybody for being so good to me. Big Jim invited me to come back at any time - with or without Willard. That got a big laugh out of everybody. As I was leaving, Belle took me aside and gave me three cakes of Cashmere Bouquet Soap. She said all her girls used it. I figured she must have daughters. Belle said the soap had a fragrance men loved. It did smell beguiling. I promised her I would use it and thanked her very much.

Big Jim walked us to the car. “Don’t forget, Willard, I get $200 a month for leasing the slots. Make me happy, and I’ll lease you more. Slots are moneymaking propositions. Get other fellows to lease them through you, and I’ll give you a cut. There is no way to lose unless you are plain stupid. You aren’t stupid are you Willard?”

“No sir, I might be a lot of things, but I ain’t stupid.”

“Just remember to pay up on time. I don’t like waiting on my money.”

Willard and Big Jim shook hands, and we started the long drive home.

“Two hundred dollars is a lot of money,” I said.

“Peanuts, Baby Girl, just peanuts. Wait and see. I’m a real businessman,” Willard laughed.

I snuggled up to Willard. I felt bad for not having anything to tell Mama about where her parents were from. I didn’t like thinking about the lies I would tell when I got home. I had never lied to Mama and Papa. I had never needed to before. But Willard had it all figured out for me. We would take them by surprise. Just outside of Boones Mill, Willard pulled the car down a dirt road by the prettiest creek you ever did see. Once again Willard asked me to look in his jacket pocket. There it was, a diamond engagement ring. Willard thought of everything!

"Enlarge the place of your tent,
and let the curtains of your habitations be stretched out;
hold not back, lengthen your cords
and strengthen your stakes."
Isaiah 54:2

RHODESSA ROSE

My engagement to Willard didn't start out so good. Mama and Papa thought I was too young and told me the wedding would have to wait until I was seventeen. That was almost a whole year! When I told Hattie it was official, I was going to marry Willard, her eyes changed quick. I had never seen such anger in anybody's eyes before. I went to hug her. She threw me hard against the bedroom wall and walked away. Hattie whispered to anyone that would listen that Willard could never be happy with the likes of me. Ruby gave me the silent treatment. I knew she agreed with Hattie. I could see it in her eyes when she looked at me.

Mama tried to set Ruby and Hattie straight, telling them that their behavior was unbecoming and no decent man would marry them if they didn't learn how to be proper ladies. After the scolding, they behaved better but that was because Mama kept her eagle eyes upon them. Neither Hattie nor Ruby apologized to me but I suppose that is what jealousy does.

Mama made Papa drive her all the way to Roanoke for just the right fabric and lace to make my sisters' dresses to wear for the wedding. Papa grumbled the whole way about money ill spent. I think Mama went to all the trouble with my sisters' dresses 'cause they were so peeved at me.

A few months before the wedding, Mama took me into her bedroom and had me open the trunk at the foot of the bed. "Rhodessa, I have kept my wedding dress in this trunk knowing the time would come for one of my daughters to wear it. I never figured on you getting married first, but it seems like this is the way it is to be. Your grandmother made this dress, every single stitch by her own hand. It takes me back to my own wedding day. I don't think I've ever told you the whole story of how I met your Papa. Seems now is as good a time as any. Do you want to hear?"

"You know I do Mama, every detail."

"Your Papa's father traveled around selling POW-O-LINE Tonic and was a circuit riding preacher on Sundays. Grandfather Hartman thought having your Papa with him was good for business. He was just four-years-old when he started helping his father sell the medicine. A lot of people believed that POW-O-LINE was a miracle tonic, and could cure anything. Truth be told it was mainly alcohol. Housewives were good customers, sometimes buying five bottles at a time. They thought they were helping the little tyke, without a mother, so they opened their purses wider.

Grandfather Hartman could gather a crowd preaching. He wasn't above telling folks about how his poor son lost his Mama when he was but a babe in a tragic carriage accident and there weren't any kin to take him in. I am sure many women had tears in their eyes knowing this wasn't the kind of life a mother would want for a child, traveling from town to town with no mother's good night kiss or a bed to call his own. The money rolled in but it became less and less as your Papa grew older.

I first laid eyes on your Papa at the General Store in Boones Mill. He had a crowd around him and he was spouting off about POW-O-LINE Tonic, which he claimed relieved all suffering. I thought him the handsomest thing I had ever set my eyes on. He had the thickest, waviest hair, and a curl that stayed right in the middle of his forehead. He was funny too, trying to sell that awful medicine. He even played the banjo as part of his act. Eligible ladies were standing in line to buy tonic. I knew they didn't have no suffering. Your Papa didn't pay them any attention, just kept looking at me with his devilish blue eyes and smiling. Well, your Papa got to really showing off and invited me to come forward for a demonstration of the miracle cure. I laughed him off but he was determined and kept trying. I never did go forward. After the crowd was gone, he came looking for me. I hung around long enough for him to find me."

"What did he say to you after he found you Mama? I want every detail," I begged.

"He found me in the General Store. He walked right up and told me I was the most beautiful girl he had ever seen and he was going to marry me! I laughed in his face knowing he was a real smooth talker so I played along. 'What about your business?' I asked him. He told me he had been traveling enough to last a lifetime and was tired of living out of a wagon."

"What did you do then Mama?"

"Well, the only thing I could do. I invited him to supper the next night. Your Papa said it was the best meal he had in his entire life. After dinner, your Papa and I sat on the porch swing. He told me his mama hadn't been killed but had run off with a man soon after he was born. Your Papa didn't want no secrets between us."

"Your Papa worked on our farm for two years to get my parents' permission to marry me. I was only fifteen you see. He had to show my parents he could make a living as a farmer not having any experience in it. They were afraid he might not take to farming. But he proved himself. It's always saddened me that your Papa feels he isn't good enough for me being raised the way he was. I suspect that's why he drinks so. He has said to me on more than one occasion that I come from good solid people and he couldn't understand what I wanted the likes of him."

"Why did you Mama?"

"I reckon the heart wants what it wants," Mama answered.

"Did Papa ever see his father again?" I asked.

"No, he never did. His father just pulled out of Boones Mill and went on to the next town. That was the last we seen of him." Mama reached into the trunk and pulled out the dress which had been folded so carefully in tissue paper. It was long and white made out of satin.

"I was a beautiful bride, Rhodessa, and you will be too. So let's see if it fits you. You'll need my help getting into it with all these buttons. If I remember correctly there is close to a hundred."

I got undressed and stepped into the wedding gown. It took a full fifteen minutes to get all the buttons done up right.

"Mama, it fits perfectly. I love it. Thank you, for letting me wear it."

"I am warning that husband-to-be of yours to be patient with those buttons on your wedding night, I want my granddaughter to be able to wear this dress too."

"Thank you Mama, thank you so much," I said hugging her neck.

Mama just smiled at me, but her eyes were not smiling. When she thought I wasn't looking I saw her wipe a tear from her cheek.

Willard didn't cotton to getting married in a church, and I insisted on a preacher. Willard liked Preacher Shiflett all right as he liked to imbibe in liquid spirits. Preacher Shiflett said the shiners were less suspicious of him when he drank 'shine with them. When Preacher Shiflett got lit up, he would really get to preaching! I know Willard's folks would have liked a church wedding, but Willard didn't follow their ways. I would have liked to have been a bride in a church with Papa giving me away but Papa didn't like churches. Our agreement would just have to do.

Preacher Shiflett had helped steer the revenuers away from Papa and Willard more than once by getting on one of his religious tangents from the good book, giving Papa and Willard time to sneak off. Preacher Shiflett could corner a person, and no one could go anywhere until he finally wore down. Preacher Shiflett said revenuers needed saving more than most, coming onto a man's land and keeping him from making a decent living for his family.

Mama and I liked Preacher Shiflett. I have good memories of Preacher Shiflett dropping by the house when he saw Papa's truck was gone. He had a way of reading the Bible that could send shivers up and down your spine, especially when he finished off a glass of 'shine while sitting at the kitchen table with Mama, Ruby, Hattie and me. Mama always wanted to hear about Jesus. Ruby liked memorizing scriptures. Hattie didn't seem to have much use for any of it but sat still like she was told. If Papa came in, Mama would send him on an errand, and he would go so Mama could get us some Bible teaching. Mama and Papa made many adjustments to one another.

Days before the wedding, Mama had us girls paint mason jars so it wouldn't look like they were full of 'shine. We painted some of the jars in pink and blue to put wild flowers in. The other jars, we painted white, so they looked like milk for the children but had 'shine in them instead. Mama thought this could fool the revenuers if they came by on my wedding day. Mama wasn't about to leave anything to chance.

It was a beautiful fall afternoon when Preacher Shiflett married Willard and me by the white rock well in the front yard. I got what I wanted, and Willard didn't get what he didn't want - married inside a church - so we were both happy.

Papa gave me away, and my sisters acted like they were pleased for us in their pretty blue bridesmaid dresses. Lots of friends came to our wedding. Some customers dropped by not knowing - or forgetting - it was our special day. Everyone was invited to stay and most did. Two of Willard's friends from West Virginia came bringing a curious wedding gift from Big Jim. It was piece of paper that had IOU written on it and it was torn in half. I asked Willard what it meant. He told me to not to fret about it, but it was the best wedding gift he could have hoped for. Willard was so excited about that piece of paper that he picked me up and swirled me around, thanking me for being his wife and bringing him good luck.

Our wedding was a good day for business as well as a wedding. It was our customers' good luck to join our wedding festivities and drink 'shine for free. We developed potential customers from the folks who stopped their cars wanting to see what all the fun was about.

Many laughs were had as Willard and I raised the dipper together from our white rock well and drank water at the same time or tried to. I was careful 'cause of my wedding dress but Willard's suit got all wet. Then Willard kissed me like crazy, lifting me off my feet and spinning me! Everyone cheered and hooted.

The men toasted us with Papa's best apple 'shine all afternoon between their chewing and spitting tobacco. The ladies, who were wearing their best dresses and hats, drank lemonade with lots of sugar from pretty fruit jars. Everybody brought a dish made from their favorite recipe. The table was brimming over with things like fruit compote, potato salad, deviled eggs and fried chicken. Mama had made a beautiful vanilla, three-layer wedding cake with butter cream icing. She decorated it herself, making flowers with pink and green frosting. When Willard and I cut the cake, he fed me, smearing icing on my face with his fingers. I got him back by smearing icing all over his nose.

When evening started to set in, the men got the fire going. It was a good thing 'cause it had started to chill down. The women gathered the quilts they had brought from home while the men got the fiddles, banjos, and mandolins out of their automobiles and wagons.

"Willard, grab that gal of yours and dance her around the fire, before the rest of us join in," called Uncle Pole Cat, Mama's older brother. Uncle Pole Cat never liked to wash, not since he was a kid. But he could play the best mandolin in these parts.

"Don't mind if I do." Willard grinned, pulling me into his arms.

I knew I was blushing beet red 'cause of all the others laughing and cheering us on. Pretty soon everybody else joined in. The dancing went on for hours until that big full man in the moon came out and Papa passed out almost hitting his head on one of the big rocks circling the fire.

Mama was looking tired after such a long day and started coughing real hard so the wedding party was ending. Everyone was a little sad.

"It's time for you and Rhodessa to leave on your honeymoon, Willard, where are you taking your pretty bride," came the teasing from Uncle Pole Cat.

"Sorry to disappoint you folks, but me and Rhodessa are havin' our honeymoon right here. All we got to do is go up those stairs," Willard said.

I thought everyone would be disappointed in that so much trouble had gone into tying tin cans, old shoes and even an old baby carriage to the back of Willard's car but instead all the men started hooting and catcalling.

"Willard, you done got yourself a practical woman and a looker too!" a male voice called out from the dark.

Willard and I commenced to take our leaving. It was time to put my parents to bed and me and Willard too!

Mama tried to make Ruby's room especially nice for Willard and me by putting new towels by the washbasin and some pretty embroidered pillowcases on the bed. Mama gave me a special lady's nightgown just before we all said our good nights. The gown was a rose pink color and felt like silk. It fit my curves in a womanly way. I made Willard turn his back and cover his eyes while I put it on. I never felt so grown up and glamorous. "Willard, you can turn around now."

I couldn't help but laugh when he did 'cause it looked like his eyes were going to pop right out of his head. "Baby Girl, I never seen you lookin' so beautiful. To think you are Mrs. Willard Grimes!" Willard swooped me up into his arms, holding and kissing me, before undressing me and laying me on our marriage bed.

The next morning when we went to breakfast, everyone was staring. I felt myself blushing from head to toe. Mama had set the table for two using her best lace placemats and napkins. She poured fresh coffee in china cups that were never allowed to be used except on special occasions. Mama set about making us her special French toast with maple syrup and bacon.

"I wasn't sure when you newlyweds would come down. Sit down, now. Your breakfast will be ready in a few minutes. Hattie and Ruby, start your chores. This morning, we want to let the newlyweds have a little privacy."

Papa got up and left without saying anything.

"Mama, it's not fair we have to leave or share a bedroom," Hattie said loudly.

"They should have gone on a honeymoon," Ruby pouted.

"We have been over this. Willard and your Papa have some big 'shine orders to fill before they can go anywhere," Mama said.

"I won't be living in my parents' house when I get married!" Hattie said with a hateful expression.

"You better find yourself a beau then. Neither one of you is getting any younger," Mama chuckled.

Ruby and Hattie mumbled under their breath about the unfairness of it as they left the kitchen.

Willard

Married life was working out pretty good for me. Rhodessa tried to please me any way she could, particularly in the kitchen. She was always tryin' some new fangled recipe for me and the rest of the family. I told her I'd rather have her help me in the 'shine business by takin' care of the customers and keepin' the books, but Rhodessa had this idea about cookin' for me, and it would just have to wear itself out. I wished she would just let Mrs. Hartman do the cookin'. Rhodessa could never match her mother in the kitchen.

Stayin' at her folks place felt a little strange at times but no one seemed to mind when I took off. They didn't ask any questions. They were not like my folks with their pryin' ways. Mr. Hartman knew I was about the family business, gettin' his 'shine delivered, makin' it possible to buy the supplies needed to increase the number of batches.

I never stayed away long, except when I had to go to West Virginia. Big Jim was trustin' me more and lettin' me in on some big deals. He liked to rib me about being a newly married man. Rhodessa had made a big impression on him with her innocence and beauty. She was a real asset to me in the business.

After a few days with Big Jim, I drove back from West Virginia. I was ridin' high about how things were going when I stopped at Maybelline's. I tried not to stay long but she liked to talk and tease me about married life. I had to go along with her as I didn't want to lose one of my best customers. Maybelline had been swell about connectin' me with her clients. She got a cut but we were both makin' money. I made the delivery and Maybelline handled the distributions using her girls. Since I had been married, Maybelline and I had the same conversation:

"Maybelline, I got your jars."

"You sure seem tired Willard. Looks like you've been driving all night. Don't you want to come in and sit for a spell?"

"No ma'am, I need to get back home."

"Back to that little bride of yours? Sure I can't tempt you with a little nap? I have a real pretty wedding present I could send to your room."

"I have to get goin' now. I'll be back in a couple weeks."

Willard, you'll be back for one of those naps. When the bloom is off the rose, you'll be back."

It was to be my first Christmas as a married woman, and I wanted everything to be perfect. Right after my wedding I had begun planning. I had Papa give me some of the cardboard boxes he used for his 'shine. Papa got his boxes at the Piggly Wiggly Store on Monday nights after the store finished putting their food on the shelves.

I drew the shape of a Christmas tree on the largest boxes, cut out the form, and painted it green. I drew stars on another box and cut them out with Mama's sewing scissors. I painted the stars red. The stars were supposed to be yellow but all we had at home was barn paint. In cursive I wrote the names of each of us on a star; Papa, Mama, Willard, myself, Hattie and Ruby. Mama wasn't happy when she saw me using her sewing scissors for cutting cardboard. After I promised never to do it again, she laughed, saying it was alright this one time. Mama and I hung the cardboard Christmas tree at the end of the downstairs hall.

Willard and I went walking the mountain in the brisk winter air, holding hands, man and wife, and found the perfect Christmas tree, a small loblolly pine that would fit well into the corner of the parlor. We had invited my sisters to come, but they weren't interested. That was fine with me; it gave Willard and me a chance to be alone. At home, there was always someone around. Cutting down our first Christmas tree, I was so happy I thought my heart would burst.

Papa and I went to Roanoke to do Christmas shopping in his old pickup truck. It was a cold but sunshiny day when we started out. Papa and I were bundled up with scarves, gloves and winter coats. I looked forward to the long stretch of road and the time to talk to Papa without the others around. There were lots of stores in Roanoke. There wasn't much in the way of Christmas shopping at the General Store in Boones Mill. Papa liked to talk while he drove. We passed apple orchards and cattle pastures. When Papa and I went by tobacco fields, he recollected traveling with his father, seeing the poor whites and negroes picking tobacco in the hot sun. He swore to himself if he ever had a wife and children, they would never do that backbreaking work. "Before you was born I used to grow a little tobacco, but the land was worn out so it didn't pan out much. Better I grow corn which I can sell and use in the business too. Farming is just like gambling Rhodessa. That's why I make 'shine. That's a cash crop that pays," Papa laughed.

We had to drive by the Virginian Railway passenger station, which was close to the city market, because Papa got excited about trains. Hopefully, we would see a Norfolk and Western train go by. Papa wanted to see what was being carried in the hopper cars. "The railroad made Roanoke by bringing in the jobs. I used to think I wanted to be a railroad man, or maybe a tobacco auctioneer."

"Why didn't you Papa?"

"I like to keep my own schedule not nobody else's. If I was working one of those jobs, I wouldn't be driving to town with my pretty married daughter now could I?"

"Papa, I want to go to the City Market Building first. Then I want to go to Campbell Avenue and look at the furniture just for fun and to go into some of the other stores to look at ready-to-wear clothes and shoes."

"Honey, we got all day. No need to rush about," Papa laughed at my excitement.

You never knew what you might find at the farmer's market. I liked overhearing people talk about the goings on in a city as big as Roanoke. Papa got the *Roanoke Times* and we looked it over in a small restaurant while we drank cups of hot cider to warm up. Then we began our shopping.

I bought a flannel shirt for Willard and a book for Mama. I have to admit I wanted to read it after Mama was through with it. Mama liked to read and we didn't have many books. For Hattie, I purchased hair clips and pretty combs from Woolworth's. I bought colored pencils and plain paper for Ruby as she was forever drawing flowers or fruit. Papa had given me special money for Christmas shopping 'cause of all the work I had done helping him with the business. It was our secret, so my sisters wouldn't be jealous, even though they had never helped Papa one little bit. It was best if they thought Willard gave me the money instead. Papa promised me not to drink until we got home, and he kept his word.

Later that evening, Mama, Ruby, Hattie and I decorated the tree. Mama had a box of special decorations, handmade from ribbons, beads and buttons that had been my grandmother's. We used great care with handling them as they were very dear to Mama. Willard and Papa sat back and drank eggnog, supervising and giving advice on decorating the tree. They spiked their eggnog with 'shine, but not us girls'. We drank it plain and ate sugar cookies. I had made the cookies, shaping them like Christmas trees and stars, with frosting in green and yellow to match the game we were going to play Christmas Eve.

I had made Willard a Christmas stocking and hung it up with the rest of ours over the fireplace. Willard said it made him feel like a real member of the family. The mantle looked so pretty decorated with greenery and red berries. I wished it could have stayed that way all year.

On Christmas Eve, I worked on my special dinner of roast chicken and gravy, mashed potatoes and pumpkin pie. I did all the cooking myself and wouldn't let anybody in the kitchen. When we all sat down for supper, Mama made her twice-a-year prayer long, thanking God for everybody and everything she could think of. She had to make this prayer last until Easter.

My first Christmas Eve dinner was delicious if I say so myself. Everyone asked for seconds and nothing was left when it was time to clear the dishes.

After super, we gathered in the hallway to play pin the star on the Christmas tree. We took turns blindfolding and spinning each other around to see who could pin their star to the tip of the tree. It was great fun. Papa had a bit too much to drink and with all spinning kept pinning his star to the wall. I accused Hattie of peeking out behind her blindfold but she claimed she wasn't. After the best three out of five games, Hattie was declared the winner.

Mama lit the red Christmas candles in the parlor while Papa went and got his fiddle. Papa played mountain tunes he learned while he and his father traveled the

Appalachian Mountains circuit preaching and selling tonic. Mama sang along with her pretty voice. Soon, we were all singing Christmas carols together. I liked Willard's singing, all smooth and gentle, but deep like a man's voice should be. Papa read the Christmas story from the Bible like he did every year. This was Papa's gift to Mama. Papa let Mama have the Christmas she wanted.

Christmas morning I woke up earlier than the rest. Snow had mixed with freezing rain and everything was dazzling white. Willard and I planned to go to his parents for dinner but now it was impossible. I was glad to stay home in this winter wonderland with Willard and my family. I knew it wasn't kind of me to think this way and for a while I felt bad about it. I went back to bed and snuggled with my husband for an extra hour before we went downstairs to unwrap our gifts.

Willard gave me an Eastman Kodak camera with lots of film and a picture album. Willard said we would start to fill the album with this, our first Christmas. For Papa, Willard had a carton of Camel cigarettes and for Mama, a bottle of Chanel No. 5 perfume. Hattie and Ruby received fingernail sets by Coty.

Papa wore the green and red scarf I made him the entire day. Mama gave me a box of recipes she had written out in her best cursive writing and bound with yarn.

"These recipes are from me, having been passed down from your grandmother. You did a fine job making this Christmas special for us Rhodessa. You make me proud."

My eyes filled with tears. I knew the long work it took Mama to write out all the recipes. On each page was sketched a different mountain flower. Mama spent hours making the box for me, and I would treasure it always.

After cleaning the kitchen and making the beds, Willard and I bundled up and went outside. Together, we made a snowman family of Willard, myself and the children we would someday have. We took pictures with my new camera. It was the most perfect Christmas ever!

It was early May, and Willard and I were still at home. It was a good thing 'cause Mama's cough was getting worse. Sometimes she couldn't stop hacking. Soon, she got where she wouldn't eat nothing but cornflakes with a little milk, claiming she had no appetite. Papa tried to get Mama to walk to the mailbox. She did it a time or two with a bit of coaxing from all of us. Then she wouldn't go at all. She sat in her rocker by the wood stove, or else she stayed in her bed. We wanted to call the doctor but Mama insisted she was getting better and didn't want to waste the money. Sometimes Mama would read her Bible. After a while that became too much, and we took turns reading it to her.

"I'd like to see Preacher Shiflett soon," Mama said. I used the phone at the apple packing plant to call him. The next morning, he was over bright and early. I met him at the door leaving Hattie and Ruby with Mama.

"Rhodessa, I want to spend a few minutes with your Mama alone. I want her to feel free to say what's on her heart. I'll call you when it's time for you and your sisters to come back in," Preacher Shiflett said as we climbed the stairs to Mama and Papa's bedroom.

Ruby and Hattie made a fuss when they were asked to leave and wait in the hall. I, for one, was glad to leave as I know Preacher Shiflett had the words of Jesus to comfort Mama.

That afternoon, I called Dr. Riddle in spite of Mama's protest. He came and examined Mama. Afterwards, he talked to Papa and me. "Mrs. Hartman is in the advanced stages of consumption. There is not a lot you can do for her now but keep her comfortable and make sure she gets lots of fresh air. I'll leave you some cough medicine and write down instructions on how to care for her. I spared Mrs. Hartman from the truth about her condition although I am sure she knows. There is not much point in taking her to Catawba Sanatorium. I don't believe she has much time left. I know she would rather die at home with her loved ones around her. All of you have been exposed to consumption and its best you stay put on the mountain. Don't tire your mother out with too much talking. Rest and fresh air is the best thing now, for all of you. I'll be back tomorrow to check on her."

Papa and I agreed not to tell Mama, Hattie or Ruby the truth for now. Hattie and Ruby were too high strung not to make it harder on everybody, especially Mama.

After that news, Papa's drinking got worse - if that was possible. He couldn't manage the business no more. It wasn't but a few days before he got fired from the apple packing plant for coming in drunk, Mr. Killgore said he was real sorry for firing Papa but that was the way it was. We couldn't blame Mr. Killgore. He had always been a fair man and done us right.

It wasn't long after the doctor came that Papa wanted to talk to me about something that was weighing heavy on his shoulders, and he was sober. Papa never talked to us girls about anything important. leaving it to Mama. If one of us had been a boy I guess things would have been different. Rearing girls is a woman's business, Papa had said many times.

"Rhodessa Rose. I want you to get Willard and come sit with me at the supper table," Papa said. Luckily Willard was working on his automobile and was able to come right in. Papa, Willard and I took our usual places at the table.

"Rhodessa, I've taught you all I know about making 'shine. If I was to pass on, I want you to keep the business going for you and your sisters," Papa said.

"Nothing is going to happen to you, Papa," I replied, hoping to stop such talk.

"Listen to me girl. Your sisters don't have no mind for business. You and Willard know how to run the still, you even better than him. Willard can help you best by keeping the revenuers away and making the runs," Papa said as he handed me a piece of paper he had written himself:

My Last and Only Will

This will, made the 18th day of May 1939, is made by me Claude Hartman leaving my farm on Cahas Mountain to my daughters Rhodessa Rose Hartman Grimes, Ruby Jewel Hartman, and Hattie Dale Hartman in equal thirds. Should any of my daughters pass away their part of the farm should be divided among their children or the closest living kin. The deed for the farm is recorded in the Franklin County Courthouse.

Signed this day,

Claude Hartman.

"Papa you shouldn't be thinking this way. It sends shivers up and down my spine. I thank you for thinking of us, but you aren't ever going away from here. You hear me?" I said with tears brimming in my eyes.

"This is all I got to leave you and your sisters. There is enough land to build on when Ruby and Hattie get married and my grandchildren start coming. I want this land to stay in the family. It's our home place. Your Mama and I will be buried in the family cemetery so we can always watch out over our girls. Give me five dollars, Willard, so we can make this all legal like and sign your name as a witness," Papa said.

"Yes Sir, I'd be more than proud to," Willard said as he opened his wallet.

"I love you, Papa."

Papa didn't say nothing. His love for me and my sisters had all been in the showing and not in the telling. It was just the way he was.

Willard and I were doing more of the business. Mama was getting worse by the day with a temperature of over a hundred and wracking coughs. She looked frail and old, not like Mama at all. I tried to keep her sitting up in bed. I gave her teaspoons of the medicine the doctor left but Papa's shine mixed with honey seemed to help more. Mama loved riddles and I tried to think up guessing games for her but most time she was too weak to play. When she was up to it, she liked all us girls to be in on the riddles.

"Mama, what is the cleanest state in the country?

"Easy," Mama said softly. Wash-ington."

"I have a harder one now. What state is a number?"

"You have me there," she said in a whisper.

"I know," piped in Hattie. "Ten. Like in Ten-nessee."

"You are right!" I said.

Mama loved it when we girls got along. When we were by her bedside we put our petty arguments aside, but outside the door, things could be quarrelsome and mean, each of us wanting Mama to love us best and scared to death of losing her. How could we exist without Mama? With the weight Mama had lost, it was if she was disappearing from us. I wondered how much longer she could go on.

Sometimes, if Papa was sober enough, he would take out his banjo and play. It wasn't like before with Mama tapping her foot or singing along as Papa did his fast picking. Papa used to serenade Mama in the kitchen while she cooked supper. He said it was the least he could do and it made Mama cook better. Seeing the twinkle in his eyes and hearing her easy laughter I saw how they belonged together.

But now Mama just lay with her eyes closed as Papa played softer, gentler, comfort songs like *Amazing Grace* and *Shall We Gather at the River*. He couldn't play for very long 'cause his eyes started brimming over, and he needed his fingers to wipe tears away. Then Papa would go get his bottle and more times than not fall out drunk in the front yard.

Time went by too quickly with us knowing that our mother's time on earth was closing. With each day Mama grew weaker and weaker, with deep coughing and not wanting food, not even the weakest soup. A box of tissues stayed by her bed. Mostly we used cloth we had cut into rags, as Mama had instructed us to do, to help her cough up the phlegm and blood. The cloth was thicker than tissues.

"Girls, what state is in poor health? Mama asked with her voice but a whisper.

"I don't know Mama," I said.

"Ill-inois. Please go now and tell Pennsylvania that I need him to get Maryland."

"What's does she mean Rhodessa?" my sisters asked me in the hall.

"Pennsylvania is PA and Maryland is MD. She needs Dr. Riddle."

Mama died peacefully in her sleep on June 28, which I thanked Jesus for and felt guilty about at the same time. Papa was by her bed holding her hand when she passed on. In death Mama looked at peace and there was no more coughing.

We were all dismayed at Mama's passing. Willard went and got Mrs. Pinkins to lay Mama out. She had been a good friend of Mama's. Mrs. Pinkins closed Mama's bedroom door and washed Mama like a baby, even shampooing her hair. I gave Mrs. Pinkins Mama's favorite dress, the one with the softest blue she wore at my wedding. When Mrs. Pinkins finished with Mama she let us girls back in the room. Mama looked beautiful. Willard got word to his folks that Mama had passed over. Mr. Grimes went to work making Mama's coffin. My sisters took to their beds. Willard helped me write about Mama for the newspaper.

"Mrs. Emily Hartman passed from this world on June 28, 1939. Mrs. Hartman lived her whole life of 46 years, eight months and twelve days on Cahas Mountain, a place she dearly loved. She was a mother and wife of exceptionally fine character and always had a bright, cheerful and loving disposition. She made warm and genial friends wherever she went. Mrs. Hartman was known for healing others with her special herbs and remedies. None knew her but to love her. None spoke her name but to praise her. Though her suffering be long, she handed her pain to Jesus. Her husband Claude Hartman, daughters, Ruby and Hattie Hartman, and Rhodessa Grimes and son-in-law Willard Grimes survive Mrs. Hartman. May she rest in peace."

Willard's parents came the next afternoon. Mr. Grimes had stayed up all night making the pine casket. I was deeply touched by the small flowers Mr. Grimes had lovingly carved into the wood. Mrs. Grimes had lined the casket with a special fabric of pink rosebuds. I had never seen a more beautiful casket. We placed Mama gently in the wooden box and took her to the parlor until it was time for the burial. Hattie, Ruby, Willard and I took turns sitting with Mama all night. Papa never left her side.

Mama was buried in the family cemetery part way up the mountain. Summer flowers were blooming in their yellow, pinks and purples, just the way Mama loved. The sweet smell of honeysuckle wound its way round the barbed wire of the cemetery fence perfuming the air. A few close friends came to the funeral but kept a respectful distance. Many stayed away for fear of the consumption which was making its claim on our mountain. Most people, including Hattie and Ruby, suspected consumption had laid claim to my mother. We were standing by the graveside when I noticed Hattie buzzing like a hornet. "Preacher Shiflett tell me the truth. Did Mama die of consumption," Hattie demanded of him. Ruby stood silent with tears streaming down her face.

"I cannot lie and disrespect Mrs. Hartman. It was the consumption that claimed her."

Hattie did not say a word but seemed to become smaller and paler as she reached for Ruby's hand. Preacher Shiflett went on to speak of Mama's goodness and how her life touched many. I could feel Mama's presence. She was watching over us.

The house was strange without Mama. Papa stayed drunk, and Hattie and Ruby were nothing but whiny brats. They kept complaining that I had somebody and they didn't have nobody. How were they going to meet fellows unless Willard and I took them to Roanoke? I reminded them of what Dr. Riddle said about us staying home because of the consumption, but with Mama gone they wouldn't listen to reason. I stopped arguing with them and tried to find ways for us to get along.

"When Preacher Shiflett comes by, I'll ask him if there is going to be a church social or something," I offered.

"How are we going to get to church unless Willard takes us? It's too far to walk," Hattie questioned.

I wondered about that myself. Saturdays were the busiest time for Willard. He stayed out to all hours and then wanted to sleep in on Sundays. Some Saturday nights, Willard didn't come in at all. Willard said he was making his best money then.

Papa wasn't of use to anyone. I pleaded with him to stop drinking and to ask Mr. Killgore for his old job back, but he didn't pay me no mind.

Preacher Shiflett came by to see how we were doing. He talked to Ruby, Hattie and Papa on the porch where Ruby was sketching a tree in the front yard. Papa was picking at his breakfast. I had taken it out to him hoping he would eat something. Willard was no where around. I finished cleaning up the kitchen then invited Preacher Shiflett in for a cup of coffee so I could talk to him privately.

"Rhodessa, you need to get your family into church. I tried to talk to Willard when I ran into him at the General Store some time back but he's got some hard notions. He's just like your Papa in these matters. Your Mama was a God fearing woman. Her greatest heartbreak was not raising you girls in the church. She loved your Papa and understood his ways, though I surely never will."

"Isn't there a revival or something Hattie and Ruby could go too?"

"There is nothing planned until next summer. People are afraid to gather for fear of the consumption. Church attendance has fallen off. You can't blame folks."

"I know we should be scared too, but Hattie is so high strung about finding a boyfriend, and Ruby goes along with whatever Hattie wants. There's got to be some way for them to meet some young men."

"There is only the Sunday morning service. We aren't even doing Sunday school classes for now. You know, Rhodessa, if I didn't visit the stills and drink with the men, I'd never get to preach the word to many men in these parts. Every now and then one of them will listen and bring his family to church. Next time I see your Pa and Willard, I'll try again. I have seen it happen before and now we have your Mama pulling for us from the other side."

Willard

I never let on how bad I felt when Rhodessa's mama died. It seemed best I stay strong for Rhodessa and her sisters. Mrs. Hartman was good to me and fair too. Rhodessa wasn't lettin' up on me about goin' to church. She said her sisters needed to go and she and I did too. I just had to get away from all of them. I felt bad about leavin' Rhodessa while she was grievin' but I just couldn't take my wife and her sisters naggin' at me.

I told Rhodessa that my Saturdays were about business. But I have to admit there was plenty of pleasure in it too. Plus if I got home in the early hours of Sunday morning, you couldn't expect me to go to church now could you? I had plenty of things to take care of in Roanoke like checkin' to see how my slots fared and going to Rex's Tailor Shop to get proper suits made.

The grand jury had just ruled that open gamblin' was an epidemic in Roanoke but so far the law hadn't cracked down. Most Saturday nights, I found a card game. I could usually sell 'shine, or trade it if I found myself on a losin' streak. Win or lose, I was able to pick up a few new customers and spread my territory.

The Perdue brothers were dirty, dark-haired hooligans from Callaway. They were nothin' but white trash and none too smart. Jasper and Angus Perdue weren't pleased when I came to the market on Saturday nights. They had 'shine of their own to sell. But business was business. What right did they have to tell me what I could or could not do? I thought of a plan for the Perdue brothers. It wasn't long before I was able to act on it at a card game.

"How would you boys like to go into business with me on a sure fire thing? I'm making hand over fist with slot machines. I got a couple of slots I can lease to you. What do you say boys?" I could see by the light in their eyes they were interested.

It wasn't long before we had a deal.

The day before Thanksgiving, Papa went missing. It was cold outside and there had been frost on the ground. For much of the day I thought Papa had gotten drunk in the woods like he'd been doing since Mama passed. He started drinking first thing when he woke up. Lecturing him didn't do no good; neither did taking his jar. There was always another to be found behind the outhouse, in the stump of a tree, or hidden in a woodpile. You didn't have to go far.

I was worried when I didn't see Papa by suppertime. I walked over to the cannery asking if anyone had seen him. Nobody had. I checked around the house, in the barn, and all his favorite get-a-way places like the willow tree by the creek where the moss grows its heaviest. Come night, I was near frantic walking by lantern light. It was real cold and a full black night. Papa hadn't had anything to eat. He hadn't eaten hardly nothing since Mama died, sometimes a boiled egg or a piece of toast if I pushed it on him. Papa was so thin he looked like one of the scarecrows in the garden, particularly since they were wearing Papa's old clothes.

During a fitful sleep in the rocking chair, it came to me that Papa was somewhere up the mountain. Before his wasting years, he and Mama would climb the mountain taking a picnic lunch. They would come home in time for Mama to fix dinner all laughing and smiling. Mama was so beautiful in those days.

Willard, Ruby, Hattie and I started walking up the mountain at daybreak on Thanksgiving, spreading ourselves out, calling for Papa but there was no answer except for our own echoes, the snapping of twigs and rustling of dead leaves under our feet.

"Papa, answer me. Please Papa, let me know where you are," I pleaded.

There was no answer except for the whip-o-wills.

Hattie and Ruby went back to the house. They were going to gather neighbors to help us look for Papa. I couldn't go back to the house. I had a feeling I was getting close to him.

Then I saw Papa, sitting with his back to an old oak tree. I called out to Willard and he came running. Willard found me sitting on the ground facing Papa. Tears streamed down my face. "He is dead, Willard, he died all alone."

"Rhodessa I am going to the barn and get your Papa's mule to carry him down the mountain. It will be like your Papa is riding Donnie Wayne one last time."

"That seems fitting, Willard, and I thank you." I could not think of anything else to say.

I was glad that Willard was gone and no others were around so I would have alone time with Papa. I got as close to him as I could and wrapped myself around him. Papa had become stiff but still carried the Papa smell I had always known. I took that smell into me so I should never forget it. No one smelled like him; no one could. I remembered back to when I was a little girl and how I nuzzled his neck when he held me. Papa smelled now like he did then. If Papa ever came to me in the night as a spook I would know him and not be afraid.

I didn't understand how Papa could have made it up the mountain. It was a hard walk in places, with continual steepness, narrow trails, rocks, and vines to trip you. A sick old man, rarely sober, couldn't manage this by himself. He had a picture of my mother in his hand, the one of her as a young bride that he kept in his wallet. Perhaps Mama had been holding Papa's hand while he walked the path they had walked so many times together. The 'shine he had with him was only half gone. Maybe his heart gave out when he stopped to rest under the tree, or maybe it just broke in two and his spirit flew to heaven so he and Mama could be together on Thanksgiving Day.

Willard came back with Donnie Wayne and we hoisted Papa up and across the mule's broad back. Willard had to tie Papa to the saddle since he was so stiff and would likely fall off. Donnie Wayne knew something was wrong. I could tell from the sadness in his eyes and the way he kept looking back at Papa.

The way down was long. Willard and I didn't speak. This would be my only quiet time for a while, on the mountain with Papa. Childhood memories of Mama and Papa came rushing back to me, flooding over me like water does rocks in Maggodee Creek.

A week after the funeral Willard tried to lift our spirits by taking my sisters and me to the American Theatre in Roanoke. Hattie and Ruby were chatterboxes in the backseat asking Willard all kinds of questions about what there was to do in Roanoke. Willard stayed good-natured with their endless questions.

I had never been in a movie theatre. Neither had my sisters. Willard had to pay fifty cents each for us to get in. The theatre was swanky with chandeliers, brocade curtains and even a hand-painted ceiling.

Myrtle and Lester joined us in the theatre lobby. Myrtle laughed at me and my sisters, saying that she and Lester went to the movies all of the time like she was some better than us. Willard bought popcorn and Hershey Bars for us to snack on during the movie. He took us up the stairs to the balcony to watch the film. Myrtle and Lester headed for the very back row while the rest of us wanted to sit up towards the front. When I looked back, before the newsreel came on, I saw them kissing. The lights hadn't even been turned off!

I will never forget seeing Carole Lombard in the picture show. She was so beautiful and funny. I hoped Willard would take me to lots of picture shows. When the movie was playing, I was able to forget about Papa for a little while.

After the show, Willard said he would take us to the Texas Tavern to eat. I thought it was going to be a nip joint from the sounds of it, but it wasn't. It was just a little place with a counter and ten stools serving hotdogs and chili. The Texas Tavern did have good hotdogs. I ate two!

"We are going to leave you folks here. Lester and I have someplace we have to be," Myrtle said trying to sound mysterious.

"You aren't taking us home now are you Willard?" pleaded Hattie.

"I was thinkin' I would," Willard replied.

"Please, Willard, take us someplace else. Take us to a real nip joint. Ruby and I have only heard stories. We want to see the real thing," Hattie begged.

Willard gave in. "I have to check on some business. I might as well take you gals with me. I hope you won't be disappointed."

As we walked downtown, Willard acted like Hattie, Ruby and I were all his dates. He made a big game of putting his arms around our shoulders, taking turns with us. Hattie and Ruby enjoyed themselves, playing along.

"If we are goin' to a nip joint, I guess we might as well do a little nippin' before we get there." Willard pulled a silver flask out of the inside of his suit pocket and handed it to Hattie, who stood there holding on to it. "Well, take a swig and pass it to Ruby," Willard said.

Hattie coughed so hard after a chug I thought she would upchuck.

I couldn't believe that Willard was having us drink 'shine in public. My sisters had tasted Papa's 'shine before, but that was at home where it was private. Neither one of them cared for it, but here, they were drinking in public with Willard!

"I don't think we should be doing this," I protested.

"Don't be such a spoil sport, Rhodessa. We just want to have a good time," Ruby scolded me.

Willard walked us to a stretch of houses behind some railroad tracks. From the front porch of one of the houses, three oil lamps sputtered. "Three lights in the window mean it's ok if we go in. This is one of my best customers. Prohibition is over but people still want to have their 'shine and a good time. Bootleggers sell here without worryin' about the revenuers," Willard told us.

Willard walked us up the steps and knocked. A muscular, dark-haired man stopped us at the front door as a drunk came out holding a bottle, stumbled and fell. The drunk managed to right himself and went on up the street.

"Willard, it's good to see you. Come on in. Who are all these lovely ladies you have with you? Looks to me like you sure are spreading the butter." The man leered at us.

"Never you mind," Willard said, locking eyes with the man.

"Well, come on in and make yourself at home. I've never known you to need an invitation!" the grinning man replied giving us girls an evil wink.

"Willard!" I said. "What kind of a place is this, and why is there a shotgun by the door?"

"Don't worry, Rhodessa. Sikes only lets in those who he knows. It's the rule of the house. There ain't no shells in the shotgun. It's just for looks." Willard reassured me but I wasn't buying it.

Ruby, Hattie and I followed Willard to the back of the house. There were small tables close together with people drinking and an over-stuffed sofa where a couple was doing some heavy necking. The house looked to me like it must have taken on boarders at one time for all the rooms. All kinds of people were milling around and music played from a juke machine. I saw two slot machines which I guessed were Willard's. Cigarette smoke hung in the air mixed with the smell of heavy perfume. Willard had taken me to some nip joints before but none like this!

"You girls sit at this table and I'll be back directly," Willard instructed us.

It wasn't but a few minutes before some awful looking cuss came over and asked us if we wanted a drink. I said no, but Hattie and Ruby let the man pour them whatever was in his bottle into some dingy looking water glasses.

This wouldn't do. I got up to find Willard. I found him in a room with a big iron bed, painted red. Willard was on his knees looking into a large trunk when I walked in.

"Willard, we have to go. This isn't no place for us to be."

"I keep this place supplied with 'shine, Rhodessa. This is one of my accounts and a good one, so don't you be sayin' nothin' about it. Besides your sisters have been wantin' a night out and now they have it. I've got to go talk a little business. You go look out for your sisters. I'll be along directly." Willard took a mason jar from the trunk and refilled his flask.

I went back to the table and sat down. Red and gold foiled packages were on the table. Sin-Sin, licorice flavored mints, breath deodorizer it said. Willard always had some of these little packages in his pocket. Now I knew where they came from. I wondered how often he came here.

Ruby and Hattie looked as though they had finished their first drink and were well into another. "We need to go to the ladies room, Rhodessa, do you know where it is?" Hattie asked.

"No, I don't," I responded sharply.

"I'll just go and ask them," Hattie said pointing to two heavily made up, loud women.

The two women showed my sisters to the powder room. They were gone for a while and I began to worry. I didn't like sitting there by myself. When Hattie and Ruby came back, they were wearing bright rouge and red lipstick.

"The nice ladies said we needed a little color on our faces to fit in here. They said we look real nice with makeup on. I think we do, don't you Rhodessa? They'll put some on you if you want them too," Hattie offered.

"What would Mama say with both of you acting like this?" I asked.

They didn't get a chance to answer as a bald, middle-aged man came up to our table. "My, what do we have here, it must be three angels passing through. I don't believe I have ever made your acquaintance," the man said.

"We are here with my husband Willard Grimes. He will be back in just a moment," I said cutting the man a hard look.

"My name is Hattie, and this is Ruby," volunteered Hattie.

"Does one of you ladies care to dance?"

"Neither my sisters nor I want to dance," I replied.

"Yes, I do Rhodessa; I really want to dance," piped in Ruby.

"So do I," Hattie chorused.

"What do we call you?" I asked the man.

"Just call me Prince Albert. Allow me to lead you to the dance floor," the man said bowing to Hattie.

Ruby looked like she was going to cry, not being the one asked to dance, but before long another man came to our table and whispered something in her ear that made her laugh.

Prince Albert took Hattie's hand and led her to the dance floor. It was a slow dance, and Prince Albert was holding Hattie real tight. I saw him try to kiss her and Hattie let him! His hand dropped and moved around to Hattie's backside where it was moving lower and lower. When he tried to kiss Hattie again, she pushed him away and came back to the table leaving Prince Albert standing on the dance floor with a bewildered look on his face. He didn't bother to come over to our table anymore, but there was a steady stream of men who did, all wanting to buy us drinks.

Ruby and Hattie continued to drink gin and gingers and to dance, coming back to the table only when someone hadn't put a nickel in the jukebox. The last straw came during one of these breaks when some loud talking roustabout wiped his hand across his mouth. "Would you looky here? There is three real movie stars in the joint tonight. Ladies, why don't you all come upstairs with me? I will make it worth your while."

Before I could say a word to him, the two women who had put cosmetics on Hattie and Ruby came over to our table. They looked bold and menacing. Red lipstick was smeared on one woman's face from kissing a man at the bar; the other woman's flaccid arm was raised in a fist. The one who did the most talking, was slurring her words through her chipped teeth: "What's this? You gals coming in to have a little fun is one thing, but when you take our business away that's something else," she said angrily.

I knew then there was going to be a fight. I ran to the back of the house yelling for Willard.

"Rhodessa, I'm just finishing my business. I got a big order tonight."

"Willard, come on. We have got to go now!"

"Well, I reckon I couldn't keep the possums away from you chickens all night. There was bound to be trouble."

Willard slipped Ruby, Hattie and me out the back door. We made a mad dash into the night until we were back to our automobile. We were all breathing hard.

"Willard Grimes, you took us to a bordello!" I yelled.

Hattie and Ruby were in the back seat laughing their fool heads off. "At least we can say now that we have been kissed," Ruby said.

"You are lucky that is all it was!" I said so mad I was spitting nails.

In the next day's newspaper there was a story about a city raid on a house on Shenandoah Avenue the night before. Roanoke City police and ABC officials had taken everyone present into custody where a number of arrests had been made.

Willard

I knew I had some serious makin' up to do with Rhodessa before I left on the biggest run I had ever made. I would be gone for a week or more.

"Rhodessa, I know you are sore at me. I planned a little somethin' hopin' you would let me out of the doghouse. Go get yourself dolled up and pack an overnight bag. You don't need much, just enough for a night."

"Really Willard? Just you and me?"

"Just you and me. Get a move on girl. I want to get where we are going by dinner time."

Rhodessa must have asked me a thousand questions tryin' to worm out of me where we were goin' until she saw us pull up in front of the Hotel Roanoke. "Oh, Willard, I can't believe you are bringing me here. Are we going to spend the night in a real hotel? Papa took me inside once to look at the railroad pictures in the lobby but I never in a million years dreamed I would be staying here. Papa told me this hotel once was a wheat field and had some of the finest rabbit hunting ever. Wait until Papa knows!"

I saw the look in her eyes as she remembered her mama and papa were dead. "Rhodessa, honey, they know we are here. They can see us from the other side," I said not puttin' stock in what I said but knowin' Rhodessa did. She believed in all the crazy stuff like angels and the hereafter. Rhodessa squeezed my arm as her way of saying thank you so I was glad I said it.

When the porter took our bags to the room Rhodessa about fell out with excitement. Her eyes were as big as saucers. I scooped her up and carried her into the room. I was wishin' I had brought her here for our weddin' night. But who's to say this couldn't be our honeymoon?

After an afternoon of window shoppin', a few purchases and a fancy dinner, we made it back to our room and had ourselves romance time. In the morning, I ordered room service. I had never seen Rhodessa so contented and happy.

I left two days later and met up with Big Jim's boys in Endicott. Big Jim wanted to supply the devil's candy to the coal miners in West Virginia, and I was gettin' in on the ground floor. I was goin' to make a pretty piece of change for makin' this happen.

We drove to an abandoned two-story, rock buildin'. I could sense apprehension comin' from the boys. I was to do the talkin' on this transaction and then drive the pilot car since I knew what to look out for on the back roads. Big Jim had two Plymouths outfitted special for hauling 'shine. I was driving my own vehicle. There were two boys for each car and another to ride with me.

It wasn't long before a Ford Roadster and two other vehicles showed up. Tom, the main 'shiner got out of his vehicle and walked towards me. All eyes were on me. I knew Tom's men were packin' heat and would use it if there was the least bit of trouble.

"Willard, some revenuers come close to getting a couple of our stills at Shooting Creek. There's fighting going on between us about who might be an informer. Hate to say, but your name's been mentioned," Tom said.

"There ain't no reason to suspect me. My name is gettin' around since I've gotten some big accounts and had cash to boot. You ain't got nothin' to worry about with me," I reassured him.

"We don't want no trouble," Tom said while taking a hard look over at Big Jim's boys. He then signaled for the Roadster and the other two cars to move forward. It didn't take long for the boys to unload and load. I paid Tom in cash. Our caravan pulled out quiet like with no lights, until we were a mile down the road and out of town.

We picked up speed anxious to get on our way. It was just past midnight. We hadn't gone ten miles when we saw a police car followin' us. We sped up, and so did the law, turnin' on his siren. Leroy, who was drivin' the last car, swerved back and forth to shake the cop. His partner leaned out the window with his .38 and started shootin'. The next thing we knew the cop's car was taking down mailboxes and headin' down an embankment.

I didn't see no more police cars the rest of the night so I knew we weren't being followed. The drive to West Virginia was dark and eerie with just the moonlight beamin' in.

"For death has crept in through our windows
and has entered our mansions.
It has killed off the flower of our youth."
Revelations 6:8

RHODESSA ROSE

Willard stayed with me the nights he didn't have business to attend to. He had set up some big deals with Big Jim, and it was his responsibility to make sure the law didn't bust them. Willard carried a .38 automatic under his floor mat. I handled all the 'shine customers that came to the house. Willard and I ran the still as my sisters had no head for business or interest in it for that matter. They weren't much help in the garden either. I had to get after them to pull weeds, milk the cows and feed the hogs. One of them was always ailing and taking to her bed. Then Hattie began coughing, and I sent for Dr. Riddle to come.

"I don't like what I am seeing, Rhodessa. Hattie's displaying some of the symptoms your mother had. Make sure she stays in bed and rests. Give her lots of broth and raise the window some so she will get fresh air. If she isn't better in a few days, get word to me. It could be consumption. Have Ruby move into your parents' old bedroom. That way Hattie and Ruby can both get better rest. There is lots of sickness in Boones Mill and all around. Stay close to home, Rhodessa. We don't want this thing spreading more than it already has."

Hattie wouldn't hear of letting Ruby move out of her room. "I couldn't stand being sick and left alone. Besides, you are never here, Rhodessa, especially when I need you."

"I am doing all I can and then some. It's up to Ruby to decide if she wants to stay in here with you," I said looking at Ruby.

"Hattie needs me with her. Hopefully, I won't get sick if I keep the windows open and rest plenty like Dr. Riddle said to do. Plus Hattie likes to watch me draw," Ruby said with a weak smile.

I knew then I would not have time for my mountain, at least for a long time. I tried to keep my mind off of Hattie and Ruby and their constant bickering. I thought about my parents while I did endless chores. I wanted to remember all the details of Mama and Papa falling in love. Each telling of their story had been a little different 'cause Papa always had something different to add. Mama was forever arching one of her eyebrows in surprise when Papa added something new into the mix. Papa sought out Mama's eyes while he talked and a tender regard passed between them. How I wished my parents were alive so I could hear their story again for I never wanted to forget.

I took Hattie and Ruby their breakfast after tending to Hattie all night. Hattie was drenched with sweat and delirious with a fever of 103 and calling out for Mama and Papa. She looked so small curled up in a ball under the flower patchwork quilt Mama had made for her when she was a little girl. I wiped her down with cold water, but it did little good. Ruby had gotten out of bed but would not dress. She sat in the rocking chair not saying a word.

Later in the afternoon Hattie's fever broke. She seemed to come round but was very weak. She wouldn't take a bit of oatmeal I made for her. I tried to lift her spirits with riddles. "What did the bride wear on her feet?"

"I don't know Rhodessa."

"Lady Slippers. Now try this riddle. What did the children call their father?"

"I don't care what the children call their father. Our father is dead. Stop your stupid riddles," Hattie cried out.

"The answer is Poppy. Poppy like the flower!" I started to sob as I ran from the room. Ruby followed me downstairs.

"Am I going to get sick too, Rhodessa, like Hattie? She's sick like Mama was and Mama died," the fear was speaking through Ruby's sunken eyes. It was then that I noticed how frail Ruby had become. I had been putting my attention on Hattie.

"No Ruby," I said, but I knew in my heart I was lying 'cause I could smell the sickness in her and felt guilty for it.

I walked over to the cannery to use their telephone and called Dr. Riddle. He came over the same afternoon. He spent a great deal of time with Ruby and Hattie.

"It is as I feared, Rhodessa. The rightful word is tuberculosis. It's going to get harder for you to care for Hattie and Ruby, and too risky. They need to go to Catawba Sanatorium where they can be looked after properly. Preacher Shiflett has helped other families make arrangements. Get that husband to help you, Rhodessa; you can't do it by yourself, nor should you," Dr. Riddle said firmly.

I made hot tea for my sisters while I got my thoughts together. I told them most of what Dr. Riddle said and promised them everything would be alright.

I had to wait for Willard before I could take Hattie and Ruby to the sanatorium. Willard was gone more than ever on business. I didn't know how many days he would be away.

Hattie and Ruby were often hot with fever. They each had a sputum cup within reach, which they needed more each day as they were hacking up phlegm and blood. I tried to give them rub downs with alcohol and begged them to eat. All I did was cook, wring out nightclothes and sheets or wait on customers wanting 'shine. We were almost out of sugar and cake yeast, too. I fell to bed in exhaustion only to awaken and start again.

Early one morning, there was a forceful knock on the back door. I thought it was a customer but it was the sheriff. "Mrs. Grimes, I'm Sheriff Greer. I had coffee with Lawyer Simpson early this morning. He said he had an important letter for you. I was coming this way so I offered to bring it myself," he said while handing me the official looking letter.

"My mother died of consumption and my sisters are both ill. I don't want you getting sick so it might be better if we stayed on the front porch."

"I'll take my chances. You can't be sheriff and stay away from the consumption, it's taking a heavy toll on the mountain," Sheriff Greer replied walking into the kitchen.

"You can't say I didn't warn you Sheriff."

"Where's that husband of yours anyway?" he asked looking around the kitchen and down the hallway.

"My sisters have been coughing real bad so I sent Willard to Roanoke to get some medicine," I fibbed. The Sheriff could hear my sisters coughing from their bedrooms, which made my lie sound good.

"I'll be on my way then. Or I can stay until you finish reading the letter in case you want to send a reply," Sheriff Greer offered.

"I don't want to detain you," I said, wanting him to leave fearful he was trying to get me to say something about Willard.

"Make sure you don't get sick too, Mrs. Grimes. It seems like you got your hands full here."

"Call me Rhodessa."

"If you have an emergency, Rhodsessa, call the office. I'm not hard to find, and tell that husband of yours I need to talk to him. He will know about what," Sheriff Greer said as he walked out the door.

I sat at the table for a time just looking at the letter. Something didn't feel right and I was scared to open it and what did the Sheriff want to ask Willard about? Finally I got up my nerve and unsealed the letter:

April 10, 1940

My Dear Mrs. Grimes,

I apologize in having to write this letter to you so soon after the death of your beloved father. It has come to my understanding that you are the one who handles most of your family matters, and to that end, I direct the contents of this letter to you.

Mr. L. K. Killgore was in my office yesterday, and in the course of our conversation I learned that the apple packing plant next to your property is using a stream, which passes near his cannery and which rises on your land. Mr. Killgore spoke of an agreement he made with your father in the fall of 1937, when your father still worked at the cannery. Mr. Killgore insisted that your father move the hog pen located next to this stream for a certain time before and during the time the apple packing plant is canning. He gave your father five dollars in good faith to do so. According to Mr. Killgore, your father, the late Claude Hartman, promised to carry out the necessary actions but never seemed to get around to it.

Mrs. Grimes you may not be aware of this but no hog pen should be on a stream for any part of a year, the water from which is used in connection with a cannery. The can goods would not be sanitary, at least they would not unless boiling the water might protect from germs. You should not place your hog pen where the excrement can get into a stream, and such pollution is an offense against the law. The penalty of this offense is fifty dollars. I hope, Mrs. Grimes, that you will remove the hog pen at once. Even to move your hogs during the specified times would hardly do as some hog excrement could still find its way down the stream. An inspector of canneries might condemn food canned under such conditions, and would certainly see to it that the hog pen is removed.

Mrs. Grimes, please be certain that you take care of this matter within the next thirty days as to not inconvenience Mr. Killgore, owner and president of the Apple Packing Plant, and to spare yourself any further distress by showing your neighbor goodwill and keeping your father's word.

Yours truly,

Joseph E. Simpson

Attorney-at-Law

"Lord, I can't move the hog pen myself or spare the fifty dollars. What bit of money I have is for Hattie and Ruby for the sanatorium. What am I going to do?" I said out loud.

"Papa is that why you didn't go to work? Were you fired for the times you were drunk at work or not moving the hog pen? Willard, where are you now and why don't you come home?"

Willard

Big Jim was takin' up more of my time. He was pleased with the Endicott 'shine operation and my part in it. We were all makin' a good chunk of change from the coal miners. I didn't figure there was any reason to tell Big Jim about the events that transpired in shooting a cop. Better to let sleepin' dogs lie.

"Willard, you have been doing fine work for me. So good that I want to invite you to one of the special parties I give my boys to reward them for their hard work," Big Jim said as he put his arm around me. I had made it. Big Jim's parties were legendary and not everybody that worked for him was invited.

Jim's house was all decked out like Christmas in April. An older gentleman met me at my car and took my satchel into the house. Belle greeted me at the door wearing a fancy red dress and a pearl necklace. I was taken aback having only seen Belle in overalls. I had to admit she almost looked pretty.

"Willard, I'm glad to see you. I'm acting as Big Jim's hostess. So are my girls. If there is anything you need just let one of us know," she said kissing my cheek.

"Is Big Jim's wife here?"

"Big Jim sent his wife and daughter to New York to visit her parents. He does that when he throws one of his shindigs. Go on in and get you something to eat and drink. You are going to have a swell time. Sometimes, these parties last for day," Belle laughed.

The food and liquor kept flowin' and Big Jim's hired help made sure our glasses and plates were always full. I wandered around the downstairs and counted four huge fireplaces with fancy decorated mantles. Fires were going and the house was real cozy. Big Jim was in rare form, all jovial with no talk of business. "Come into the ballroom, Willard. I got some of the finest musicians playing the latest tunes. I even got some dance teachers to make us all look like Fred Astaire and Ginger Rogers," Big Jim laughed.

Big Jim offered me a glass of champagne from Paris, France! It wasn't five minutes before one of Belle's girls was pullin' me to the dance floor. I must have danced with every female there. People just kept switchin' dance partners and carryin' on. I finally broke away sayin' I had to relieve myself and have a smoke. Big Jim was takin' people around his house showin' them his artwork collection. He was excited about somethin' new he just bought called a Picasso.

I was there for three days I think. I don't remember much. I do remember goin' upstairs with one of Belle's girls and several bottles of French champagne. I must have had a swell time. Parts of it I remember others I don't. I do know I can jitterbug with the best of them now.

Since Willard had gone off for God knows where I didn't have a way to the store to post a "Hogs for Sale" notice except to ride Donnie Wayne. This wasn't gonna be no easy task 'cause Donnie Wayne had these fat pockets on him and his saddle didn't fit so good. Donnie Wayne was a good mule for turning over the soil, but he don't like to walk fast. Donnie Wayne had ridden the trail to Boones Mill with Papa but he was a younger mule then, and Papa was a younger man. Donnie Wayne must have been about twenty-three years old now. There wasn't a time for me when there wasn't a Donnie Wayne.

"Donnie Wayne, you and I have got to go to the store and post a notice tomorrow," I said while tossing him some hay on the ground. "I know you are Papa's mule and you miss him dreadfully, but you and I have to work together. I wouldn't ask you to do this if I didn't need to get some supplies and need your help carrying 'em back up the mountain. I am gonna leave you some extra hay in your bin and some clean fresh water. It's good clean hay, no rocks or varmints in it. Think about what I'm saying and I'll see you in the morning."

I was up extra early to give me and Donnie Wayne lots of time. Donnie Wayne is big, about sixteen hands high and spent his life totally devoted to Papa. Papa traded a shotgun for the mule and then named the mule after the man. Papa claimed Donnie Wayne looked just like his previous owner and both of them was butt ugly.

Donnie Wayne wouldn't stand still for me to get the saddle on, so I stopped trying and brushed him for a while just like Papa used to do. After a while, we seemed to make our peace, and he let me put the saddle on. Starting out, Donnie Wayne moved so slow I had to constantly urge him to keep at a trot, which was near impossible, so we settled for just plain walking. Sometimes he would just stop and go no further. This was no fun at all. I cut a switch from a hickory tree to encourage Donnie Wayne to move along. My hitting him didn't seem to do no good. He'd just turn that big head of his around and look at me like I had plumb lost my mind.

The trail had about grown over from not being used. I knew Donnie Wayne wasn't about to walk on hard-packed gravel, going the long way the automobiles go, but we were able to follow the weedy ruts into the woods and stay on the hint of a trail to the General Store and filling station in Boones Mill. There was nothing more beautiful than being in the woods on Cahas Mountain on a spring morning, which improved my mood on the way down.

A fire was going in the potbellied stove in the corner of the store when I walked in, and it felt good. Several men I knew from here and yonder were joking and boasting while a mostly neglected game of checkers went unnoticed. Dalton, the store manager, was in the back unpacking some deliveries.

"Hey Dalton. Can you help me here? I got some pigs I got to sell, and if you could manage it, a little store credit. I'll pay you soon as Willard gets home. I promise I will," I said hoping not to sound desperate.

"I know you will Rhodessa. You're a good girl with a lot on you," Dalton replied as he wrote down what I needed to say and posted it on the store bulletin board:

Hogs for Sale –
Best Offer
Come to the home place
of Claude Hartman
Cahas Mountain.

"You might not get many folks to buy hogs. Dr. Riddle says there's too much sickness for people to be out and about. This consumption is killing some. Must be at least five have died so far on the mountain. The Kennys just lost their boy Timmy," Dalton said as he was getting the coffee, sugar and other things I needed.

I couldn't believe it. Mr. and Mrs. Kenny had been up to our place several months ago buying 'shine. Mr. Kenny was coughing and spitting some but I didn't think much of it then, I just got him a drink of water with the dipper. Timmy was only eight-years old and seemed fine. My head started swimming and I had to sit down.

"Rhodessa, are you alright? I didn't mean to scare you. I just want you to be careful with Willard gone so much. Here sit down and drink this Coca Cola before you start back up the mountain. It's on the house."

"Thanks Dalton." I sat there taking small sips wanting the Coca Cola to last as long as it could. After a while, I did feel better. I gathered my purchases and placed them in the burlap bag I had brought from home.

A couple of the men delayed my leaving, asking me questions about Willard's whereabouts. They said the sheriff had been asking questions about him. Then I got a bit of teasing about riding Donnie Wayne to the store, coming right through the woods the way I did. But it was all good-natured.

Having accomplished what I set out to do, Donnie Wayne and I started our long climb back up the mountain with me mostly walking and leading Donnie Wayne. I was aching tired when I got home. Hattie and Ruby were full of complaints for me being gone. Their lists of wants was a mile long. Going up those steps to my sisters' bedrooms, toting this, getting this, it seemed about like climbing the mountain with Donnie Wayne all over again.

It wasn't a few days before two hog farmers came by and bought the piglets, their mama and porker daddy. One old sow, named Lulu, nobody wanted. I was out of time and I didn't want to pay the fifty-dollar fine. I would have to kill Lulu myself.

At daybreak I set about filling the old drum with water and heating rocks on an open fire just like I had seen my parents do. The last time there was a fire like this was when Willard and I got married. Now it had come to this. Willard was gone to who knows where, and I was butchering a hog. I never did like hog killing. Mama and Papa usually spared me from this farm chore.

I don't know what I was thinking or not thinking that day. I didn't have nobody to help me hang the old sow up by her feet so her throat could be slit. I did have Papa's bolt-action 22 rifle. I would have to shoot her; there weren't no other choice. I didn't know how this shooting a hog in the head was going to work, without all the blood draining out. I wish I had Papa to ask.

"Oh, Papa why did you have to go and die? I need you here to help me. Willard is of no use to me. It might as well be him I shoot for the good he does around here," I said out loud.

It was hard shooting Lulu right between the eyes at close range, and forgive me Jesus, for thinking about Willard while I fired that shot and for just a split second wishing it was him. Lulu took the bullet while looking at me square on. Perhaps she knew it was coming, and that's why she stared at me the way she did. It gave me the shivers. It was like Lulu knew something I didn't.

I started thinking about Mama and Papa. We always had hogs. I felt like I had chopped off a part of my parents' life and my own with getting rid of the hogs and piglets. I couldn't stand feeling this way. Tears came to my eyes and fell down my cheeks. I began sobbing for Mama and Papa and from my tiredness, which had gotten the better of me.

"Get a grip," I told myself. "You've got too much to do here to feel sorry for yourself." But the tears wouldn't stop coming and soon, I was sobbing like a baby wanting Mama and Papa to make everything alright.

"Rhodessa, you here gal? I heard a shot fired!" a male voice called out.

Lord, it was Sheriff Greer!

"Good God Rhodessa, what are you doing shooting a hog in the head and crying too? What's ailing you?"

I couldn't think of a good answer so I just told him the truth about the letter from the lawyer and the fifty-dollar fine.

"You don't have Willard here to help you?"

I couldn't think of an answer and I was tired of lying so I didn't say nothing.

"Rhodessa, you can't do this yourself. I'm gonna call one of my deputies over here. Ain't no way a pretty mite of a girl can get that hog in that scalding water. Go sit down on the porch while I make the call on the radio and get someone over here to help us."

I wondered how it was that Sheriff Greer just happened to be passing by and heard the shot fired. I was too tired to ask. I sat on the porch and tried to rest when I heard both Hattie and Ruby calling for me wanting sponge baths, fresh gowns, and something to eat.

When I got back outside, the deputy had arrived. He was a muscular young man and well versed in hog killing. I had heard rumors about Sheriff Greer when he got elected. Seemed he had two years of college at Ferrum, unlike his father who was the sheriff before him for many years. People around here wondered if going to college helped any with being a sheriff.

I went into the kitchen and fixed cornbread, leftover pinto beans, and lemonade while the two men dropped Lulu in scalding water with the ashes in it.

While looking out the kitchen window I watched the sheriff unbutton, take off his uniform shirt, fold it and place it over a chair. Hog killing was messy business for sure. It would be a lie for me to deny that for a moment or two I let myself admire his manly build: strong shoulders, muscular arms and dark hair peeking out from his undershirt. The hair on his head was thick, dark and wavy. I had never seen such beautiful hair on a man. Sweet Jesus forgive me. I felt the steam rise in me just like the kettle Lulu was boiling in. Luckily, my sisters were sleeping and didn't see me take leave of my senses.

It was early evening when the deputy went home to his wife and children. Sheriff Greer stayed on. He and I worked side-by-side scraping the old sow clean. He helped me with the butchering and getting the ham all trimmed up. It seemed the Sheriff didn't have no place to go, and I didn't ask. I just plain needed his help. He didn't ask anything else about Willard, and I wasn't about to volunteer nothing.

"I'll be back to check on you tomorrow and get this ham strung up for you in the smokehouse. Don't you be trying to do it by yourself, you'll hurt something. Then we can tackle tearing down that hog pen."

Sheriff Greer kept his word, coming back this next afternoon and hanging the ham. I had already gotten it salted and the sausage made. We tore down the hog pen, working side by side like God intended man and woman to do.

When I had gotten Hattie and Ruby settled down for the night, Sheriff Greer and I sat down to a supper of pork on biscuits and applesauce. I didn't care if Willard walked in right then, I was so mightily peeved at him. I knew Sheriff Greer would give Willard a piece of his mind for not being around to help his wife and to care for her sisters. I didn't care about the judgments that would surely come from my sisters' mouths about having a man in the house who was not my husband.

Sheriff Greer continued to come by and check on me. Sometimes he would bring me wildflowers he picked on the side of the road. I got to calling him Jethro. He began to call me Dessa. I looked forward to his visits.

Willard

I was lookin' to hire a fella I could trust to help with deliveries as I was gettin' more and more customers. Hopefully whoever I hired would collect on my slots and make sure they were workin' like they were supposed to.

I was itchin' for a game of cards. It wasn't long before I found a game in one of the upper rooms over the meat market in downtown Roanoke. The regulars had been drinkin' and playin' a good while before I got there.

"Well, look if it ain't Willard Grimes come in the door. You here trying to steal more of our business or trying to cheat somebody else with those worthless slot machines?" Jasper Perdue said to anyone who would listen.

"Ain't lookin' for any trouble, just want to play some friendly cards," I said.

"Well, you won't mind playing a few hands with us then," Jasper said.

I looked around the table: Angus, two regulars and Jasper. The pickings looked good. Angus was watchin' when he wasn't noddin' off. Drunk as a skunk he was. I pulled a chair over to the table. We played on in the night, hand after hand, drink after drink. Lady Luck was bein' real kind to me. My winnings were pilin' up. "Reckon you lost again. Jasper, you can't play cards any better than you make 'shine. You owe me fifty dollars and you're a month past due on the machines," I said laughin'.

"I ain't paying you nothing. You and them damn slots machines. You think you're something coming into town like you a somebody. You ain't nothing but a hoodwinking cheat with all your bragging and billfold full of money," Jasper knocked over his chair as he stood up.

Some of the men started laughin' and eggin' us. Angus and Jasper were drunk as coots and could barely walk. Jasper took the first swing at me but I was ready for him. I swung back at Jasper and knew I had him when I saw his knees buckle and give way. Some of the men pushed Angus towards me but he was too far gone with his own rot-gut 'shine to 'cause me any harm. Jasper got up from the floor.

"I've seen that pretty little wife you bring around some times. One of these nights, I'm going to get me some of that. You wouldn't mind that now would you Willard? Letting her have what a real man can give her?" Jasper taunted.

Somethin' hard took hold of me when he mentioned Rhodessa like that. I went at Jasper with everythin' I had. After a few blows he was on the floor screamin' with pain. I kicked him in the head and gut again and again. There was a deep red gash runnin' down his face. I couldn't stop kickin' him. Some of the fellas pulled me away from him. By then, Jasper wasn't movin' or makin' a sound.

"Willard. You better get out of here before the law shows up," one of the boys said. After a brief moment I understood what was meant and ran down the steps and into the street lookin' for my automobile. I could have killed Jasper and maybe I did.

We had moved into fall. Without the leaves on the trees I could see straight to the cemetery from the kitchen window. I liked the feeling of my parents looking down from their hillside graves, like they were still watching over me. For the past few days, Ruby and Hattie had seemed to feel better. Maybe it was the cooler weather and leaving the windows open that helped them breathe easier. I wanted to take them to the sanatorium, but Willard had not been around enough to take them. Hattie was being particularly quarrelsome.

"Ruby, do you wonder if the sheriff is gonna come call on Rhodessa today?" Hattie asked with me standing right in front of her.

"Perhaps he is just trying to help, Hattie. He seems like a nice man," Ruby replied weakly.

"It's not fair we are sick. If I could stop this coughing, I'd get the sheriff to turn his attentions to me. I think Willard needs to know the sheriff has been sitting at his kitchen table, and it isn't about official business either," Hattie said.

"Willard isn't here, and I need the help the sheriff is offering. I can't take care of everything or you two are gonna have to do housework, sick or not. Ruby why don't you draw something with the new pencils Jethro brought you or write letters? Maybe you could teach Hattie to draw. I have work to do in the kitchen," I said as I left their bedroom.

I stood at the sink peeling potatoes. I needed some quiet time without their bickering. I was lost in thought when I heard a loud knock on the door. It was Jethro.

"Dessa, I'm here on official business. Come over and sit down," he said.

"Let me get you some coffee, Jethro," I replied, wondering if he had found Willard's still.

"This isn't time for coffee, this is serious. Where are your sisters?"

"They are in their room. I think they are sketching or maybe napping."

"Good. I have something to tell you, and you don't need Hattie and Ruby giving you grief about this. Turn the radio on to drown out our voices so nothing gets overheard," Jethro directed.

"It seems your husband had an altercation with Jasper Perdue. Willard beat Jasper up bad almost killing him, and left him lying on the floor in a pool of blood. Willard ran off when he realized how bad he'd hurt him. Jasper and Angus Perdue are bad news. It runs in their family. I need to pick Willard up before Angus and his clan find him and do God knows what."

"What's this mean, Jethro? What will happen now?"

"He's running from the law. Lock the doors, gal. From now on, you always lock your doors. I wouldn't be surprised if the Perdue clan don't come here looking for Willard. Not Jasper though, he will be in the hospital for a long time. He might not make it."

Jethro reached into his uniform jacket. "I want you to take this pistol and don't tell anybody where you got it. I'll be around watching out for you and your sisters. You won't see me, but I'll be close by. I'm not stupid, Dessa; I have been watching Willard for some time. My main priority now is to figure a way to keep you and your sisters safe."

Jethro didn't give me time to speak but rose from his chair pulling me up with him then tilted my chin so I was looking up at his strong face. I could read worry in his eyes. "I'm serious Dessa. I don't know what I would do if something happened to you."

With that said Jethro moved his head close to mine and kissed me tenderly and I let him.

Willard showed up in the middle of the night looking like a dirty-faced devil in muddy boots, eyes burning with a crazy fire. Sweat was running down his face and a bottle of 'shine was in his pocket. I knew Willard was in a heap of trouble 'cause Jethro had brought me the newspaper to show me:

"Battery charges against Willard Grimes of Cahas Mountain have been filed in the beating case of a Calloway man, Jasper Perdue. The altercation took place in a room above the meat shop on the Roanoke City Market. Willard Grimes is thought to be dangerous. Anyone with the knowledge of Willard Grimes' whereabouts is encouraged to contact the local authorities."

Willard stood in the kitchen looking at me funny. He could see the paper lying on the kitchen table.

"Rhodessa honey, I'm in a heap of trouble. You gotta help me out. I need some fast cash so I can lay low awhile. I'm not plannin' on spendin' any time in jail or worse. Go get your pearls and diamond ring. I never told you, but I won 'em gamblin'. I promise to get them back or buy you a bigger diamond from a real jewelry store, one no woman has worn before."

I walked to the bedside table, opened the drawer and retrieved the pearls. I pulled my engagement ring off my finger. "I don't want them anymore." I placed the necklace and engagement ring in Willard's outstretched hand.

"Rhodessa, things will get better real soon you'll see."

"Willard, stop talking and listen for once in your life. Take my wedding band too. I won't be needing it. You have sowed your oats before and after our marriage. I will no longer be humiliated. Now be gone with you." I was as surprised as he was at the words that came out of my mouth, but they were perfectly true. Willard left as fast as he came. Five days later, there was an article in the paper:

“Battery charges against Willard Grimes, a Country farmer and businessman from Cahas Mountain have been dismissed by a Roanoke City General District Court Judge. Quoting Mr. Jasper Perdue the victim of the alleged crime, ‘It was just a big misunderstanding with tempers flaring, no harm done.”

Soon after, Willard came home with his tail tucked between his legs.

"For the lips of a strange woman drop as a honeycomb,
and her mouth is smoother than oil."
Proverbs 5:3

Willard

Sippin' from a Mason jar always made things less ragged around the edges. I couldn't take much more of Rhodessa's sisters' bein' sick and carryin' on. I couldn't take no wailin' women. Rhodessa was still peeved at me for not bein' around when she got that letter from the lawyer to move the hog pen. She barely spoke to me, tryin' to freeze me out. I wasn't goin' nowhere though, I didn't care how cold she got. I had a business to run and Rhodessa's bad mood wasn't about to ruin it for me. The Sheriff comin' round made me nervous. He might have done some snoopin'. You don't have to walk too far up the mountain to get to the still. It was pretty well hidden in the woods but if you knew what you were lookin' for, reckon you could find it.

After a day or so at home, I had to get out of the house. Usually I went to the still to get away and have me a drink. It warmed my insides. After I drank a while I got to feelin' a little randy. Rhodessa was always too busy carin' for her sisters, customers or the house to pay attention to my needs. She didn't have time to walk up the mountain anymore, and she knew I liked the mountain about as good as she did. We had ourselves some fine times on Cahas Mountain, but it seemed like a long time ago. Some days, I plain got mad. That's when I put on my pinstripe suit and went to one of the juke joints. She didn't try to stop me 'cause she knew if she did I would stay gone longer and there would be more for her to do. All she wanted to do was work anyway so she could have at it.

When I walked into a joint I tipped my hat down over one eye as that seemed to be what the ladies liked. After I bought the ladies a drink or two they seemed to appreciate me. I wasn't one of these cats who was gonna spend his life wipin' his greasy hands on his overalls in some piss poor garage or waitin' for his woman to make time for him. Not me! I had plans, big plans. I wasn't meant to be no small potatoes!

Usually I told Rhodessa I had someone I had to meet or I was goin' on a run and didn't know how long I'd be gone. Sometimes it was true but mostly not. Mostly I didn't say nothin' and just left. Rhodessa didn't say much about my takin' off. It was like she expected it. She was so serious and no fun. She was always worryin' about money and who was goin' to take care of her sisters. Rhodessa Rose that's who! Hell, I was just out tryin' to have a little fun. Can't blame a chap for that!

I did my best ponderin' at joints. I had been thinkin' about Dr. Riddle's idea about the sanatorium. I could be rid of Hattie and Ruby and have a little peace at home. Maybe Rhodessa would do for me like a woman was supposed to do for her man and I wouldn't have to find my enjoyment elsewhere. I thought I'd take a little ride to Catawba to check things out and conduct a little business on the way. Kinda kill two birds with one stone.

Hattie and Ruby took a turn for the worse. I stopped listening to Hattie and moved Ruby into my parents' bedroom. Hattie's breath was shallow. She kept her arms folded over her chest in an attempt to protect herself against the violent coughing spells that come upon her. A pitcher of water stayed on the nightstand. I continually tried to make her drink.

It wasn't long before Hattie's cheeks had turned pale even with a running fever. I dampened washcloths and wiped her face. I placed pillows behind her back to help her breathe easier but time and time again she slid down into her bed and I had to pull her up again. Ruby was relieved to be in my parents' room although she did not say so. She seemed to rest better without Hattie in the bed with her.

I washed their sheets and nightclothes daily, sometimes more, as they were frequently soiled. I tempted my sisters with buttermilk biscuits, offering bites soaked with honey - to no avail.

I waited on my sisters while trying to keep up with the other chores. I was forever running up and down the stairs going in and out of their pale painted rooms tending to the pale women. Dried flowers in white vases sat by their beds for I had no time to change them and the seasons had changed. Lace curtains blew from the bedroom windows which stayed open all the time as Dr. Riddle had said to do.

All was ghostly pale except for the color of Hattie's blood. My sisters' health left me nervous and exhausted yet I could not stop caring for them. The house seemed haunted by our troubled sleep and nightmares. It was as if it was sick and grieving too. Like a tree, bending from prevailing winds, I felt myself weakening and knew that soon I would fall in this seemingly endless storm.

"Handsome is as handsome does;
Fine words butter no parsnips"
Proverb

Willard

I carried Ruby into Hattie's room where I could talk to both of them at the same time. I didn't want to have to repeat myself. Placing Ruby in bed with Hattie I told them what I had been rehearsin' all day. "You gals will get plenty of fresh air and sunshine at Catawba Sanatorium and all you can eat. You don't have to do nothin' but get well. Catawba used to be a mineral springs resort called Red Sulphur Springs and it's only eleven miles from Roanoke.

"We are not going to any sanatorium. People get sicker there, not better. Rhodessa's not sick, she can take care of us," Ruby said softly.

"Dr. Riddle says you have to go. Rhodessa can't take care of you anymore, and you are both too sick to take care for yourselves. When you are better, you can come home," I explained.

"Some folks never come home," said Hattie.

"Many do and there are men there. Maybe you two will come home with husbands," I teased. Ruby and Hattie seemed to take this comment into consideration so I knew I had struck the right chord.

It was noon the next day before I started drivin'. Ruby and Hattie fell asleep in the backseat for most of the ride. Rhodessa didn't say a word on the drive. I reached over and put my hand on her knee but she would have none of that and pushed my hand away roughly. I thought Rhodessa would be pleased her sisters would be at the hospital. There would be less work for her, and she could get back to runnin' the business. I tried to joke with her but there was no use when she was in one of her moods.

Just before we got to Catawba Sanatorium, I began talkin' to Hattie and Ruby wantin' them to wake up and be alert. I needed to make sure they were willin' to stay and be treated. I didn't want no problems.

“Yes sir, ladies I’ve already been here and checked it out. I came up here last week. Good thing the kind doctor who runs the hospital likes my blue jars. That did the trick, no waitin’ list.

“You will both get your breakfast on the front porch every mornin’ at seven sharp. No beatin’ that. You will have porch mates and can sit outside gabbin’ and readin’ magazines for hours like you girls like to do. They have sleepin’ porches so you will get plenty of mountain air and that will help you get better faster. Before long, you two will be gainin’ weight and be out on the croquet court. Might even find you some fellows and take to courtin’. I wouldn’t be a bit surprised. Bein’ at this place is like being on a fine vacation. It looks like we are here now. That ride didn’t take so long now did it? Take a look ladies. Did you ever see a finer place?” I said turning in to the entrance of the large brick sanatorium.

“Look at the sign girls. It says Catawba Sanatorium opened for business in 1909. See that iron pavilion over by the mineral spring and the gazebo? There are people in the gazebo right now. Have a look. You’ll be enjoyin’ that in no time at all. Now let’s go find the good doctor and get you ladies settled in.”

Willard and I helped my sisters settle in the small room they were to share until it was time for them to move to the screened-in sleeping porches. The doctors at the sanatorium thought it best for patients to get all the fresh air they could despite the weather. I promised to visit as often as I could but would be depending on Willard or Preacher Shiflett to bring me. I didn't think Hattie cared if I came or not because of her dislike of me, but Ruby would want me to come. Finally, a nurse told us we had to leave saying my sisters needed their rest. "Give them a couple of weeks before visiting. This will give them time to get used to their surroundings and build up the strength," the nurse said.

I had a queer feeling all the way home in the car. There would be no one but me at home when Willard was gone on business. Only me. I had never spent a night alone in the house before. That very night Willard told me he'd be leaving for a few days. The revenuers were making arrests in our area busting up stills and seizing vehicles.

"I got to lay low for a while, Baby Girl. I don't need any of revenuers comin' here and questionin' me. They won't be thinkin' you have anythin' to do with 'shining if you don't answer no questions. Many the woman don't know nothin' about her man's business. It wouldn't do if anyone got to thinkin' I was a snitch. Don't be takin' nobody to the still or sell any 'shine until I get back. It's a wonder they haven't searched our place yet."

"What will I do here all by myself? What if something happens and I need to get in touch with you?" I asked.

"You just rest. When I get back we will have some fine times, just you and me livin' here alone. Now let's go upstairs and do some spoonin' before I go," Willard said taking my hand and leading me to the bedroom. When I awoke the next morning, he was already gone.

Willard stayed away for the better part of two weeks. Several stills were busted up real close to us while he was gone. I saw revenuers walking our land but they didn't find nothing cause Papa and I had hidden our little house good. It wasn't the same at home without my parents or my sisters. I was not used to the silence.

Preacher Shiflett came by and checked on me. We sat at the kitchen table and talked. I liked it when he held my hand, and we prayed together. He offered to take me to church on Sundays as I didn't have a way to get there. I told him I didn't want him going out of his way.

"It's not a problem, Rhodessa. We would just have to leave early. My wife and I would like to have you in church," Preacher Shiflett offered.

"I don't want to be one of those women who attends church without her husband, and have everybody feel sorry for me."

"If you change your mind, let me know. Until then we can have our own little prayer meetings at the table."

I was getting comfortable with Willard's absences. It was peaceful, and I didn't have to work so hard. I had time to sit in the rocker, to read Mama's Bible and listen to the radio. I pondered on what a foolish girl I had been when Willard breezed into our lives. How I wished Mama and Papa had seen through him and kept me from marrying him, but Willard was a smooth talker and deceived them as well. I felt bad that I had stopped loving Willard. I wished it wasn't so but it was. It seemed like it happened suddenly but maybe it hadn't. Maybe my eyes just opened up a little bit at a time. Days would pass before Willard breezed in with some big adventure story of where he'd been and how much money he made by spending time with important people like Big Jim. Sometimes it looked to me he spent more money than he made.

"I've been to Baltimore, Baby Girl, that's where I got this Stetson hat. I had a grand time and wished you were along."

"Funny Willard, you didn't ask me."

"I didn't think you were up to it with you lookin' so tired."

"It would have done me good," I shot back.

"I brought you somethin', a pure silver hairbrush and mirror so you can brush that long hair of yours. Take out those damn pins now, and let your hair down a like it was I first laid eyes on you," Willard ordered me.

"Willard, you know Mama didn't allow mirrors in the house, she said they brought bad luck."

"That's just an old wives tale, Rhodessa, nobody believes that stuff anymore. You need to stop believin' such foolishness!"

"Where did the brush and mirror come from Willard? They don't look like something you would have picked out for me."

"I was in Wheelin' conductin' business with Big Jim. I ran into Belle Adler. She gave me the idea."

"How is Belle?"

"Fine. She was askin' about you."

"Next trip I want to go. I'd like to see Belle and Big Jim. They were real nice to me."

"My business ain't safe. You are better off here. I'll be leavin' here tomorrow to get a new automobile, probably a Buick Roadster or a Hudson Touring Car. I'm needin' somethin' that can run faster. Big Jim thinks it's time."

"Willard, you are talking about a lot of money! There are things we need more than a new car! We owe on our account at the store."

"I need the car for work, not that it is any of your concern!" Willard said with his voice raised.

I knew not to say anything else and went to bed where I faked sleeping.

It got where every night I sat at Mama's dressing table with that silver hair brush stroking my hair a hundred strokes, wondering what Mama would think of me now. I left the mirror on the dresser, glass side down, remembering Mama's warning. Every now and then I would be tempted to look in it, and sometimes I did, but I felt guilty for it. Before going to bed, I said my prayers and wondered if God knew where Willard was, 'cause I sure didn't.

Willard

Things had taken a turn with me and Big Jim. I had trouble runnin' shine from Endicott to the coal mines as the revenuers were on to me. I couldn't get Big Jim the quantities he wanted. I also couldn't keep up with my 'shine customers at home and the men who were leasin' slots from me were behind on their payments.

I had seen firsthand what happened to people who owed Big Jim money and didn't pay. I couldn't rest. Just the same, I had to keep up appearances. The 'shine contacts I had couldn't think I had fallen on hard times lest they stop sellin' to me. There were a couple revenuers who would look the other way, but that cost plenty and I didn't have the cash.

Word got to me that Big Jim wanted to see me. Big Jim and two of his men were waitin' for me in his parlor. They were listenin' to the radio and drinkin' scotch when I entered the room. I wasn't offered a drink or a chair, but just stood there as Big Jim gave me a dressin' down.

"I'm keeping tabs on you, Grimes. You are into debt with me, and I don't like it. The revenuers are your problem not mine. You got a job to do for me and if you can't, you can be replaced. Consider yourself warned." Big Jim looked at me directly.

Big Jim had no sooner finished his words when a radio broadcaster broke in. There had been an attack on Pearl Harbor. Big Jim and his goons turned to the news report with full attention. I took the opportunity to sneak out the back door and headed home to Rhodessa. Maybe this attack on Pearl Harbor was a good thing – for me anyway.

I was at home by myself listening to the radio when I heard the announcer say, "Japanese bombers have attacked the naval base of Pearl Harbor on the territory of Hawaii."

I didn't know what to think. I wished Willard was here to talk to but of course he wasn't. I was too tired to ride Donnie Wayne to the store so I just sat in Mama's rocker and listened to the radio. No one came by for 'shine. I was so relieved when Jethro walked in the kitchen door mid-afternoon. "Jethro, you don't know how glad I am to see you," I said hugging him hard. Jethro grew alarmed when I started coughing.

"It's nothing but a cold coming on, there's no need to worry," I told him. Yet I had my doubts. I had been coughing for about a week, and my head felt warm. *It will pass*, I told myself. It had too.

"I wish I didn't have to leave you, but I have police business I have to handle. Fix yourself some hot tea and take a nap. I don't want your cold getting worse," Jethro said, kissing my cheek before he left.

On the 8th of December 1941 I sat by the radio listening to President Roosevelt's speech.

"Yesterday, a date which will live in infamy – the United States of America was suddenly and deliberately attacked by naval and air forces of the empire of Japan. The United States was at peace with that nation..."

I heard someone knocking at the kitchen door. It was Myrtle and Lester. I was surprised 'cause they seldom came to see us, even though Lester's parents didn't live far away.

"Come in quick, the President is talking. Willard's not here, it's just me," I said. The three of us stood spellbound listening to every word coming through the radio.

"...so help us God. I ask that Congress declare that since the unprovoked and dastardly attack by the Japanese on Sunday, December 7, a state of war has existed between the United States and the Japanese empire."

"I am going to enlist in the Marine Corps tomorrow. I've talked to my folks about it. They took it hard but weren't surprised either," Lester said.

"Lester, you have to change your mind. Do it for me!" Myrtle pleaded.

"This is something I have to do, Myrtle. I want to be a Marine and I want you waiting for me when I come back."

"Take some time to think about it. In a few days you will see things differently," Myrtle said her eyes wet with tears.

"The Jap's didn't wait, no sir. Neither will I. No one does this to our country and gets away with it!" Lester declared. His face was red with rage and his voice loud.

Myrtle sat at the kitchen table, her face drained of all color. Just maybe Myrtle liked Lester more than she ever let on.

On December ninth, when Willard came into the house, he was blistering drunk.

"Willard, have you heard? Our country has declared war!" I attempted to tell him.

"They are just a bunch of blowhards in Washington. Nothin' will come of this, you'll see. Nothin' to worry your little head about," Willard said while holding on to the kitchen table for support.

"Don't you think you should serve your country? Lester is enlisting in the Marine Corps probably as we speak. Myrtle must be proud of him even though she's scared. I know his folks must be too."

"The war will be over before it starts. I need to stay close to home to take care of you and your sisters. I have responsibilities. You don't want me killed off do you?" Willard said raising his voice as he spoke.

"I don't need much looking after. You are never here, and you haven't visited Hattie or Ruby once," I fired back.

"Rhodessa, it sounds like you want me to enlist. Do you?"

"We don't have children and your parents are running their farm just fine. Jonah and Michael are plenty old enough to help them. It's not like you help your Pa anyway."

"I'm not needed here. Is that what you mean?" Willard said as he knocked over a kitchen chair in anger.

"What I am saying is that your country needs you more." Then I had a thought I knew must be true. "Willard, you haven't even registered for the draft have you?" Willard looked at me with such rage I stopped talking. He had never hit me before but it felt like it could happen tonight.

Willard stumbled off to bed. The next day, he took off again.

Day after day, I sat in the kitchen, with my morning coffee going cold in the cup. It seemed all I could do was gaze out the window at the large oaks where Mama and

Papa were buried thinking of the people who were gone and wishing Willard would go away for good.

I lay awake during the night with the sound of the rain keeping my thoughts company. It had turned to morning, and the rain had stopped. The house seemed quiet, as though it knew it was Sunday and a day of rest. A gentle melancholy had taken over it and me. I had been coughing during the night and felt cold some of the time and then too warm. I must have had as many thoughts as there were raindrops falling on the tin roof of this house my grandparents built.

There was no one here but me. There was nothing I had to do. I felt lonely for my parents, sisters and especially, Jethro. Now that the rain had stopped it came to me: I would fix myself a picnic of bread and cheese - and walk up my mountain. I would make myself do it. It would be good for me in spite of my tiredness.

The day was a cold but sparkling one with droplets of water still falling from leaves. They were soon gone for the sun was shining bright. I walked the trail from the barn, past a large fallen pine, which had come down during the previous day's storm. The crows were loudly talking to one another as if to say I was out among them and they welcomed me to share their day. The wind stirred ever so gently. Then I was with them. My family.

"Mama and Papa, I have come here to talk. There is no place on earth that is more peaceful than here with both of you. I am sorry it's been a while since I have visited. I have not been feeling well lately. I say prayers that I do not have consumption but am just worn down from all the caring I did for Hattie and Ruby. I know you feel my love coming your way when I look at the cemetery from the kitchen window. So many things are coming undone. Ruby and Hattie are sick, the country is at war and Willard is never home. I don't know what is going to happen next. Can you help me understand it? I envy you being in this peaceful place quietly covered up in your earth quilts. I brought some lavender with me. I know it's not time for planting but I wanted to bring you something. Hopefully, it will thrive and give a fragrance that will carry all the way to heaven and grow deep roots where your bodies are. Mama, am I going to live to be an old woman, able to sit and talk with you like I am doing now? I know you understand me, you always have. I pray for everything to be well with Hattie and Ruby and our country. Mama, I know you are praying and I bet you have Papa praying too, now that you are both in heaven."

The longer I stayed, the more peaceful I felt. At times I thought I should go home but what for? There was no one there and nothing to be done. I took the quilt from my shoulders and spread it out by my parents' graves. I wrapped my shawl tighter around even though I barely noticed the cold. After a bit, I grew sleepy and closed my eyes. A deep sleep came over me. I felt like a small child again in my parents' arms and safe from the world. I dreamed of banjos, guitars, fiddles and mandolins playing mountain melodies, and Mama and Papa dancing. I heard Papa's voice calling me his little Indian princess, which felt to me like warm molasses.

I awoke to moonlight melodies faintly swirling in the night air while the brightest of stars pulsed their messages of love calling Rhodessa Rose, Rhodessa Rose. I would be alright whatever else may come.

I had been tired before but not like this. My clothes were getting loose, and I didn't want much of anything to eat. I continually listened to the radio broadcasts of the war. Myrtle came by in her Pa's truck to see Willard. But of course Willard was gone. Myrtle didn't bother to hide her agitation that it was me home instead of him. Willard had told Myrtle I thought he should enlist, and she resented me for it.

"Lester was accepted by the Marine Corps. He's leaving for Parris Island at the end of the month," Myrtle informed me.

"Do you want me to go with you to see Lester off?" I asked.

"I won't be going."

"You have to Myrtle. You are sweet on each other. His parents will be there and so should you!"

"I will not be blowing any goodbye kisses to Lester. He shouldn't be fighting in the war but staying here working at the bank. If he really cared for me, he wouldn't go. We don't need Willard enlisting either and you had no business telling him so. Our family is Church of the Brethren and don't believe in war. If Willard gets any foolish notions, you talk him out if it. You heed what I say!"

Myrtle stared at me hard for full minute, her eyes blazing. Then she turned and left.

There wasn't much to celebrate New Year's Eve. Willard was gone as usual; New Year's Eve was the best night of the year for making money. I was in the parlor listening to the radio. It was almost midnight when there came a light knock on the door. "Dessa, it's me. Let me in."

My heart skipped a beat. I hadn't heard from Jethro in days. I threw the door open.

"I couldn't let the New Year happen with knowing you might be sitting here all by yourself. I know it's not right, but here I am."

"Oh, Jethro," I said throwing my arms around him.

"I've never seen you without your uniform! You look so handsome are you wearing your church clothes?"

"Something like that. I wanted everything to be special. I brought us a bottle of champagne with real champagne glasses. We will toast to the New Year, to the end of the war and your sisters getting well, Dessa."

"Thank you Jethro, for coming. I shouldn't say it but I have missed you. Your coming tonight means everything," I said with tears in my eyes.

"I've left you alone too long thinking I was doing the right thing. I can't deny how I feel about you anymore. You always made excuses for that no count husband of yours. You may think he loves you, but he doesn't. He only cares about himself. I don't mean to hurt you, but you need to hear the truth. Come with me tonight. Leave Willard, and don't look back."

I tried to breathe but couldn't. The coughing came on hard and fast. I could see fear on Jethro's face. Finally, the coughing stopped.

"Let me take you away tonight. I want to take care of you," Jethro pleaded.

"I can't think straight; this is all happening too fast. You had better go now."

Jethro did not leave but took me in his arms and carried me to bed. I wasn't as strong as I wanted to be; my resistance was weak. I fought hard against my desires but not so hard.

I suppose all adulteresses say it began innocently enough. Perhaps we convince ourselves we didn't see it happening. I wasn't loved by Willard, and I desired love. Willard claimed to love me, yet betrayed me again and again. Yet had I not done worse than he by sharing my body and my love with another man? I did not leave with Jethro. The costs for everyone would have been too high. Yet, I could not turn a deaf ear to what Jethro was asking me to do. I was tired and needed rest.

“Be aware that a halo has to fall
only a few inches
to become a noose.”
Dan McKinnon

RHODESSA ROSE

Jethro came by every day he could, checking to see if Willard’s car was in front of the house. He was always bringing something to tempt my appetite like Coca Colas and candy bars. He brought me magazines hoping I wouldn’t continually listen to war reports on the radio. One day, Jethro sat with me in the parlor and talked about what was in his heart.

“Rhodessa, I want you to know I’d be serving my country if I could. Being the sheriff I’m needed here, least that’s what the recruiters say. I’d go in a moment if it was up to me. My dad was shot when he was sheriff causing him to be crippled in one leg. That’s why he had to step down. My folks’ run a small farm, and I help them as best I can. It’s a hard life for them but they never complain, I’m their only child. Plus I need to keep an eye on you,” Jethro said then kissed me lightly on the forehead.

“What about other women? Why haven’t you married Jethro?”

“Jessie Meador and I grew up together. Her parents and mine were best friends. Jessie was an only child like me. We were always at each others’ houses. We started dating in high school. I assumed we would end up together, but she had other ideas. When we graduated from high school Jessie got a job at the bank, and I went to Ferrum College. It wasn’t long before she was going out with a guy that worked at the bank. She said she didn’t want to be married to a sheriff and worry about me being shot or killed. I guess I was blindsided. She married the guy at the bank and has a couple of kids now. She seems happy.”

“There’s not been anyone else?”

“Just a cup of coffee with a pretty girl now and then, until now.”

On days I felt poorly, Jethro made me lie on the sofa, plumping pillows under my head. He pulled the rocking chair up close to me and held my hand while we talked. He wanted to take me to the doctor but I wouldn't let him, raising a fuss anytime he brought up the subject. On the days I felt strong enough, we took a blanket to the woods and explored every facet of our love. I wanted to be outside so I could see and smell my beautiful mountain. If I had consumption, I didn't want to know it other than to protect Jethro, but he and I both knew it was too late for that.

We were in the parlor when a fit of coughing racked my body. Jethro pulled a bottle from his jacket pocket and got a spoon from the kitchen drawer. "Dessa, take this paregoric. I got it from a doctor I know in Roanoke," Jethro said while giving me a teaspoonful.

It didn't take but a few minutes for the coughing to stop and I could breathe again. "I have to lay down Jethro, the medicine is making my head swim and the coughing has taken a toll on me."

Jethro carried me to my bedroom and put me to bed. I started crying and couldn't stop for the gentle ways he showed his love for me. He held me until I was all cried out and then made me eat a candy bar, convinced I wouldn't eat anything once he left.

I'll be back to check on you when I get off duty. Don't turn the radio back on, Dessa. Get some rest," Jethro instructed me.

Jethro and I both knew I would turn the radio back and listen to news about the war. We also knew I was not getting any better and I was not strong enough to run off with him.

Jethro hated it when Willard was home, thinking the man a monster for his treatment of me. Nothing a husband and wife did in the bedroom passed between Willard and me as I was too sick or at least I had Willard believing so.

"Pack a bag and let me take you home with me," Jethro asked again and again.

"This is the only home I know. I can't leave my home place and the cemetery where my parents are. When I am stronger, we will find a way to be together," I promised hoping Jethro would understand.

Jethro made sure I had plenty of paregoric. He made special trips to Roanoke to get it for me. He had seen the night sweats and the terrible coughing that came on suddenly. Jethro could not bear to see my coughing spells and the toll it put on my body afterwards. After he gave me my paregoric, he would stay until the medicine calmed me enough to sleep.

"Dessa, you can't be left alone like this. That no account husband of yours hasn't been home in days. I'll take you to Catawba myself if I have to. When Willard gets back from God knows where, I am going to beat some sense into him!"

"Don't Jethro, it will just make things harder on me and you as well. I'll go to the sanatorium if I can't pull out of this soon. Promise you won't say or do anything!"

Jethro was afraid to leave me at night. The best sleep came when Jethro held me in his arms and rocked me in Mama's oak rocking chair. At times like that, I surely believed in angels.

Willard

I heard moaning the moment I walked into the house.

"Rhodessa, are you alright? Where are you?" I called out. Then I saw her, asleep in her mama's rocker in the middle of the afternoon. A cup of tea gone cold and an untouched plate of scrambled eggs at her feet. I knelt beside her takin' her hand. "Rhodessa, wake up. You're havin' a nightmare."

But she didn't wake up. There was a cold stillness to her until she began to cough. The sound of mucus had her in its grip. The color of red was down her dress, blood from the coughin'. I saw a bottle of paregoric by her chair and the spoon. I didn't recognize the bottle but was grateful for it being there. I poured the syrup into the spoon and into her mouth. "Drink this, Rhodessa. Take it all down." She was too weak to swallow, the syrup formed rivulets down her chin. I left her and ran to the cannery to use their phone. Dr. Riddle answered and within the hour, he arrived.

"I haven't seen Rhodessa recently though God knows I should have. She is one sick gal. She shouldn't have been left alone. She could have hemorrhaged," he said with a hard look on his face.

"You didn't leave the paregoric?"

"You ought to thank who did. Willard, you don't have a choice. You have to take her to Catawba Sanatorium. If you don't, she could die. I'll call the sanatorium and make the arrangements."

"My confusion is continually before me,
and the shame of my face hath covered me."
Psalms 44:15

RHODESSA ROSE

I don't remember Willard bringing me to the sanatorium or staying with me for the first two days. Once he knew I was doing better he took off, telling the nurses he had business to attend to. After a few days sleep, I began to improve. I was very weak and run down from not eating and constant worrying. I had consumption there was no doubt.

Ruby and Hattie seemed to be doing better. They had picked up their bickering where it left off at home. Patients were told to remain positive in their thoughts and in their talk, as part of the cure. Hattie and Ruby were reprimanded constantly by the nurses to watch what they said and how they said it.

The hospital grounds were beautiful even if it was still winter. The snow gave a brightness to the day and a stillness at night that sometimes took my breath away. For the first few weeks, I stayed in bed. After one week without a temperature, I was able to sit on the porch. It took another two weeks before I was allowed to wander the grounds. I felt as if I had been set free. Eventually I was able to take some light exercise which helped with my melancholy. How I longed to see Jethro. My thoughts were always with him. In truth, I don't know when I first fell in love with Jethro. I feel as if I have always known him, his kindness, his tender eyes and the smile that lighted my heart. I want to sleep in his arms, to bear his children and grow old with him. In my heart I know it was wrong for me to feel this way for I had taken an oath for life. In my prayers I asked Jesus for answers for my conflict was always with me.

I cried out in delight when my beloved appeared before me. It had been weeks since I had seen him last. He found me sitting on a bench along the walking path reading the poetry of Robert Frost.

"Rhodessa, you look so beautiful. There is color in your cheeks! How I've missed your smile. I would have been here sooner but had to be in court testifying against some big time 'shine operators and I knew you needed time to get well. I want you to know my thoughts never left you."

"I can't believe you are finally here! I am so happy I think my heart will burst!" I said as our eyes gazed upon each other.

Together, we walked the loop toward the barn even though men and women are not allowed to walk together at the sanatorium. In the mornings women walk toward the store and the garden, while men walk toward the barn and loop around. In the afternoon the paths are reversed. We did not care who came upon us. Jethro kept his hand on my elbow as we dared not hold hands for I was a married woman.

No one spoke to us, either sensing our need for privacy or because we were breaking the rules. I wondered if they could feel the secret longings that passed between us. I showed Jethro the flower gardens outside the patient pavilions although it was too early for anything but daffodils. We admired the view of the mountains and the serenity of the grounds. How I wanted to kiss his mouth, his brows, his eyes! There were rules against kissing as not to pass this horrible disease.

We slipped into the gardeners' shed. Jethro took me in his arms, parted my aching lips with his tongue and kissed me deeply. There were no thoughts of the sanatorium and the consumption that plagued so many of us here. I felt a moment of guilt knowing of my illness, but it was known that not everyone exposed to the consumption was overtaken by it and so far Jethro showed no signs of it.

A blissful afternoon was spent, our limbs entangled, among the potted seedlings and other growing things never letting go of one another except to breathe.

Will I be judged for loving a man with my total being who was not my husband? Am I to be found guilty in desiring to fill emptiness with what could be mine were it not for my husband? Did Willard's wrongdoings give me the right to my own misdeeds?

When the gray clouds gathered, patients assembled in the parlor. There were jigsaw puzzles, checkers and other games for amusement. On days like this it was difficult to escape my sisters. A tray with three cups of tea was set in front of us along with oatmeal cookies the nurses encouraged us to eat.

"It's not right for the sheriff to visit you. You are a married woman and people talk. People have seen you walking with him," Hattie rebuked me.

"He is my friend and has been a friend to you as well. He watched out for us when Willard was away." I say defending myself.

"We are not fools, Rhodessa. He loves you and so does Willard. It is shameful the way you act," Hattie continued as Ruby kept silent.

"It's not like that," I protested, but I knew it was. I could not hide my smiles or love filled eyes when my thoughts went to Jethro. Yet here I was pretending not to love him by keeping my face stone set. What a liar I was!

"You bewitched them both, that's what you did, leading them both on! We know you entertained Jethro in the house when you thought us sleeping!" Hattie said, her voice escalating.

"I don't deny it."

"Willard does not know the kind of girl he married." Hattie spit out the words.

"And you don't know the kind of man I married." I replied without thinking.

As soon as I spoke those words, I regretted it.

Spring gave way and so did the health of Ruby and Hattie. The weeks passed slowly. Summer was upon us. My sisters had improved, but it was only remission, and now, they were slipping away. A wild rose vine, blossoming with petals of red graced my bedroom window. Orange and yellow day lilies profusely bloomed as Ruby and Hattie's health deteriorated. It did not seem right somehow. I sat with my sisters helping until admonished by the nurses to let them do their jobs and take care of my own health.

The doctors and nurses did what they could and I was never far away. My sisters were given cornflower tea and chicken broth. Every day they had treatments for breathing. Hattie had spots on her left lung which showed on an X-ray. An operation called pneumothoraxy was performed with the doctor putting a needle through her ribs, injecting air to fill the chest cavity causing the lung to collapse so as to get the rest it needed. Soon after, Ruby needed thoracoplasty, for the spot on the top of her right lung had formed a hole. Three ribs were removed from her right side causing the right lung to collapse. My sisters could not speak afterwards as talking agitated the lungs causing more coughing. With the drugs they were given, they slept their days away. It was terrible to witness the wasting away of their bodies and not be able to do anything but pray. So tiny they were in their beds. Towards the end I had to place my ear close to their mouths to hear what they had to say the few times they had the strength to whisper.

Fall turned chilly and my sisters got no better. Willard came rarely and when he did, his visits were brief as he was always in route to some other place. I did not care. Time passed and winter was upon us. The birds stayed huddled deep within the evergreens for warmth. In the bleak coldness of winter, nothing moved. Infrequently my sisters found their way to consciousness, through drugged sleep, finding it all but impossible to breathe. They gave up hope of living and waited on the angel of death.

Hattie passed away on December 4, 1942 from a hemorrhage. Ruby followed one day later. The funeral service was brief, given by Preacher Shiflett. One service for two sisters. It was held in the chapel at the Sanatorium. I was too ill to go having fever and chills. Three staff members were in attendance as well as a handful of patients who insisted on being there. Doctors frowned upon patients attending a funeral because sadness took its toll on consumptives and could have dire consequences on their health.

The nurses gathered Hattie's and Ruby's things, meager as they were, and gave them to Willard. They did not want to leave me with remembrances of loss when I should be concentrating on my recovery.

Preacher Shiflett borrowed a Hearse from a funeral home in Roanoke and secured my sisters' bodies in the back with blankets. Willard's father made two more caskets for my family. Willard, his parents and Preacher Shiflett buried Ruby and Hattie in the cemetery, side-by-side, like they had been in life. Mama, Papa, Ruby and Hattie would be together in heaven for Christmas. I was a lamb lost from her flock. I had no more family. There was only Jethro, and loving him was a sin.

The darkness of the evergreens was all there was when I looked from the window of my room at the sanatorium. The air smelled like snow. Christmas was a few days away, but I could find no joy. I was lost in thought when Jethro came upon me.

"I got here as soon as I heard, Dessa. I am so sorry for the loss of your sisters. Are you strong enough to walk with me? You look so thin!"

No one questioned us as we left the building. The nurses saw what went on. How could they not? Yet they turned a blind eye when Jethro came. We walked on the path until we were out of sight.

"Rhodessa, you are shivering, wear my coat," Jethro said putting it on me.

Jethro helped me inside his car and took me into town where we had a cup of hot tea. It felt good to be with him in a normal way. It did not last long, as I started to cough. People looked at me as if to say, I was one of those people from the sanatorium, so we left. Once in the car, Jethro drove us to a quiet setting where we talked.

"Rhodessa, I have something to give you. It's an opal ring my grandmother gave to my mother. When you are well and can leave the sanatorium, we will face what lies ahead together. Wear my ring and know that I want to take care of you always," Jethro said putting the ring on my left ring finger.

I silently thanked God that my finger was bare, having returned my wedding ring to Willard where it undoubtedly lay in a pawnshop. I believed in Jethro's love for me. The ring told me all I needed to know. One day I would be Jethro's wife.

Willard came for me in the middle of the night throwing rocks against the screen next to my bed on the sleeping porch. He demanded I come outside and follow him to the gazebo. Once there, he bundled me in a blanket – I had not taken the time to put on warm clothes, thinking I would only be a minute - he carried me down the long drive. Willard wouldn't let me go back and get my things, the picture of my family, a poem Ruby had written, my small treasures. I should have protested, should have raised a fuss. I tried to talk to him, but he slapped me across the face.

"Nothing you can say matters now," Willard said in a cold voice.

I went quietly in the night, obeying my husband and letting him lead me down the lonely dark road, feeling rough pebbles through my bedroom slippers. Willard had parked his automobile by the side of the road where no one could hear it or me. There, Willard snatched the blanket from around my shoulders and pulled me into my dark night of terror. I could only protest weakly as he dragged me deep into the woods. He forced me on the cold, snowy, hard ground lifting my nightdress above my head. He ripped away my undergarments while using his other arm to pin me down. I yelled for Jesus to help but Willard slapped me harder this time. He used me with a roughness and carelessness that I did not know possible. I begged for mercy as only a pathetic creature could do, but he only laughed. I thought this would be my last night on earth. When Willard was finally through with me, he got up, zipped his pants and lit a cigarette.

"I found a letter, addressed to me, in Hattie's belongings. I suppose she died before she had a chance to mail it. She tells me about the sheriff a visitin' you in our own home and here at the sanatorium. Hattie wrote that Greer came to the house at all times of the night while I was gone and you thought your sisters were sleeping. If I find out any of this is true, I'll kill him, you know I will. You better hope I find that Hattie was lying in that letter. But I can't much ask her about it now can I?"

I tried to reason with Willard, but he placed his hand over my mouth so I could not speak.

"I got it planned out for you to live with my parents so I know Greer won't be sneakin' to see you. I got my draft notice, just like you wanted. My parents are goin' to watch over you while I'm gone."

I shall never forget the roughness of Willard tearing into me with his cruel hands and unwashed flesh. I still smell and taste the stench of him from the liquor on his breath when he forced his mouth on mine. I did kiss Willard deeply and with as much saliva as I could manage, not from the wanting of him, not from desire, but from loathing and my own wickedness that he should become as ill as I and die.

I never got to say goodbye to the doctors and nurses, the friends I made at the sanatorium or Jethro. How I wished I had yelled for someone to keep Willard from taking me. Dear God, why was there no one to help me? Mr. and Mrs. Grimes were kind to me, bringing me meals and speaking kind words. But they couldn't understand. How could they? If I spoke against their son, they would only believe it was because I was ill.

I am sure Willard told Myrtle things he suspected about Jethro and me. Myrtle relished her role as keeper of my shame. She had changed for the worse since Lester went missing after battling with the Japanese in the South Pacific. Lester's parents had been notified, but no further information had been given to them by the military. Myrtle's eyes blazed at me as if the war was my fault. I did not know her anymore.

My coughing got worse after leaving the sanatorium and the treatments I had there. Willard went to Roanoke and got several bottles of paregoric. It made me sleep. It seemed like now someone was always giving me a teaspoon of it. I didn't care. I wanted to sleep; it was better than being awake.

Willard told me he would have to report for induction soon. I did not care that he went, in fact the sooner the better. The people he was leaving me with felt like strangers. I feared Jethro would never find me here. How could he? I would write to him when I had the strength, hoping somehow to get my letters to him. If only someone I trusted would come to visit me, Preacher Shiflett perhaps. I would have to be careful. I had caught Myrtle sneaking into my room when she thought I was sleeping, trying to read what I wrote. I left papers with Bible scriptures written down for her to find hoping to fool her.

I saw nothing of life except through the bedroom window. I prayed but I heard no answers. Sometimes my thoughts were cruel and heartless, wishing Willard harm. *Jesus forgive me for such thoughts and keep my Jethro safe so he may come and rescue me from this dreadful place.*

"The wind bloweth where it listeth,
and thou hearest the sound hereof,
but canst not tell whence it cometh,
and either where it goeth;
so is everyone that is born of the spirit."
John 3:8

RHODESSA ROSE

Mrs. Grimes thought it was a good idea to bundle me up and have me sit on the front porch swing and breathe the fresh air like they do at the sanatorium. Myrtle was standing in the yard gazing at me like I am some despicable creature as an automobile turned down the road to the house. Myrtle took off in a flash calling for her mother.

"Aunt Nancy and Uncle Henry just turned down our road!"

Mrs. Grimes came to the porch to see what Myrtle was hollering about.

"Lord Jesus, the fireworks are about to start," Mrs. Grimes said as she wiped her hands on a dish cloth.

"Myrtle, do as I ask and take the boys down to the creek. I don't want them to hear what's going to be discussed. When your Uncle Henry gets out of the car, take him to the sawmill."

"Rhodessa, go to the side porch. Whatever you see or hear, I don't want you to make a peep. There's no time for you to go anyplace else. I don't know what Nancy would say to you, and I want to protect you, child," Mrs. Grimes ordered.

Mrs. Grimes gathered my blanket and quickly settled me where I wouldn't be seen. I wanted to know what all the commotion was about. Mrs. Grimes left and went to the kitchen rattling pots and pans as if nothing had transpired.

"Is it true what I heard Ida, tell me it's not true," said all 250 pounds of floral print entering the kitchen. This had to be Mrs. Grimes's sister, Aunt Nancy.

"It's true," Mrs. Grimes said.

"I knew something was wrong with you missing church. I had to call the Pollards to find out what was going on. They didn't know much, with Mavis staying in bed with a troubling pregnancy. You and Mavis have always been there for each other and this should be no exception. You should be caring for Mavis not Rhodessa! I don't know what you are thinking letting Willard bring Rhodessa here! You have other children to think about. Consumption kills people, Ida, old and young alike," Aunt Nancy's tone was stern.

"Willard hardly gave us notice he was bringing her here," Mrs. Grimes said.

"Well you should have had Willard turn around and take her back to the sanatorium, if you ask me," Aunt Nancy said.

"I didn't ask you. The poor child has lost her parents and her sisters. The first night she was here, I heard her sobbing through the bedroom door. Willard had taken off somewhere and left her alone. I couldn't bear the crying I heard coming from her room. When I looked in on her, she was leaning against her pillow, propped up to ease the coughing. Her face was streaked with tears, and the dark shadows under her eyes broke my heart. I asked Jesus to forgive me for not wanting Willard to bring her here. I gave my heart to the girl then, for I am one of those women who is at her best caring for the sick. Caring for Rhodessa is what I am going to do!"

"How long has Rhodessa been here?

"Almost three weeks," Mrs. Grimes answered.

"Three weeks and you didn't get word to me? If you would get a telephone, I wouldn't have had to bother the Pollards. No wonder there's dark hollers under your eyes. You are working yourself to death and worrying too!"

"I knew you'd get aggravated and I didn't want to hear it although I am sure enough hearing it now," Mrs. Grimes said as she set dishes on the table.

"At the risk of saving one life you could lose all and do I need to remind you there is a quarantine?" Aunt Nancy questioned.

"Yes, of course. Who doesn't? There's plenty of food in the root cellar. Not to mention canned goods and hams in the smoke house. We will make do, we always have."

"It's a lot of work caring for someone with consumption. You can't be asking anyone for help without putting them at risk. You are going to be all alone in this, except for whatever family gets exposed."

"We will do the best we can, and leave the rest up to the Lord. I know I won't be going to church for a while or seeing anybody except those that live here. You stay away too, sister. If I had known you were coming, I would have kept you away. Please don't come back until I say so, and pray for us. With any luck, by spring, this will all be behind us and Rhodessa will be well." Mrs. Grimes said putting cabbage on to cook.

"So there is no talking you out of this?"

"No, sister, there's not."

"I'm going to help you string this mess of beans. If I can't do anything else, I can do this and then I'll be on my way. But you can't say I didn't warn you. Plain foolishness this is."

"There is one more thing. You might as well know it all now," Mrs. Grimes said.

"What else pray tell?"

"Willard's been drafted into the army. He will be leaving soon for basic training and then shipped off most likely."

The room fell into silence except for the sound of two grief worn women snapping beans. The smell of cooking cabbage flowed through the air.

Myrtle

The creaking of my bedroom door woke me from the deepness of sleep. Then I heard the familiar sound of a Diamond match striking against the wooden walls that made up this home our Pa built. The smell of smoke moved towards me and circled me like a specter in the night. All I could make out was a bright orange burning circle and the familiar odor of a Camel cigarette.

"Willard is that you?"

"It's me, Myrtle," he said.

"Come sit on my bed. It's so cold in here and the fire has gone out."

"You know I can't. This is as close as I dare come. No use whinin' about it. I just came to say goodbye."

"You're leaving now! You told us you didn't leave until next week. You can't do this to us, sneaking away early," I said tears stinging my eyes.

"I don't like goodbyes. I have to do this my way."

"How long will you be gone do you think?"

"No telling. War is war. You got to promise me something Myrtle. Promise you will look through the bedroom door at Rhodessa. Talk to her and keep her from being too lonely."

"I'll sneak in to see her. I'm not afraid," I said not letting Willard know I already had.

"Mama would have your hide, and keep Jonah and Michael out of her room too. Have Michael look through the window and make funny faces at Rhodessa. See if he can make her smile. He's good at funny faces."

"I promise. I remember what you told me when you brought her here."

"Write me and tell me everythin' especially if she gets visitors."

"I don't want you to go. I think about Lester all the time. I may never know what happened to him or if he could still be alive. I couldn't bear to lose you too," I said starting to weep.

"Lester was brave to enlist. There ain't no pride in being drafted like me. I didn't even register until Rhodessa figured it out and called me on it. The way most people see it, you're a coward if you get drafted. What was I to do, Myrtle? I couldn't leave Rhodessa at the sanatorium with Jethro Greer wantin' her, but it ain't fair of me to leave her here either. Ain't nobody gonna understand what my real reasons are but you. What if somebody gets sick and dies by me bringin' her here? There ain't no fair choice here. I'm damned every way I turn."

There was a change in Willard's voice. It sounded like something in him broke in two. The sun was barely up as I watched him walk up the red clay road leading away from our home. I wanted to walk with him, but he made me promise not to. Willard turned one time to look back at home. I could make out the eerie glow of his cigarette, and I got this spooky queer feeling all over me that what I had seen was Lucifer's light. Then the glow was gone. Willard's hand went into his pocket and reached for his bottle. I could see his head tilt back and heard the sound of glass shattering as Willard used his best pitching arm to hit one of the quartz rocks on the way up the hill. I ran after him, but he was too far ahead. I picked up the shattered glass as best I could and laid a rock over it. A shard of glass cut my finger and I sucked the blood, the same blood running in Willard that runs in me.

I picked up the butt of his cigarette and walked far down the road away from our farm. I didn't want to think of it, lying on our land cursing our family if it was Lucifer's light. I took the paper off what was left and laid tobacco and paper in my open palm. Just then the wind began to swirl around me, picking up the tobacco and bits of paper, scattering them to the wind.

"Maturity is a bitter disappointment for which no remedy exists, unless laughter can be said to remedy anything."
Thomas Edison

RHODESSA ROSE

Willard was gone and I could not say I was sad about his leaving. He came into my room in the darkness of night and tried to hold me and kiss me goodbye. I wanted no part of it and turned against him. My heart was cold as stone. In the passing of the days, there had been no softening in me, nor would there ever be. It was Jethro I wanted. But would Jethro want me if he knew what had been done to me? I was damaged in body and soul. Willard was a man who did as he pleased and gave no thought to the misery he caused others. It was not the same for me. I tried to do what was expected, to be a dutiful wife, daughter and sister, but at what price? Maybe the life I was living now, ill and cut off from my beloved Cahas Mountain and all I cared for, was punishment for loving a man who was not my husband.

I tried to imagine walking up my mountain plucking wild raspberries and tasting the tart juiciness. Every rock and tree had meaning as I saw myself as a little girl climbing the wandering dirt paths. Sitting by a stretch of water that made up Maggoddee Creek, I could look up and see the morning mist clinging tightly to the mountain peaks. Remembering my mountain was a haven for my tired soul but then, my thoughts returned to the shadowy dimness of this room where I was held captive.

Myrtle left a letter by my bed while I was sleeping. I prayed the letter was from Jethro but it was not.

Dear Myrtle,

I bet you didn't expect a letter from me. There ain't anybody around here I can talk too. Not anybody that knows about home anyway. Maybe you could read the parts you think are ok to Rhodessa and the folks. Plus it saves me from writing separate letters.

I don't remember much about my last night of civilian life. I made it to the station just as the train conductor was yelling all aboard. It was hard to believe I was on a steam locomotive heading to basic training. I remember passing through some small towns, looking out the window and thinking that fellow is free and I am caught as I smoked the last of my cigarettes. It was Ft. Bragg, North Carolina I was going to if I didn't tell you before.

The army thinks I didn't enlist 'cause where it said religion I put down Church of the Brethren. I wrote it down 'cause of what the folks believe in. You know me, I don't believe in any of that malarkey. I'm letting the army think what they want about me and the Church of the Brethren. At least there is one thing the church and I agree on. They don't believe in no war. Me neither. Ain't my fight, ain't my war.

Getting a razor cut and being deloused was about more than I could take. Who do these people think they are, treating a man like that? I never seen so many fellows in one place before, most of em' babies. I know the army likes them young. I'm 27 years old. Hell, I'm a civilian at heart and ain't no army gonna change that. They might break those young ones, train them the way they want them. I've been out in the world. I know how things are.

Reveille at 0455 is bullshit, but I know what they do to fellas that sleep late. The barracks is bleak but it does have heat and running water. Some of the boys eat that up, plus getting an issue of clothes, like they never had nothing before and maybe they ain't.

The second week was better when I went through training on the Browning Automatic and the M1 Rifle. The drill instructor couldn't believe I shot a score of 292 right off the bat. What did they expect with me being a farm boy? I shot rabbits and squirrels every day. I knew then your big brother wasn't about to go unnoticed. Before long they are gonna be calling me Sir!

The paper the army had me fill out about life insurance kinda spooked me. I thought about being killed. I figured out the odds of me making it out of the army in one piece and it looks pretty good. I don't want Rhodessa collecting on that life insurance policy!

Willard

“My breath is corrupt, my days are extinct,
the graves are ready for me.”
Job 17:1

RHODESSA ROSE

I have fallen worse since Willard left. I am weak and haven’t the strength nor desire to eat. My throat feels ravaged, and I can no longer swallow without pain. I have been passing blood. Mrs. Grimes knows since it is she that carries out my slop jar and dumps it down the hole in the Johnny House so won’t nobody see, especially the children. I suspect Mrs. Grimes knows, like I do, that I don’t have long in this world. Sometimes I trace Willard’s postcards with my fingertips. Mrs. Grimes and her husband think it is ‘cause I miss him. If only they knew that I am glad he is not here.

Sometimes I heard my home calling for me, searching for me, wailing for me. My house on Cahas Mountain needed to be consoled. It needed footsteps and laughter. I knew the house was physically sick without having me and my family in it. I couldn’t bear the thought of it, suffering a long and painful death without me to love and keep it alive. My house needed me, and I needed to return to it. I tried to imagine Mama cutting mixed roses and placing them on the kitchen table. I could almost smell the sweetness of the flowers. I thought of the freshly baked bread Mama baked as she hummed in the kitchen, and her wonderful pies so warm and delicious. Maybe if I imagined this enough it would help the house to hold on until I returned. One day Mrs. Grimes brought me a letter.

“Looks like someone has written you from home, Rhodessa, the postmark is Boones Mill,” she says smiling at me.

Jethro knows where I am! I tear into the envelope the moment Mrs. Grimes is gone.

My Dearest Rhodessa,

Imagine my surprise at going to the sanatorium to find you were not there but had disappeared in the night and no one knew where you were. I was at my wits end to know if you were safe and to find out what had happened to you. I asked questions and found an old gardener who said he had seen Willard on the grounds and you with him in only your nightclothes. He would tell me no more. No one at the sanatorium would offer me more information than that. I drove to Hardy on a Sunday morning and visited the Church of the Brethren, having remembered you speak of how Willard's family were members there. I pretended to be a friend of Willard's. Churches are good places to gather information. That is how I found out where you are. I was glad to hear Mr. and Mrs. Grimes are good Christian folks and thought of highly. I know that Willard is now in basic training and that his folks are helping you to get well.

Rhodessa, I will not come to see you or write again as word would no doubt get back to Willard and there would be too many questions that could make life hard on you in your weakened condition. I feel as if I am putting you at risk by writing this, but feel it is necessary to give you some peace of mind. Please my dear, take rest and if you are able to write to me without raising suspicion please do. There will be time for us and we will figure a way to be together.

Yours truly,

Jethro.

If Jethro only knew what happened the night Willard took me from the sanatorium. He would have come and taken me from this wretched existence. There had yet to be a way to get a letter to him!

Knowing Jethro loved me kept me from going mad. I lived in a house full of people but I had no one. I feared in my heart that my time with Jethro had already passed, but I daydreamed and smiled when I reread his letter. Sometimes when I slept, he was here and we walked hand in hand in the greenest of meadows.

"Even in our sleep, pain which cannot forget falls drop by drop upon the heart until, in our own despair, against our will comes wisdom through the awful grace of God."
Aeschylus

RHODESSA ROSE

It grew tiresome forcing a smile for Willard's youngest brother when he looked through the window. I did not have the inclination or the energy. I did not want him to see me coughing up blood and wasting away so I asked Mrs. Grimes to keep the window shade down. Mrs. Grimes has been good to me on account of Willard, but I could tell she didn't want me here though she tried to hide it. She was right not to want me. She had to think about her own family and the infection I had brought into her home. How scared she must have been for her children! What had Willard been thinking bringing me here, except that I should not see Jethro again?

I believed Myrtle was watching me, for things to tell Willard. Some nights, she snuck out and went to the top of the road but I did not know what for except that I heard an automobile stop and male laughter.

I gave myself extra spoonfuls of paregoric during the day to sleep and not be bothered by anyone. At night, I lay awake with my thoughts, undisturbed by the others. It was then that I re-read what Jethro had written and I wrote my thoughts to him in a letter he would probably never see. I placed the letter in a hole I had made with a letter opener in the mattress and tucked it down in the feather ticking.

I looked for letters from Jethro but they did not come. If there had been any, Myrtle would have destroyed them. I had friends at the sanatorium, people that knew me and my sisters. How I would have liked to hear from them but they did not know where I was. I tried to think about sitting on the porch at the sanatorium, listening to the piano playing and watching the birds at the feeders. Although my sisters were close only to each other, they were still my family. Jethro came to visit me there.

My mind traveled in endless circles until my thoughts gradually slowed down enough for sleep and if lucky, dreams of my mountain. Sometimes my dreams were lovely as I walked the mountain paths where rhododendron bloomed. I stopped and dangled my feet in the cold mountain water of Maggodee Creek and in the trees the sparrows sang in the forest shade. At the top of my mountain, I raised my arms to the morning sun and the breezes from the mountain caressed me and told me I was home. I never wanted to leave these dreams.

Willard had told me that if I stayed at Catawba I would have died and that it was for my own good he took me away. He did not want me to dwell on the savagery of the night he stole me away, but instead used consumption as an excuse for kidnapping me.

Living in this house, with only my memories, I knew there were things worse than death. I tired easily. I was skin and bones. Whatever force was left in me must be spent for the secret life. Often I feared if I should get well, Willard would come home and again I would be his wife or instead, I would pass to the next life without seeing Jethro again.

I wanted to be left completely alone. I had no desire for nourishment or the prayerful murmurings of Mr. and Mrs. Grimes. I yearned to go and be with those I loved. It would not be long.

Often I fell into fitful dreaming. I would awaken with lips parched and my tongue feeling thick but sapless like a broken branch baked by the sun. Sometimes my dreams were of meadows, with ripening apple trees and I was a young girl with Mama. More than ever my breathing offended me by offering only a thread of air, drawing in and out ever so slowly. In moments of surrender I heard an undertone within me saying I was becoming a gentle breeze which soon would blow no more.

Sometimes I hear my mountain calling me to a narrow path that is my own to walk. Am I shedding skin? Am I coiled in this bed to strike at death and have it take me? My grief and loneliness have become my shroud. When will my redeemer come for me? Please, I am in a hurry. Take me now! But I am not baptized! Jesus forgive me.

Today, Myrtle came by with another letter from Willard. For some reason she thinks I need to read his letters. Perhaps if she knew the truth of what her brother had done to me she would feel different. Perhaps she would not, I do not know. The letter lies for days by my bedside table. It is not Willard I want to hear from. It is only Jethro. I read the letter in order to be done with it.

Dear Myrtle.

I know it has been a while since I wrote home, but I sure was glad to get your last letter. I wish you would write more about Rhodessa. What I am gonna tell you here ought not to be read to the others except for certain parts but I'll let you decide which ones. I reckon much of what I write will be censored and blacked out. Hopefully you can get the jest of what I am saying.

I have found myself in some hard fighting, killing krauts in Italy. Sometimes I get to thinking about how much it costs to kill one German and how much it would cost to kill me? Is one of us dead worth more than another? If Uncle Sam is gonna have to pay up for dead krauts, I'm owed something big. A real marksman, the army is calling me. They told me I qualify as an expert and will get a five dollar a month bonus.

I got a pass in Rome. I don't care if I get passes or not. I am partial to cognac now and I get the other fellas to get it for me when they go into the town. In the beginning, the men tried to talk me into going with them. A few times I went and blew off some steam, shooting pool and drinking. The others spent time with whatever women were there. All that made me do was think of Rhodessa. After a while, the boys stopped asking me to go. I'd rather lie down on a cot, if I am lucky enough to have one, and re-read letters from home. Some men have no one write them, nor no one to write to. Often I try to imagine Coopers Cove on a cold frosty morning, the quietness of the water and tall trees naked of leaves except for the evergreens. I see the fallen down chimney and sunken graves of the long deserted

Cooper farm, perfect for hunting. I'm a young boy with Pa and we are shooting rabbits instead of where I am now. I remember the 22 rifle Pa gave me the first time he took me hunting and how I laughed every time our pack of beagles howled wildly, hot on a rabbit trail. I felt like a man when I killed my first rabbit, and Ma cooked it and served it for dinner. I'd like to be there now looking for rabbit droppings, thick clover and teeth marks instead of hunting Germans to kill.

Do you know if Mama and Rhodessa got their cards? I sent Rhodessa a handkerchief with sewed in flowers. I mailed it hoping she would like it and it would make her think fondly of me. I wrote on Rhodessa's postcards about swimming holes, loafing around and how lousy the rations are. I make out like I have a pal or two. I made up lies so Rhodessa won't worry about me. Truth is I don't want to be chummy with any of the fellas. Why? To see them blown up to bits?

I didn't mention the cow barns I stay in, or sleeping under wagons where the rats stick their whiskers in my face or the days spent in foxholes filled with cold, steady, icy rain. Every day is about staying alive, wanting news from home, a good drink or a plug of tobacco. I've seen many a man lay dying calling out for his mama.

Most often we travel by night. I ride on top of the truck mainly. I like it up there, on top of the supplies away from the others. But I almost froze to death traveling through Italy. I ain't never been so cold in my life. I went numb.

The Germans laid many towns flat on into Northern France. We keep going, fighting, killing and getting killed through the Low Countries. Soon we will be in Germany.

Ma writes, but not often. Rhodessa never does. I wonder if things aren't going so good and nobody is saying nothing to me about it? We are told mail is hard to get through and not to be discouraged if it's a long time in getting letters. Part of me is glad you have moved in with Aunt Nancy and Uncle Henry since it is closer to your new job at the weaving mill. Whoever thought there would be so many women going to work? I guess you feel like you are helping since the mill has shifted to making nylon for parachutes. It's probably better for you to be working than being at the farm wondering about Lester. To my way of thinking Lester should have stayed with the bank. I shouldn't say this but if he had, he might be with us today instead of missing in the South Pacific. I could have told him he didn't have what it took to be a Marine, but didn't nobody ask. Still I am rightly steamed at you for not staying at home watching after Rhodessa like you promised you would.

Tell my little brothers I am thinking of them. I'm glad they are too young to see the hell of this war and they are still at home to be a comfort to our folks.

Your brother,

Willard

The days crawled by. I tried to read the Bible in my room but found it hard. I could not concentrate on the words of Jesus. I comforted myself with thoughts of my mountain and how it looked during the seasons. I loved them all. There was nothing so beautiful as Cahas Mountain in all its fall splendor of orange and gold, except maybe summer with the chirping birds, bright sunshine and wildflowers.

Mrs. Grimes thought I was sleeping when she came into my room with Mr. Grimes. Often I play possum not having the energy to engage with anyone nor the desire to do so. I hear things this way, sometimes things I would rather not hear.

"Myrtle came by today. She brought a letter from Willard. She told me not to read it until you and I were together. It's on the table by Rhodessa's bed," Mrs. Grimes said.

"Tell me how Rhodessa's doing before I read the letter out loud," Mr. Grimes replied.

"Her fever is worse, and she's been talking out of her head. I've been putting cool cloths on her face since this morning. Maybe hearing something from Willard will get through to her and pull her out of this," Mrs. Grimes said.

"Has she eaten anything?"

"Not so much as a sip of soup. I'll go fix her something else while you read scriptures to her. Don't start reading Willard's letter until I get back," Mrs. Grimes said.

Mr. Grimes read from the Bible. I couldn't concentrate on his words 'cause my thoughts were on Jethro. It was Jethro I wanted by my bed. I heard someone come into the room.

"Jethro, is that you?" I asked confused from my daydreaming.

"No Rhodessa, it's me, Mrs. Grimes. Take some of this soup, it's good for you," she said as Mr. Grimes pulled me up in the bed so I might eat.

I took a spoonful then shook my head no. I wanted no more. Mr. Grimes began reading as I fell back into my daydreams of Jethro and happier times.

Dear Myrtle,

It seems like years have passed since I was home even though I know it's not been that long. I will try to catch you up on what has happened since you haven't heard from me in a while. I have had time to ponder on many things, and I ask you to put up with me as I ramble on. I am in the hospital with a nurse writing what I speak. I am getting better but will tell you more about that as this letter goes on.

While I was in the Vosges Mountains, I thought of Cahas Mountain and Rhodessa Rose especially as the fruit trees were blooming in white, red and pink along the hillside and mountain paths. A couple times, I thought I got a glimpse of Rhodessa, teasing me, hiding behind a tree, then another tree, her footstep just ahead of me, taunting me to follow her. I wanted more than anything to catch her and pull her down on the mossy grass and to hear her sweet giggle. For a minute I was back home but it was just my mind playing tricks on me. The truth was General Hodges had us American and British ground forces attempting to take bridges over the main rivers of the German occupied Netherlands. That's when I shot a young German soldier right between the eyes. I walked into the woods to take a leak, and there he was. He just stood there looking at me. I didn't have no choice. He would go back and tell others where we were. What was he doing out by his self any way? Had he been scouting us or was he a deserter? I took aim at him and as I did I remembered shooting a pig like this when I was a boy just 'cause I could. The pig and the boy looked straight on at the barrel facing the bullet coming perfect and true taking them into the black pitch of death with its dark hole and oozing blood. I don't know if it was right, me killing the boy. I could have taken him as a prisoner. I know what Pa would say. But Pa wasn't here. Pa never had to be a witness to the likes of war. I searched the boy and found a picture of a woman, must have been his wife or sweetheart.

I took a silver cigarette lighter from his uniform. I took it 'cause I needed it and not 'cause I wanted it. That seemed to make it ok. I took his smokes. He wouldn't need them where he was. I pulled the boy into a thicket so not to be found, at least not for a while. There were wild animals there and men that are no better.

I've spent time thinking how it is that the Church of the Brethren was started in Germany and how the church spread to be a place where I was born and reared. Look where I am now having been shelled and shot at. It's a laugh, all this religious stuff. Me, I got the odor of dead soldiers swirling in my head and try as I may, I can't never seem to get the stench out.

Christmas came and my mind strayed to home. I felt myself homesick. The army tried to serve us a turkey dinner. I got a good laugh off that. I spent the day smoking cigarettes, having my blistered heels tended to by the medic and sleeping. I couldn't help thinking about my own bed, with Rhodessa Rose in it and Ma's cooking. The day after Christmas we were back to soggy potatoes, onions and beans. The fighting went hard for days. Sometimes the rain fell in torrents with cold winds blowing. Many the day I went from tree to tree in heavy fog looking for snipers, trying to get them before they got me, crouching in a trench, just me and my rifle, sometimes wet to the bone. I remember not being scared until the shelling stopped and the silence was all there was. We got orders we were heading for the front lines in Epinal, France. The Germans were putting up a stiff resistance. I just wanted to go home. Like I said this ain't my fight.

I didn't know how much time passed when I came to in the 59th Evacuation Hospital. I can't piece much together except for what I'm told. I've got head injuries 'cause of the shells blasting trees making branches and tree trunks go every which way. At least my skull wasn't blasted open and my brain wasn't sticking out like what happened to most of the boys in my unit.

I remember waking up in a clean night shirt. I kept looking at my hands and feet being glad they were there. I was glad feet didn't hurt me anymore and that I could go back to sleep in a real bed. I slept for days.

General Hodges came to see those of us that was left. He was concerned for what we had been through. Hodges had been an enlisted man and thought of himself as one of us. He told me I charged up a hillside and crawled behind enemy lines hurling grenades into German machine gun nests. There were 185 of us in the forest that day but only seventeen came out. He told me I was a hero, and the military was gonna give me a Purple Heart and maybe a Bronze Star.

I am given pills to swallow and the pain stops for a while. Sometimes I forget where I am. Often I dream of a thin misty rain on frozen roads and it is raining dead birds. While my head wounds are being treated and the bandages changed, the nurse holds my hand. She is going to help me write letters to Rhodessa and the folks telling them when I will be discharged. The doctors don't know how much time I need before I am well enough to leave. There are a lot of men here worse off than me. I will leave it to you to tell Rhodessa and the folks the parts of this letter they should hear.

Somewhere in the Bible, I remember Pa reading that at times the wicked man is spared in the day of calamity. It hardly seems fair that others who don't do nothing wrong die and the likes of me comes out alive. Maybe some people, like Rhodessa's sisters are born to the grave.

Your brother.

Willard

Mrs. Grimes' weeping caused me to arouse. I was confused about where I was. I opened my eyes and saw the worry on Mr. Grimes face and a sloop in his shoulders that wasn't there before. This much I had gotten from the letter. Willard would be coming home.

That night passed slowly, fitfully, as I alternated between wild thoughts and snatches of dreams. The ground was full of apples, some golden, some red, having fallen from branches bearing down under the weight of the heavy fruit. Then the apples all rolled away. The branches were bare. The bees and blossoms never came again and the orchards stayed empty except for a single rotten apple which still hung on.

I wanted to be alone, but Mrs. Grimes would have none of that. Her son was coming home, and she thought for him I would rally. I pulled the sheet over my head hoping Mr. and Mrs. Grimes would go away. *Leave me alone! Don't touch me! No more prying fingers or voices. Let the sheet be!*

"Too small to meet Jesus," I hear a voice say and then recognized it as my own.

Mr. and Mrs. Grimes were in the room. "Rhodessa what did you say?" Mrs. Grimes asked.

I raise my head from my pillow and sit up suddenly with a strength I had not possessed in months. "Do you see HIM? Do you see Jesus, look there? He is looking through the window!" I say pointing my index finger.

"No child, the shade is down. There is no one looking in. You are tired and have a fever. You need to rest now," Mrs. Grimes said.

Mr. Grimes silently left the room. He returned with a black cloth and covered the mirror. I knew what it meant. He wanted to make sure my soul didn't stay on earth when I left my body.

I knew it was the next morning 'cause I smelled the fire. I fooled Mr. Grimes and lived through the night. Like most days, Mrs. Grimes was boiling water to wash my nightdresses and linens in the large kettle behind the house. While the water heated up she changed my night dress and linens.

This morning, there was blood on my pillowcases and sheets. I had had no strength to reach for the slop jar, much less use it.

I studied my hands so thin with the blue. My belly was swollen large, mucus and fluid gathering there. Could it be? Was I with child? I had not had my lady time in months. *Oh, please Jesus, don't let it be Willard's!* There was a fire rising in me. I surrendered to sleep and rode blue veins through my large belly and into my heart where Jethro waited for me and his baby.

I awakened to Mr. and Mrs. Grimes talking. They were saying prayers that

Willard would be home in time to say goodbye to me. That evening, I managed to take a bit of broth. Not near enough for Mrs. Grimes, but something. I had been changed into a clean gown. I heard Mrs. Grimes say my brow is warm but not as hot as before. She thanked Jesus my fever had broken and I should live to see another day.

"Through the tender mercy of our God,
when the day shall dawn upon us from on high
to give light to those who sit in darkness
and in the shadow of death,
to guide our feet into the way of peace."
Luke 1:78-79

RHODESSA ROSE

"Jesus, is that you? I know it is! Thank you for coming for me. Yes, I can do that. I will follow you! Wait, let me put on slippers." I was so glad I woke up. I had heard something so gentle, so persistent. It was Jesus outside my window peering in through the glass! I was so very glad to see Him. I quickly wrapped a quilt around me anticipating the cool night air. With every bit of strength I had, I raised the window and climbed out onto the porch. Jesus was giving me the strength I needed. Jesus would show me what to do. I just had to follow him!

There was a chill in the night, a full moon, and stars shining bright. Jesus stayed ahead of me. He was easy to follow. Down the path behind the house, we went, past the sawmill, the grape arbor and the garden where the cornstalks left from summer still stood. I was so happy, laughing like a child. I knew where Jesus was taking me. I was to go down to the creek and follow it to where the water was at its highest; where children from times past had piled up rocks, damming up the water to make a swimming hole.

I tried to catch up to Jesus, to touch him, but I never could. He stayed just out of reach. I could feel myself getting tired and wanting to slow down and rest, the soft moss under my feet seemed to invite me to lie down, to spread out my quilt. But I kept on as my Spirit was on fire with the Lord, and Jesus beckoned me still.

When I got to the swimming hole, Jesus was standing in the tall pines. I could hear a voice from nowhere and everywhere speaking to me:

"He maketh me to lie down in green pastures; he leadeth me besides the still waters, He restoreth my soul; he leadeth me in the paths of righteousness for his name's sake."

Jesus, with an outstretched arm, gestured for me to get into the water. "Go in Rhodessa Rose, go in, wash yourself free of sin," the voice said.

Was that Jesus that was speaking to me?

I dropped my quilt on the ground and walked into the water, slowly feeling the smoothest of pebbles with my toes, then under my feet. The water was deeper toward the middle, as I walked toward Jesus. My long white night dress billowed as the creek water swirled around my hips. I placed both hands on my belly. My baby belly. I was being cleansed. I was forgiven and the life within me was being blessed. My baby and I were being baptized! I slowly laid back into the water until I was floating. I could see Jesus' face, with such tender eyes, hovering just over mine, smiling. I was at peace, flowing free! There was no more pain. My baby and I would go to heaven.

Mrs. Grimes

"Come now! Rhodessa is gone. Disappeared from her bed!"

My husband came running into the bedroom. It was the middle of the night.

"The window is wide open. She must have crawled through it or someone has taken her!" I said in a panic.

"There is a torn part of her gown hanging on the nail. Her quilt is gone. Get your shawl and a flashlight. I'm going out into the yard. The moon is full. I might be able to make something out," my husband ordered me.

I hurried as fast as I could and met my husband in the front yard. "I found a slipper on the porch. The other slipper is beside the house," he told me.

"Do you think somebody is carrying her? Who could have done such a thing? Rhodessa couldn't have done this herself. Why the window? She could have gone out the front door."

"Wait here. I'm going to get my pistol, and please be quiet in case someone does have her. They don't need to hear us coming." He said as he went back into the house.

Waiting for my husband to return with his pistol, I listened to the night sounds. "Listen, do you hear it? It sounds like a child's laughter coming from the woods behind the house."

We knew then to take the path that led through the pasture to the creek. I shuddered to think what we might find. Rhodessa had not the strength to raise her head to eat. She was a shadow of the girl she once was. *What harm may have befallen her? Who was that laughing and who had her?* My husband and I hurried down the path. Within minutes we found Rhodessa lying still under the moon's soft light.

Rhodessa was lying on the creek bed, by the deepest part of the swimming hole, completely soaked, with an expression of bliss upon her face. She had no fever. I could not comprehend what I was a witness too. My husband collected her quilt.

Kneeling by Rhodessa's side I brushed the long wet hair, away from her face. I placed my hand gently on her wet gown which clung to the roundness of her belly. I felt a movement. A baby. It could not be possible! "Rhodessa is pregnant, and I think her time is soon!" My astonished husband and I stared at Rhodessa for what we now knew to be true. So small and frail Rhodessa looked under the moonlight, but so peaceful.

We wrapped her tenderly in the quilt and carried her back to the house easily for she weighed no more than a child. I dressed Rhodessa in a dry nightgown as my husband closed the window. We tucked pillows under her back and head least she begin coughing. I fixed her chamomile tea but she roused not to drink it. Rhodessa slept quietly through the night, the next day and night as well. We did not leave her side. For the next three days she did not cough at all. She had no fever. Yet she glowed.

"Who are these that fly as a cloud,
and as the doves to their windows?"
Isaiah 60:8

RHODESSA ROSE

Mrs. Grimes tried to tempt me with chicken cooked tender in her big soup pot. She made broth with herbs the children collected. I did not have the strength to eat and because of me I was afraid my baby suffered. The pains had been coming all night, but I was too weak to call out for help. I prayed for my baby to live and that I might hold my child before I died.

Mrs. Grimes found me before the sun came up. I heard her call for her husband to come quickly. It wasn't long before I heard a gentle mewing and Mrs. Grimes placed my tiny precious daughter in my arms.

"Rhodessa, I need you to hold on just a little longer. It appears another baby is to be born." This time there was no sound except for the sobbing of Mrs. Grimes. "A son, Rhodessa, a perfect little man no bigger than the palm of my hand."

I had a daughter who lived and a son who would be with me in heaven. Somehow this seemed as it should be. From somewhere deep within me I was able to whisper words that were in my heart: "Don't let Willard know about my daughter. Promise me he will never know about her birth. Give her my opal ring as a remembrance of me. Take her someplace safe and give her to someone who will love her all the days of her life. When she is older make sure she knows of Jethro Greer." I was able to kiss my daughter's beautiful face before my eyes closed for the last time.

The peace of Jesus comforted me.
I needed nothing else.
Alas the winds came,
With visions of loved ones whirling,
I was neither here nor there.
My breath flew up and out of me
Traveling thru the window,

Making clear circles,
That ascended towards heaven.
A snow dove, of icy white appeared
Showing me steps,
I climbed them,
A door opened,
Mama and Papa, luminescent,
Beckoning me to come with them,
As I walked into the Light.

Mrs. Grimes

Rhodessa was so beautiful and brave as the pains overtook her, yet she did not cry out. It was as if she was being given help from the other side. I sensed angels or maybe it was Jesus who was with us. I had no time to ponder what I was feeling as there was much to do. With a few pushes, Rhodessa's tiny daughter was born. I placed the baby girl in her mother's arms and witnessed the look between mother and child. Such a look of love to behold! Then I saw that this was not the end of it. There was something else, another push and a tiny boy, born dead. As I was cradling him, Rhodessa slipped away from this world.

I instructed my husband to bring a wash bowl and a pitcher of water. I bathed my beautiful granddaughter through my tears. She was so small, I could not believe she lived. I wrapped her in a tablecloth my own mother spent hours stitching. I laid the child in a dresser drawer I placed on the floor, then washed my sweet grandson, held him and rocked him for the first and only time.

How I loved that baby girl when I first held her and what grief I had for the baby boy already gone. Feelings of joy and sorrow filled my body as I prayed for what to do. Why did Rhodessa want me to take the baby girl away from Willard? What had my son done to this lovely girl? A shudder ran through my body as I thought this. Even so why shouldn't my husband and I raise her? She was our own flesh and blood. Then a thought came into my head. Perhaps she wasn't Willard's daughter. Where did that thought come from? Could this be why Rhodessa wanted this child to know of Jethro Greer?

My husband came in the room after Rhodessa was cleaned and clothed. Together, we said prayers over our grandchildren.

"I trust Rhodessa knew what's best for her daughter even though Willard's our own flesh and blood. It is probably best we honor her wishes," my husband said, his eyes red rimmed with tears.

We talked and prayed for hours asking for guidance of what to do and then the answer came clear. With heavy heart our decision was made. I collected my egg basket from the kitchen and placed my granddaughter in it. Walking through the woods, my husband and I delivered Rhodessa's daughter to her new home with a shared faith that the good Lord worked in mysterious ways.

Mrs. Grimes

We got word to Preacher Shiflett about Rhodessa's passing. My husband then went to work making Rhodessa's casket. He never made a casket until someone actually passed over saying who was he to start carpentering before the good Lord decided to take a soul to heaven. For years, people came to see my husband about a casket for their child or infant. Most people offered to pay what they could but he would not take a penny. This was work the Lord called him to do.

From my cedar chest, I took the lace shawl I wore as a bride. I dressed Rhodessa in her best night dress. I knew why Willard loved her so. She was but a girl in the bloom of life.

We tried to bring the casket into the house, but it seems when my husband built our home the doorway and hallway were too close for a casket to make the turn. We had no choice but to bring Rhodessa to the front yard. My husband carried her outside and placed her in the casket made so lovingly with carved rosebuds, a cross and a baby sheep. I carried the infant boy, wrapped in my wedding shawl and placed him in his mother's arms. We didn't want to risk anyone touching Rhodessa or the baby for the fear of illness and thought it best to close the lid. How hard it was knowing we would never see her beautiful face or our grandson again.

It wasn't right or proper to have the girl laid out in the yard with chickens scratching all around and not in a parlor for people coming to show their respects. But these weren't normal times. I wondered if Willard could feel it in his bones that Rhodessa had passed on.

We borrowed a team of horses and a wagon to take Rhodessa's body to Cahas Mountain. Soon after daybreak, my husband and I began the sorrowful journey to take Rhodessa home. We didn't speak much as we drove the wagon, each caught up in our own grief. There were many sharp turns, people on horses and automobiles. We could have used the funeral home in Roanoke but it was a far piece for them to come to Hardy then to take Rhodessa Rose to her homeplace. It would cost money too. It seemed right taking Rhodessa and her boy home this way.

Coming upon Cahas Mountain I felt shivers run through me. There was something about it that seemed to speak to me, giving me comfort to get through the day. Purple violets grew wild and full, overlooking Rhodessa's family home. I could tell it had been a while since anyone had lived in the house. It needed a good scraping and painting as the white paint was peeling off. The weather had taken its toll. It had been a lovely home and could be made so again. I could see why the girl loved this place. Rhodessa would be pleased to be buried in her family cemetery.

There was a small gathering of folks when we pulled up at the house. Two ladies were in the kitchen having brought food. The ladies had cleaned the kitchen well. I thought the house welcoming with pretty wallpaper in the dining room. It had started to come loose in places and would fall down if something wasn't done soon. There were sketches framed on the walls of trees and flowers. I remember Rhodessa telling me that her sister, Ruby, liked to draw. I could almost imagine Rhodessa and her sisters playing on the staircase and sliding down the railing like my children did when they were little. I liked thinking of Rhodessa in this way. It made me smile on such a sad day. Men had gathered at the graveside preparing the burial hole. At noon, Preacher Shiflett began the small service:

"Rhodessa Rose Hartman Grimes was born on April 2, 1920 right here on Cahas Mountain. No one knew her but to love her. None spoke her name but to praise her. Though Rhodessa's suffering was most intense she bore it with Christian faith. Surely we know she has gone home to Jesus with her baby son. Although Rhodessa Rose and her child cannot return to us, we can be with her again in the home above, where all is peace and love. Heaven grows sweeter and brighter to each of us as one by one our loved ones gather there. With her sweet baby son in her arms, Rhodessa Rose will now rest peaceably with her sisters, Ruby and Hattie, her mother and father on this the 23rd of July, 1943."

Preacher Shiflett had more to say, but I don't recall the words. There was too much suffering in the day. Preacher Shiflett had us sing Rhodessa's favorite songs, the ones her mother taught her. There were no eyes without tears and no joy in the words as we sang *I'll Fly Away*, and *Go Tell It On The Mountain.* In spite of our sadness, the mountain shone bright with a purple hue. Looking up, I admired the steep but gentle nature of the mountain with its hardwood trees and flowering shrubs. A black crow sat watching us as if to say we had better do right by Rhodessa or else. I sensed deer and small game watching us, possibly loving Rhodessa as much as she loved her mountain, and they were there to welcome her home.

I saw the local sheriff standing at Rhodessa's grave after everyone else had left. His head was bowed as if he was praying. I tried not to question what I was seeing. Rhodessa's daughter was an infant and no good would come of telling Jethro Greer about her now. Time would tell me what to do. One thing I was certain, this was not the time. Mr. Grimes hitched up the horses. We had a long ride ahead of us with much to think about.

Once home, Mr. Grimes and I dropped to our bed but neither of us could sleep. I got up, and stripped Rhodessa's room bare: clothes, linens, even the window shade and made a pile of them in the yard. I found a tip of a letter coming out of Rhodessa's mattress. It looked to have been stuffed into the feather ticking. I pulled it out. It was addressed to Jethro Greer. Why was she writing to him? I would ponder on what to do with the letter later. I was too tired to think on anything. I placed the letter in the bottom of my cedar chest for safe keeping and went to bed.

The next morning, Mr. Grimes made a fire near the garden. Everything of Rhodessa's was burned to ashes. While the fire was burning and through my tears, I scrubbed the room with lye soap and then scrubbed again. I opened the window. I needed to let the sunlight in.

PART TWO

WILLARD COMES HOME

"Who hath woe? Who hath sorrow? Who hath contentions?
Who hath babbling?Who hath wounds without 'cause?
Who hath redness of eyes?
They that tarry long at the wine;
They that go to seek mixed wine.
Look not thou upon the wine when it is red,
When it giveth its colour in the cup,
When it moveth itself aright.
At the last biteth like a serpent,
and stingeth like an adder."
Proverbs 23:29-32

Willard

I didn't get word that Rhodessa and the baby were dead. Didn't nobody want me to know she was as sick as she was until I was back home. Claimed they were afraid of what I might do if I knew the truth. Keepin' secrets that's what they done. Keepin' secrets about my own wife and son. It weren't right.

I didn't let anybody know when I was gettin' home. I wanted to see the look on Rhodessa's face when I walked in the door. It was high noon when I hitched a ride from the train station in Roanoke. I met a fellow on the train whose Pa was meetin' him. They were goin' my way. I got dropped off a couple miles from our farm. They would have taken me all the way but I insisted on gettin' out when we got to their turn. I thanked them for their kindness. I wanted to get my bearings before I walked in the house and greeted Rhodessa and my folks. I was in uniform and carryin' my duffel bag. I can't tell you what kinda day it was or if I saw anybody in the fields. I was walkin' as fast as I could to get to Rhodessa. By now, she would be glad to see me and would welcome me home. We would go back to the way things were when they were good between us. We would let bygones be bygones.

I turned down the road to our house. Everythin' was the same as when I left. It was like time stood still but not for me. War changes a man, I knew this now. Nobody was in the yard when I got there. I walked into the house, to the bedroom, where Rhodessa was when I left. She wasn't there. "Rhodessa, where are you?" I called.

"Rhodessa, I'm home!" I yelled louder.

Ma and Myrtle came runnin' at the sound of my voice. "Willard you're home! Why didn't you let us know?" Mama was huggin' me tight.

"I didn't want to ruin the surprise," I said laughin'.

"Well you did that. It's good to have you home son."

"Ma, where's Rhodessa? I want to see her."

A funny look came over on Ma's face. "Myrtle, run get your father. He's in the sawmill." Ma was quiet. A feelin' of dread washed over me as she began to speak.

"Son, Rhodessa's gone from here. She's in a better place."

"What do you mean, has she gone visitin' or somethin'?"I asked as Pa came into the room.

He put his hands on my shoulders lookin' at me square on. "Son, we have some bad news. Rhodessa didn't get any better after you left. She got much worse. Jesus took her home to be with him. She's buried on Cahas Mountain with her parents and sisters."

"How come nobody got word to me?" I felt my anger risin'.

"Your mother and I thought it was best you got home safe, so we could tell you ourselves. We aren't fools, son. We know you like your drink. We were afraid you might start and not stop. We didn't want you driving and going off the road and hurting yourself or somebody else. We wanted you home where we could help you get through this."

"You should have let me know. I'm a grown man not a boy. You had no right not to tell me how things were with my own wife!"

"There's more and no other way to tell you but straight on. Rhodessa gave birth to your son. The baby was stillborn," Pa said with a look on his face I had never seen before. It was like he had somethin' more to tell me but stopped himself.

"Rhodessa would have told me she was pregnant, wouldn't she? She never wrote nothin' about it. But all of you knew and didn't tell me! It's not right you didn't tell me," I said wantin' to cry and put my fist through the wall at the same time.

"I'm sure she didn't want to worry you while you were fighting the war. You don't know the way it was. It's difficult to put in words what went on here. We didn't know Rhodessa was pregnant until the end. She didn't gain weight with the pregnancy. I thought she was swollen in the belly cause of the consumption. Perhaps Rhodessa didn't know herself; she was so sick. I should have noticed the signs more when I was tending to her. But we are here to tell you everything you want to know now." Tears fell down Ma's cheeks.

"Where are the postcards I sent Rhodessa?" I asked Ma.

"We put them in the casket with Rhodessa and your boy."

"She liked the postcards didn't she?" I asked noticing how Ma had aged while I was gone.

"She read them and looked at the pictures. They were by her bedside," Ma said with sadness in her voice.

"I did good by her didn't I, by sendin' them?"

"I'm sure it brought her a measure of comfort to think about you comin' home."

It was a warm evenin' and I went out on the front porch and smoked cigarette after cigarette. I drank what liquor I had left in my duffel bag. Word was out that I was home. A few of the fellas I used to run 'shine with came by.

But one of my headaches was comin' on. After a while I couldn't talk for the pain. The boys left me with my grief and enough 'shine to last for days. The days passed, one much like the other. I was lost in thought rememberin' some things and tryin' to forget others. Rhodessa was gone and so was my son.

It rained for days and then it stopped. The clouds had broken and showed a sky dotted with stars. I was in the swing when my folks came out to the porch to talk to me. They stood there just lookin' at me before Pa started speaking.

"Willard, you can't sit drinking and smoking on this porch day after day. Your ma and I have left you alone long enough. You know we don't abide drinking. I don't want your brothers seeing it. They look up to you going to war and coming home a hero. You need to set an example for them. Myrtle cared enough about you to move home. We want to see you get through this, son. I've looked the other way while you drank your liquor, but now I am telling you to stop. Your ma has something important to talk to you about and I expect you to do what she says," Pa said in his stern lecturing voice.

"What is it Ma?"

"We have to discuss naming your child Willard. I've waited for you to come home so I can put the child's name in the Bible, least he be forgotten down the years," Ma said softly.

"I can't do it right now, Ma. I don't even want to think about it." A sharp pain exploded in my head.

"Willard I don't want this to wait any longer. It must be recorded that there was a child born into our family. I insist on it," Ma said.

"I can't think about it now; my head is hurtin."

"Do what your mother asks Willard!" Pa said. Both my parents were hell-bent I give the baby a name right then and there, and they wouldn't let go of it.

"Ma, you do it. Makes no never mind to me what my boy's name is. He and his mother are dead!"

I had to get out of there. I needed a drink, to pass out, to stop the pain. I went to my bedroom, grabbed a full bottle of 'shine and headed for the woods. Pa had the good sense not to follow me. Ma named the child after me, Willard Grimes. I thought later that Ma put no junior after his name. I reckon she forgot.

"He that is good for making excuses
is seldom good for anything else."
Benjamin Franklin

Willard

All I could think about was Jethro Greer and the letter Hattie wrote while at the sanatorium. Probably made up lies about Greer and Rhodessa. Her sisters were always jealous of her. But where there is smoke, there is fire.

The letter claimed Greer had been at our house all hours of the day and night while I was gone doin' business and he had been at the sanatorium to see Rhodessa as well. What business do you reckon he had in visitin' her there? No sheriffing business I could think of. Many a man had looked at Rhodessa. I had watched them watch her. Nary a one would try anythin' knowin' she was my wife.

This was Rhodessa's guilt as well as his. A woman knew to be virtuous and let no man enter her home without her husband present. The porch was good enough to stand on and talk with her sisters present. There was no good to come from him being in my house, with my wife, alone. No good at all. Jethro Greer had to pay for what he had done.

Thinkin' about Greer put a sour taste in my mouth and I needed to get rid of it. Some of the fellows had told me about a gin joint in colored town. I thought I might as well check it out and see if they needed 'shine or a slot machine or two. It was time for me to get back into the business.

Pa had taken good care of my automobile while I was gone. He kept it covered up in the barn. I had $300 in service pay I had saved up. I put a couple of bottles of 'shine under the seat. My pistol was still there from before. I was grateful Pa had let the gun be, though it surprised me. I thought for sure he would have taken it, but then Pa would have seen that as thievin'. I sat in the car and had a few swigs while I thought out my plan. I knew how and where to find Greer, and I had my gun.

As I was drivin', I was feelin' the need to have a woman. It had been too long. I reached under the seat for my bottle. I poured some 'shine in my mouth and let it roll around on my tongue before I let it slide down my throat. By the time I finished the first jar, I had found the place. I parked my car a block off and walked towards the joint in the colored section of town. It was right where I was told it would be. I knocked on the door and told the colored man that answered who my buddy was that sent me. He let me in with no questions asked. I hadn't been there but a minute when a fine lookin' high yellow gal wrapped her arms around my neck. "Buy me a drink Mr.?"

"Sure thing darlin'."

She sashayed to the bar knowin' I was watchin' her walk with that ripe rear end of hers swingin' from side to side. She had some mighty fine curves and she knew it. Sittin' our drinks down at the table, she started runnin' her fingers up and down my arm. I liked her perfume, and admired her soft pouty lips, which were painted red. We had us a couple more drinks and were gettin' along swell. She seemed to know what a man needed before gettin' to the bedroom.

People around us were having a fine time, white and colored alike. Jazz was playin' in a back room. The guy on the horn was plenty good. A few card games were goin' on. I recognized several bootleggers I had done business with so there was lots of wisecrackin' and backslappin' between us.

The pretty gal and I had a few more drinks, danced, then ate us some big steaks. Before long I was kissin' her on the mouth and she was leadin' me upstairs. I woke up the next mornin' wonderin' where I was. The girl entered the bedroom in a short nighty bringin' two cups of hot coffee. "Come on back tonight, we can continue the party."

"Sorry, sweetheart, no can do. This evenin' I got to kill myself a sheriff."

Willard

When I got in the car, I reached beneath the seat makin' sure some 'shine was still there. I threw the empty jar in the backseat and opened a full one. I took a long swig for the road and began to drive. It was rainin' hard by time I hit Boones Mill. Just a few more miles and I would be at Cahas Mountain. I took another long, slow swallow. It was goin' down smooth. I laid down the jar and picked up my gun. I liked the feeling of cold metal in my hand. I was feelin' good. I was ready for anythin'.

"Where are you Greer? Come out and play!" I shouted.

I pushed the accelerator hard, fifty, sixty, seventy when I saw the bastard behind me all sirens and flashin' lights. Greer knew my car and that it was me drivin' it, of this I was sure.

"I bet you think you got me, you bastard, but you've got another thing comin'," I yelled out the window.

I wasn't about to let Greer come to the car with his gun drawn. I wasn't givin' that bastard any advantage. I'd keep the fool in my side mirror as long as it took. "Come on Greer, pull on up next to me so I can blow your fool head off," I yelled out the window. Greer stayed right behind me. The asshole must be thinkin' I was gonna pull over, can you beat that?

I'd shoot back at Greer, I remember thinkin'. I knew I was weavin', but I could drive, hell I was a good driver even drunk. One of the best! I leaned out the window, got me a good aim and fired one off but I didn't figure on the road takin' a turn just then. I went off the road slammin' the brakes, into a deep gully. My car rolled over, and I hit my head hard on the steerin' wheel. Before I knew what happened I heard the cockin' of Greer's gun. Lookin' towards the sound, I saw the barrel aimed straight at my head.

"I should let the Perdue boys finish you or kill you now claiming you resisted arrest. Nobody would know the difference, and I would be doing the world a favor. In memory of Rhodessa I won't, but know that the Perdue boys aren't finished with you. You almost killed Jasper after your card game at the city market. They won't be forgetting that. It might be in your best interest if you moved away from here and don't come back. Do you understand me Grimes?" Greer was starin' at me hard.

He turned and walked back to his patrol car. I had a clear shot at his back, if only I could have found my damn gun.

"Hide our ignorance as we will,
an evening of wine reveals it."
Heraclitus of Ephesus

Willard

I got a job at the American Viscose plant workin' in the cloth room. I needed to save up for an automobile as mine was too far gone to be fixed. Pa let me drive his truck to work. Standin' up most of the day and doin' work that was boring as hell, might be ok for some knuckle heads but not for me. I wasn't cut out for punchin' no time clock or having a boss over me. I needed to be my own boss. For a while, I had tried working with Pa in the fields, in the hard packed Franklin County red dirt, but there wasn't enough money in it and I had to put up with Pa's sermonizin'.

I was given to drink every chance I got, except when I was under my parents' pryin' eyes, but Pa knew I could tell. More often than ever he was quotin' me something from the Bible. "'Wine is a knocker, strong drink is raging, and whoever is deceived thereby is not wise.' This is from Proverbs 20:1, Son. You take heed and read your Bible," Pa pontificated.

I couldn't take Pa's preachin'. Sometimes, my head would start to throbbin' and a bad headache would take over. I needed to get to Big Jim. I knew that I had to buy 'shine and get myself established again.

Sometimes at night when I was in bed, I would start recollectin' Rhodessa's voice, soft like whisperin' wind. It was like Rhodessa was a ghost callin' me in, laughin' and sweet smilin'. Sometimes I wondered if I was livin' in Rhodessa's dreams and wishin' I was. But there wasn't no way to go back to the way it was when she and I lived on Cahas Mountain.

Willard

I drove Pa's truck to the feed store to pick up supplies. I don't remember skiddin' off the road and hittin' a tree. I must have gotten out of the truck on my own or been thrown out. I don't know which. All I remember was pain comin' on quick and HIM havin' a hold of my head. Blood was comin' out of my flesh from the thicket of blackberries I was tangled in. All I could do was be still. I was afraid to move 'cause if the pain in my head got worse, I would go crazy. The damn bullfrogs wouldn't shut up, gettin' louder and louder mockin' me as I lay there wantin' to die.

It was gettin' cooler as the sun was goin' down. It had been noon when I started out in Pa's truck. I made myself crawl up the creek bed, through the weeds and briars, over the cracked red dirt to the truck. There had been a pocketknife and a can of pork and beans in the floorboard when I left home. I hoped they were still there. They were. The keys were still in the ignition but the truck wouldn't start. There was still some 'shine left under the fake bottom I had made in Pa's truck. I checked my pockets for cigarettes and my lighter. Smokes no, lighter yes. Damn, my lucky rabbit's foot was gone. I never went anywhere without it in my pocket!

With the last of my strength I picked up enough kindlin' to start a small fire to keep off the chill. There wouldn't be anyone passin' this way after dark. I cursed myself for takin' the back road. I sat by the fire and took some swigs of 'shine. I fingered the cigarette lighter, flickin' it again and again. My hands didn't seem able to stop messin' with the damn lighter. The face of the German soldier I killed was before me with his dead eyes and the devil's slow grin. He was smilin' at me as if to say "I got you now boy!"

I was sweatin' in shiverin' skin as the shakes took hold. With my head turned up, I guzzled what was left in the bottle, to kill the pain and the visions, and to silence the talkin' tongues in my head. With my eyes wide open, hungry flames danced, lit up blue and red, as skull-like heads with devouring mouths circled round me.

"Jesus, I ain't ever called on you before but if you are out there, make it stop!" Instantly the pain, the visions and the voices in my head disappeared.

Willard

I came to, hearin' voices but not the ones in my head, men's voices. There were two of them. It was the Perdue brothers. Flashlights beams were gettin' closer. I was face down with red mud in my nostrils and mouth. My breath was ragged. Hell, what happened?

"Looks like Willard's making it easy for us to find him with his Pa's truck being off the road. You know his Pa ain't the one out drivin' this time of night." Jasper Perdue said in a deep slow drawl that was only his.

"Good thing we're going coon huntin' or we never would have seen it. Ain't that right Bo?" Angus, the other Perdue brother, said as the Bluetick hound dog got himself a head scratch.

"Maybe we can get Bo to flush him out and tree him for us," Jasper said laughin'.

"Even a good coon dog like Bo don't want nothin' to do with the likes of him," Angus replied.

I lay as quiet as I could as the voices came closer.

"We were fools to drop the charges before we went to the pawnshop. They wouldn't give me next to nothin' for that diamond ring and pearl necklace since they weren't real," Jasper said.

"We should have known better after he leased us those worthless slot machines. Willard Grimes has lost us a lot of money, and when I find him, I'll get it back one way or another," Angus replied.

"You look in the direction of the creek. I'll stay around here and beat the bushes. He's around here somewhere. Smells like he had a fire, so he's gotta be close. Good thing we got moonlight," Angus said.

The crunch of feet was getting close. Before I knew it the dog was right on me givin' out a long hollow moan. Angus's boots were in my face. "Well speakin' of the devil himself. I found myself a grimy bastard. Jasper get back over here and see what's in the brush. What do you make of the great Willard Grimes now?"

"I heard tell Willard came back from the war with his head all messed up. He looks like somebody that's escaped from the penitentiary or the nut house," Jasper said shining his flash light on me. Both brothers laughed.

"His chest is still going up and down and it looks like he pissed himself so he must be alive," Angus said.

I didn't move hopin' they would think I was dead or passed out and leave me there.

"Let's roll him over and see if he's got any money on him," Jasper said.

I continued to play possum as their hands searched my pockets.

"Ten dollars is all he's got and this here shiny cigarette lighter. I'll be takin' that. Damn you Grimes. We want our money. Guess we will just have to take it out of your hide," Jasper hissed.

I felt the first kick to my gut, the pain searin' through me. I tried to get up to fight but I couldn't stand. I made it to my knees. That was all I could do. They took turns kickin' me and laughin', sayin' I was gettin' my comeuppance. I curled into a ball tryin' to protect my gut while they continued to kick me with their heavy boots. Then they stopped.

"What should we do with him now? There ain't much sport in just kickin' a man when he can't fight back," asked Jasper.

"Hell, I don't know. He ain't movin' none. Just dead meat," Angus said.

Lyin' there in the dirt all twisted and broken the taste of blood filled my mouth. I could no longer see.

"We did a good job of workin' him over. He'll think long and hard about messin' with us," Jasper said.

"I noticed a fence post that's almost falling over up on the road. I suspect there's enough barbed wire to go around Willard three or four times if we do it tight," Angus replied.

"He deserves the barbed wire and more for putting me in the hospital."

"Yeah, let's have a little more fun with him, like he done you, little brother. Grimes will feel it plenty. He's getting his due don't you worry about it none."

"Well, let's get started then," Jasper replied.

Jasper held me upright while Angus wrapped the wire around me. The pain was such that I could not speak or cry out but prayed for death. I pitied my folks when my body was found after man and animal had finished with me.

"I told you the wire would go around him three times," Angus said.

"Yea, you were right. That's real handiwork," said Jasper.

"Let's have some 'shine to celebrate, Grimes ain't goin' nowhere," Angus said laughing.

"You are right about that. But now that we got him tied up good, I don't reckon we should just leave him a lying here," said Jasper.

"He's alright just where he is. Let's you and me get some shuteye. When it's dawn we'll put him in the back of the pickup and let him roll around while we make the curves. We'll throw him out at his Pa's farm," Angus said.

"Yeah, let's take him home to his Mama.

Myrtle

It was first light when I heard the dogs barking. Something was wrong. Fast as lightning I jumped out of bed and ran to where the dogs were. I found them growling over my brother's body at the top of our road.

On my God, Willard!" My heart was racing in my chest. I couldn't tell if he was breathing. There was so much blood and barbed wire. But then he moaned real loud.

"Ma, Pa, Come quick. It's Willard. He's bad off," I yelled running to the house as fast as I could.

My parents both came out of the house in their night clothes. We all three ran to Willard.

"We have to get this barbed wire off of him before we can carry him home. Run, Myrtle, get the pliers and the wire cutters in the barn then go to the house and bring me rubbing alcohol and a strong blanket. We'll need it to carry him home in. Have the boys go to the neighbors as fast as they can and call the doctor. Go now, girl!" Pa ordered.

I returned as quickly as possible after doing what I was told. I forbade my brothers to see Willard. This was no sight for young boys.

When Ma poured alcohol over Willard's wounds he screamed like someone possessed. Pa slowly and gently began cutting the wires every few inches. Ma and I both had to hold Willard still so Pa could get the barbs out.

"Grit your teeth boy and think about the pain of Jesus on the cross. Jesus will get you through this," Pa commanded.

One by one Pa pulled the barbs from Willard's mangled flesh, ripping away at his bloody clothes. When Pa got too tired to go on Ma pushed her long hair behind her ears and took up where Pa left off. Her gown was soaked through with Willard's blood. My mother was always dressed proper with her hair in a bun; I never wanted to see her this way again. Taking turns, Ma and Pa worked on Willard until the last barb was out of his sorrowful body. I stood by watching, helplessly not knowing what to do.

"If I never knew it before, I know now that there is evil in the flesh. My lineage, my son, lost to deprivation. The devil himself caught up with him," Pa said looking down at Willard.

"We have suspected Willard has been doing things he ought not be doing which are against the law. We have heard rumors about his being involved in 'shine. I now believe it to be true," Ma said as tears ran down her face.

Willard lay naked and bleeding on the dirt road, on a quilt Ma's mother had made. I had never seen a naked man before. Willard's bloody clothes, torn to shreds were discarded all around him.

The doctor arrived and examined what Ma and Pa had done. He said there was still much for him to do. He wanted to take Willard to the hospital in Rocky Mount but Pa would not hear of it, claiming Willard would get better care at home. The doctor kept insisting but Pa held firm telling the doctor Willard needed to have the scriptures read to him night and day.

The doctor, Ma, Pa and I each took a corner of the quilt and carried Willard into the house to his room and placed him in the very bed he was born in.

"My house burned down but anyway,
It was after the flower petals had already fallen."
Tachibana Hokushi

Willard

The doc gave me somethin' for pain and I slept for four days. Four ribs were broken, my shoulder dislocated, and my eyes were swollen shut. Three of my teeth had been knocked out and there had been internal bleedin'. More than 300 stitches were in my face and body. It took the doctor more than four hours to stitch me up. I was covered in bandages. The doctor came to see me several times, checkin' my stitches and givin' me pain medicine each time he came. Pa stayed up all night, sittin' in the rocker by my bed readin' scriptures out loud. By day, Ma sat with me as much as she could. Myrtle cared for me in the evenings after workin' all day at the Weaving Mill. She fed me my suppers and did all she could so my parents could rest and spend time with my little brothers and stay caught up with their chores.

A couple weeks passed, and all I did was lie in bed. Ma changed my bandages every day. It hurt like hell. She wouldn't let me get up until the bleedin' and oozin' stopped, rubbin' salve all over my wounds, like the doctor told her to fight infection. Myrtle continued feedin' me what Ma cooked. I couldn't eat without spillin' most of it on myself. After nothing but broths and chicken soup Ma starting fixin' soft stuff like soup, eggs and boiled down vegetables. After I was feeling better Myrtle started readin' to me from some ladies' magazines, mainly recipes. I think this got me to eatin' more, and I started to get my strength back. Sometimes Myrtle and I would listen to radio shows and laugh over the Blondie and Dagwood comics in the Sunday paper.

"You're a good kid Myrtle. When are you gonna get married and have a family of your own? You are plenty old enough, that's for sure," I teased her.

"After you get well, and I can stop worrying about you, which might be forever. Plus all the good men around here are fighting the war."

"You will find someone else, Sis. You've got to get on with your life."

"There is a saying Willard, that you can't step in the same river twice. I don't know who said it, but it's true. I won't never have peace of mind until I find out what happened to Lester. He could still be alive as a prisoner of war or just lost somewhere in the jungle."

"You know there's almost no chance of that."

"You know, big brother, if you hadn't taken' up with Rhodessa, wouldn't none of this ever happened to you."

"You don't mean that Myrtle!"

"Without Rhodessa, maybe things would have stayed the same and you never would have left home." Myrtle stared at me, her eyes as dark as coal.

I tried to talk to her. I wanted to know how she could be thinkin' like that but she turned and walked out of the room. She didn't come back for three days.

I got out of bed and started walkin' around a bit, mostly to the front porch. After a while, I could tolerate the swing which became my day long restin' place. Like a pendulum, I swung, waitin' for somethin' to break the rhythm of each endless day. My little brothers were full of questions. I didn't have no answers young boys should hear so I stayed quiet. Pa got me some tobacco and papers though he thought better of it. He wouldn't let me have nothin' to drink, nothin' I wanted anyway.

"How long is it gonna be like this? I need to get out of here and get on with my life. I'm almost well," I said to Pa.

"Patience is a virtue."

"Patience is for old fools," I countered.

Pa slapped me hard across the face, his eyes blazing with anger. Our eyes locked hard for what seemed like minutes and then Pa spoke to me in a gentle voice: "Son, you cannot fix an egg once it's been cracked; only Jesus can."

Then Pa turned and walked away in the direction of his sawmill. He was goin' to read his Bible.

I didn't speak another word to anybody for days. There weren't nothin' to say. I was gettin' thirstier by the day. The doctor came to see me one last time, pronouncin' me a lucky man to be alive. I had scabs and bruising all over me. The itchin' was drivin' me crazy. I hadn't had a drink for what seemed like ages except for the small amounts Myrtle brought me hidden in her purse.

Pa managed to find his old Chevy truck where I had wrecked it and hauled it home. Jonah and Michael spent several days in the barn helpin' Pa fix it and get it runnin' again after all their chores were done. They were his good sons, nothin' like me. They liked church and workin' with Pa on the farm. They were a help to the folks and not a bit of worry.

The next day before the sun was up I took my money from where I had hid it in a tin can behind some loose boards in the barn. I was behind the wheel before the old rooster crowed. Pa's run-down beaten up truck lurched and rattled as I drove away. Good riddance was all I had to say.

Willard

I took off to West Virginia to see Big Jim. I needed a good time and to make some money. I had to blow off steam. Pa would be rightly ticked about me takin' his truck but he could get by. He bought the horses he used to carry Rhodessa and my son back to Cahas Mountain from Old man Simpson who was only too happy to sell. Pa often said he would like to have a couple of good horses instead of Jack and Rowdy. Rowdy wasn't a good plow mule; he was always in to somethin', and Jack was the slowest walkin' mule you ever did see.

It must have been four in the afternoon when I rolled into Wheeling, West Virginia. My belly was growlin', but my thirst was worse. I needed me a shot, hell a whole bottle, of somethin' strong. I heard music comin' from a juke joint and ambled on in. The room was badly lit, and the air was heavy with smoke. People stared at me then looked away goin' back to their own business. I squinted my eyes to adjust to the tobacco haze and the dim light, surveyin' the scene. My head was poundin'. The scabs from the barbed wire were itchin', particularly around my ears. Some of em' was infected I could tell. I asked for a bottle and the bartender was happy to oblige.

"Anybody up for a game of cards?" I asked the bartender after the alcohol calmed my nerves.

"Son, from the looks of you, you ain't got money to bet, much less lose," came his reply.

"That ain't no way to talk to somebody with almost 300 dollars in his pocket, ripe to spend, and a friend of Big Jim's to boot. Anybody seen him?" I asked loud enough for the other men at the bar to hear.

"No, but I know where he is. There's a big race today. Wheeling Downs. He'll be at the track. His horse, Devil Darling, is racing," a man at the bar answered.

"Then I know where to find him." I said payin' my money, takin' the bottle and walkin' out the door.

A day at the race track was what I needed. My mind was full of big ideas when I pulled in the parking lot at Wheeling Downs. I parked as far off as I could from the main entrance so no one would see me drivin' an old beat up pickup truck. I had a reputation to maintain.

It didn't take me long to spot Big Jim. He always had a crowd around him. At his size he was hard to miss. Big Jim always wore a bright colored suit and a necktie, didn't matter where he was. He was usually smokin' a big cigar. Belle was there too, larger than life, in her bib overalls and cowboy hat. I caught Belle's attention before Big Jim had a chance to see me in the crowd. I signaled for her to come over to me. I saw her whisper something to Big Jim, and I got nervous. I didn't want Big Jim to see me yet but he didn't look my way.

"Damn Willard, what happened to you? You look like hell," Belle said when she got to me.

"Just a little trouble with some barbed wire."

"What did you say to Big Jim?"

"Just that I was going to the ladies room and would be back directly. Big Jim's been asking around if anybody has seen you since you got home. It's probably a good thing you showed up today before he sent his boys out looking for you. It's time you got things straight with him. He doesn't care if you have been in the war or not." Belle warned.

"I'll work my way to him in a bit. I wanted to talk to you first."

"Make sure you do. There's a couple of fellas never been seen again that didn't settle up with Big Jim."

"Belle, can you do me a favor? I don't rightly know the full amount I owe Big Jim. Do you think you could find out for me before I talk to him?"

"Give me a few minutes, and I'll see what I can find out. I'm sorry about Rhodessa's passing. I can see things haven't been right for you since. She was a sweet girl."

"Thanks Belle, whatever you can do, I would appreciate," I said meanin' every word.

"Let's see if we can't make this day a better one for you, honey. Walk over this way with me. I want you to meet some of the girls from my house. I have a whole flock of my beauties out for a fun day. It's good for business."

"This is swell of you, Belle," I said as we made our way over to her girls.

"You remember Maude?" Belle asked me. Maude was a brunette in her thirties. She was wearin' a lavender dress that showed her curves to their best advantage. She and the other girls were lookin' at the racin' forms and pickin' out horses to bet on. Maude could sure get a man's pulse to racin'.

"Maude, you are as beautiful as always. Maybe more so," I said teasing her.

"There's a few more pounds of me, since you seen me last. I recall you kinda like a full-figured gal," Maude said laughing.

"Some things never change. You are an eyeful for sure, Maude."

"Here's Danny Jo," said Belle. "I don't think she was working for me when you were here before. Danny Jo's known for, well I'll let her explain it to you herself," Belle said.

"Good to meet you, Danny Jo."

Danny Jo nodded to me as her mouth was full of what looked to be greasy sausage.

"Let me introduce you now to Bobby Jean, she's my special girl. You be extra kind to her Willard," Belle admonished while giving Bobby Jean a knowing wink.

"Belle, I never met a one of your girls that wasn't somethin' special."

"Damn straight," Belle said, and we all laughed.

"Willard, you can introduce yourself to the other girls while I go talk to Big Jim about what we discussed."

When Belle returned, she took me aside. "Big Jim says you owe him $5,000 and more everyday because of interest. He said you should have settled up with him before you went overseas, serviceman or not. He didn't take kindly to it Willard."

I must have turned white. I didn't have that kind of money, but I didn't tell Belle that.

After a while, I made it over to Big Jim havin' thought over what I was goin' to say. Big Jim was still smokin' a cigar and was surrounded by his boys. I was glad Belle had greased the wheel with him before we met face to face.

"Well if it isn't Willard Grimes. Belle told me you were here. It's been a long time since I laid eyes on you. You sure enough look like hell. You ready to settle up with me son? You better have my money if you know what's good for you."

"Sure Big Jim, my money is in the truck. Thought I'd just hang out with you at the races, play some cards tonight, and pay you tomorrow. I'm good for it." I tried to bluff him.

"I've been keeping watch on what you owe me and I told you there would be interest. Nobody gets by without settling his debts to me." Big Jim said putting on airs by waving a fist full of money. The good life was catching up with Big Jim. He looked like he had eaten too many good meals and drank too much hard liquor. It showed in his belly and the puffiness in his face.

"Leave the boy alone, Big Jim, can't you see he's been through a lot. He said he would pay you." Belle came to my rescue.

Not many people could talk to Big Jim this way, but Belle had always made Big Jim a lot of money with her various enterprises.

"Willard, if you got the money to pay me back and some extra, you need to place a bet on Devil Darling. I got me a Man o' War on my hands, and he's gonna make me some big money," Big Jim said.

"Yes, sir, I'll do just that." I was tryin' to work my way into his good graces.

"I'll go to the window with Willard to place his bet. I'll be back to sit with you in a while," Belle said to Big Jim.

"See that you do and keep a good eye on Willard. I don't want him disappearing on me until I collect my money," Big Jim said giving Belle a hard look.

Belle got out of her seat and I followed her through the crowd.

"You are into Big Jim for some serious money. Have you got it?" Belle whispered in my ear once we were at the betting window.

"Hell no, Belle. Not by a long shot."

"Well you better have some serious luck about you. You don't have much time to get it and when Devil Darling loses, Big Jim acts like the devil himself," Belle warned me.

"Today's my lucky day Belle, you just sit back and watch."

I knew I couldn't go wrong when I saw Rose Runs on the Daily Racing Form. This was sure to be a sign from Rhodessa Rose. I bet on five horses to place. First out of the startin' gate, with the jockey barely hangin' on, Rose Runs placed second. I did about as good bettin' on Easy Street, a three-year-old that looked good on paper and on Hardy Rascal too. I was on a winnin' streak. No holdin' me back! Five races and I placed in three! People were watchin' me place my bets and followin' what I did. I was makin' everybody money! I was feelin' good and not so uneasy about payin' Big Jim back. Big Jim's horse Devil Darlin' didn't do so good, not even placin'.

Belle left Big Jim to come warn me. "Stay clear of Big Jim. He's been drinking hard all day. I'm gonna stay with him 'til the races are over and drive him home. You make sure you see him at his house first thing in the morning and settle up if you know what's good for you."

Belle's girls stayed with me makin' sure I had a fine time. I was gonna have Big Jim's money by mornin', I was sure of that. Lady Luck was with me. Belle's girls kept me in booze and I kept them in dollars. Bobby Jean was lookin' prettier as the evenin' went on. She sort of reminded me of Rhodessa in some kinda of way, maybe it was the long dark hair and her soft laugh. Maybe Bobby Jean was my Lady Luck.

"Bobby Jean, have you been to any of the nightclubs around here?"

"I've never been in a nightclub. I wouldn't know how to act but I know where they are. Belle has pointed them out to me," Bobby Jean replied.

I always liked it when Belle's girls acted a little coy and hard to get.

"You feel like a little ride, doncha' sweetheart? We can do us some dancin'.

Have some real fun. Later we can find a card game and get back into the action."

"I guess that would be alright, if we aren't gone long."

"You meet me out front in about twenty minutes. I got a few things to take care of and then you and me gonna have us a real big time."

I had me a problem though. Bobby Jean was gonna think I was a real country hick if she saw what I was drivin'. I couldn't be seen goin' to a nightclub in Pa's old truck. I had an image and there was plenty of business I could do in Wheeling but I had to look the part. That's when I got the idea to borrow Big Jim's car. He wouldn't miss it since Belle was drivin' him home.

I cashed out the rest of my winnings. All combined I had $1,700 in my pocket. I saw a couple of boys I knew and bought two bottles of 'shine from them as I left the track. Big Jim's automobile was easy to find. It was hard to miss being Big Jim owned the only bright red convertible anywhere around. It was easy as pie gettin' into Big Jim's car with my Barlow whittling knife. I put my 'shine in the floorboard. I needed not to bother 'buyin' any shine as Big Jim's had a full case sittin' in the backseat.

"There you are darlin', get on in," I said spottin' Bobby Jean in the parking lot.

"Willard, this is a mighty fine car you got. It must have cost you plenty," a wide-eyed Bobby Jean said as she got in the car.

I was afraid Bobby Jean would recognize the car as Big Jim's but she didn't.

"Well scoot on over close to me and I'll let you steer some. I'll tell you all about what a fine businessman I am and how I make my money," I said all important like.

Bobby Jean and I drove in the direction of the nightclub with her pointin' out the way. She and I were sippin' a little as I drove the crooked dirt roads, not much more than paths in some places, with Bobby Jean helpin' with the steerin'. Every now and then I would 'cause us to weave extra. I liked makin' Bobby Jean squeal. It made me laugh. I was also makin' sure Bobby Jean stayed snuggled up to me real close. It wasn't hard to weave on these roads, play actin' or not, with all the curves and trees comin' out of nowhere. Bobby Jean and I were havin' a fine time, and the night was gonna get better yet.

"Looks like we gotta stop at the fillin' station, Bobby Jean, and get a little gas," I said lookin' at the gauge.

"I could use the little girls' room."

"You go on ahead then."

Behind the station I spotted a long row of small, run down cabins tucked in the woods. There was a sign posted with black chipped paint. Vacancy.

Bobby Jean came out of the bathroom and got in the car.

"Bobby Jean, our good luck, while you was freshin' up, look what I got from the attendant," I said holdin' up a shiny key. "Come on darlin', we'll hit the nightclubs later."

"I don't know Willard. We are almost at the nightclub. Let's just keep going," Bobby Jean whined.

"We won't stay here but just a little while. Have us a few drinks and I need to freshen up. You don't want me goin' lookin' like this now do ya?"

"This place gives me the creeps Willard, especially in the dark. There's no other cars here either. I don't feel good about this."

"Come on girl. Live a little." I tried to lighten the mood.

"Just for a little while. I got to get back to Belle. She will be lookin' for me. I didn't tell her I was taking off."

I helped Bobby Jean out of the car, just like she was a real lady, takin' her arm as we walked to the cabin. Bobby Jean was feelin' the liquor and stumblin' some. I opened the creakin' door into the cabin.

"Willard this place is horrible. The paint is all peeling, and the curtains are torn. This place smells something awful. There isn't anything in here but a bed!" Bobby Jean said looking horrified.

"That's all we need," I said puttin' my arms around her and pullin' her down on the mattress.

Bobby Jean struggled, and attempted to get away from me. "Let me go, Willard, you let me go now!" Bobby Jean said fighting against me.

I held on to her, as she turned her head from side to side smearin' her cheap lipstick all over my beat up face.

"I'm not one of Belle's girls. I was just along for the fun. I ain't never been to the races before. Belle is my aunt!" she cried out.

I let go of her then. "What are you tellin' me girl?"

"I'm staying with Aunt Belle while my parents are in New York. She let me dress up in the other girls' clothes. They did my makeup and hair. Aunt Belle's gonna be real mad. She never would have let me go off with you. You better take me back. I only went with you so I could go into a real nightclub."

"Hell, how old are you?"

"I'm not but fifteen."

Before I had the chance to think there was the sound of thunder on the door.

"Open up in the name of the law," called the voice from outside.

"I don't want no trouble," I yelled back.

I opened the door. Two deputy sheriffs stood there with their guns drawn.

"That's him boys, the lout that stole my car. Bobby Jo is an underage girl and in there against her will," Big Jim said pointing his finger at me.

The deputies put me in handcuffs and threw me in the back of the police car. "If you get out of this you had better never come around here again, Willard Grimes, or I will shoot you myself," Belle yelled at me while holding on to a weeping Bobby Jean.

I reckon Big Jim wanted me alive so I could pay off my debt; otherwise, he would have had his goons kill me. For this I was grateful.

The next day, in jail, a deputy let me read his paper:

"A Franklin County, Virginia man, charged with kidnapping of a minor, automobile theft and the transporting of untaxed liquor in Virginia and West Virginia is being held in the Wheeling jail. Willard Grimes, 29, of Hardy, Virginia faces a total of six felony charges and five misdemeanor charges in connection with the theft of a prominent West Virginia man's automobile, $1,700.00 cash taken from the glove box of the vehicle, and the transporting of a case of untaxed liquor for distribution. Grimes was found in the company of a fifteen-year-old girl. The young woman in question claims to have been held against her will and forced to drink alcohol. Grimes was apprehended in a cabin behind Ferrell's Service Station. The girl appeared to be unharmed. Mr. James Amos of Wheeling, West Virginia is the owner of the stolen vehicle. Mr. Amos is the owner of several of Wheeling's finest dining establishments and known as a philanthropist to the children's orphanage in Wheeling."

Willard

I was held in the Wheelin' jail until I got my court date. Myrtle had managed to find a lawyer who would take my case. I felt real bad about this 'cause I knew Pa was havin' to pay for my defense. Only capital crimes, like murder, were granted the right to legal counsel if the defendant couldn't afford a lawyer, at least that is what Harold Jones, my attorney, said.

Without tellin' me, Jonesy sent for my folks. Jonesy thought it might be helpful to the court if it showed what a good family I was from.

Ma, Pa and Myrtle made the long trip to see me. Pa even bought a used automobile so he wouldn't be beholdin' to anybody for the drivin'. Mostly he didn't want anybody to know our family business. My folks had never been so far from home. I knew it was an ordeal for them to make the trip. Jonesy took my family into his own house to stay the night which was real good of him. He wanted to get to know my family to see if it would help my case. Jonesy took a likin' to Pa right off. They talked far into the night.

The mornin' of court Pa wanted to see me alone. Jonesy asked me if it was alright. I owed my father that much. Jonesy brought Pa into the small windowless room I was being held in with the same woeful green cinder block walls all jails seemed to have. I knew I would never forget this room. It was the last place I would see my family for a long time. Pa stood stiff and erect before he began to speak in low clear words. "Son, there has never been a crime laid at our door, and I never expected there to be one. But now there has, and we will deal with it the best we can with the help of the Lord." Pa's expression was grim.

"I know, Pa. I didn't intend for none of this to happen."

"Willard, I saw my pickup truck last night. Jonesy took me to where the court was having it kept. I had figured on Myrtle driving the automobile home and me driving the truck if I was allowed to have it back. There won't be no need for that now. Every part of the truck has been shot up with bullets. Those bad people you have been dealings with have sent you a message."

"I'm sorry about your truck, Pa. I am sorry I took it and for all the trouble I have caused."

"Willard, be a man and plead guilty to all your sins. Take your punishment and come out of this a better man. Then come home, son. We will be waiting for you," Pa said and then he hugged me.

I didn't know what to say. Pa wasn't one for huggin'. I could feel tears comin' to my eyes and that wouldn't do. A thought passed through my mind that this might be the last time I saw Pa. He wasn't a young man anymore, and he had aged a lot since I had seen him last and I knew that to be my own fault.

"I'd like to see Ma and Myrtle for a few minutes if I could," I asked Jonesy when he came back into the room.

"Sure, Willard, but you only have a few minutes before they call your case."

Ma came into the small room wearin' her black funeral dress with the white collar. She thought she was wearin' what she needed for court but it spooked me. Ma had a couple other church dresses with flower prints. I wish she would have worn one of those instead. It was hard to see Ma and Myrtle with so much pain in their eyes. I could tell they had been cryin'.

"Do what you are told to do and don't make no trouble for yourself or no one else if you get sent to prison. It would be best to find a way to make yourself useful as quick as possible. You are my son and I love you no matter what. I have a picture here of your family. Keep it with you if they will let you." Ma said while pressing the picture into my hand.

"Thank you, Ma. I'll do my best to keep the picture safe. Don't worry about me. I'll be alright and home again in no time, you'll see."

Myrtle was sobbin' like her heart would break. "Willard, don't you know you are likely to go to the state penitentiary for what you have done? Tell me you are not guilty and you will be coming home with us," Myrtle said hugging me hard.

"Jonesy is gonna get this whole mess straightened out. Don't worry about me."

We all knew I was lyin'. I wouldn't be goin' home anytime soon. I was caught in a web and Big Jim was the spider.

"Three-six-nine, the goose drank wine,
The Monkey chewed tobacco on the street car line."
Children's rhyme

Willard

I entered the court room in handcuffs. I hated my family seein' me this way. I looked around for Big Jim and Belle. I didn't see Big Jim but Belle was there. I knew how this was goin' to go down; Jonesy had told me what to expect as he had been in the judges' chamber earlier. Judge Wilks mounted the bench for the mornin' session. The court was called to order. The clerk called the case: "The United States vs. Willard Grimes."

I took my place on the witness stand and was told to put my hand on the Bible and to swear to tell the truth, the whole truth, so help me God. I knew my family was watchin' every move I made, and I could not lie with them watchin' me.

The prosecutor, a big man by the name of Michael Mason, began askin' me questions.

Q. "Can you give the court your full name?"

A. "Willard P. Grimes."

Q. "What is the P. for?"

A. "Ain't for nothing, just P. That's all my folks named me."

Q: "Willard Grimes, have you any connection with the liquor business?"

A. "Yes, sir I have been known to from time to time."

Q: "Were you transporting untaxed liquor in the automobile belonging to Mr. James Amos?"

A. "Yes sir, it was in the backseat of the automobile I was drivin' so I was transportin' it."

Q: "Were you aware that concealing intoxicating liquor is in violation of the internal revenue laws?"

A. "I have been told that before."

Q: "So you were aware it was against the law?"

A. "I reckon I knew."

Q: "Mr. Grimes, did you steal the car belonging to Mr. Jim Amos from the racetrack parking lot?"

A: "If Mr. Amos said I did, I must have done it. I didn't think of it as stealin', just borrowin' it a while."

Q. "Did you ask Mr. Amos's permission?"

A. "I didn't think he would miss it. I planned on returnin' it the same night."

Q. "Let me get this straight Mr. Grimes. You went on a joy ride with an under-aged girl, taking her to a motel room against her will and with sexual intent? You also had untaxed liquor and stolen money in the automobile?"

A. "Yes Sir, that's about right. Except for the money part. I won that gamblin'."

Q. "Do you have any way to prove that money was your own?"

A. "I reckon not."

Q. "So you ask the Court to take your word for it?"

A. "No, I reckon not."

Q. "Mr. Grimes, did you steal $1,700 from the glove box that belonged to Mr. Amos?"

A. "If Mr. Amos said I did it, I must have done it. I don't remember a whole lot. I know I did win money at the track."

Q: "Mr. Grimes were you aware of Bobby Jo Hartman's age?"

A: "No sir, I didn't know her age but I took her for at least eighteen."

Q. "Mr. Grimes, did you force her to drink alcohol?"

A. "No sir, though I did encourage her a bit."

Q. "Whose idea was it to go into the motel behind Ferrell's Service Station?"

A. "I reckon it was mine."

Q. "Did the young lady in question put up any resistance?"

A. "She didn't much like the idea at first but she went along with it."

Q. "Did she refuse your sexual advances?"

A. "Yes, sir she did and I stopped too, when she blurted out her age. I didn't know she was Belle Adler's niece. I never would have taken off with her had I known that."

Q. "There are several witnesses here today. Do you wish them to be called for your defense?" Prosecutor Mason gestured towards the other people in the court room.

A."No, we do not," my attorney stood up and replied.

Q. "Mr. Grimes do you understand that the purpose of the criminal prosecution today is to ascertain the truth of the events which took place on the night of June 12th, 1947?"

A. "I understand what you said.

Q. "I have no more questions," Prosecutor Mason stated.

"

Judge Wilks turned to Jonesy. "Mr. Jones, have you had an opportunity to present all testimony to your client which would protect his rights guaranteed under the law?"

"Yes, your Honor, we have."

Judge Wilks turned to me: "Willard Grimes are you guilty of the charges filed against you?"

I hung my head. "I was drunk and stupid, Judge, so I figure I'm guilty."

Two hours later, Judge Wilks had me stand while he read his ruling. "Willard Grimes, although you have not been in trouble with the courts before, the crimes you have committed are serious and leave me little choice but to rule as follows: In the charge of abducting a minor the court finds you guilty. In the charge of transporting untaxed liquor the court finds you guilty. In the charge of grand larceny auto theft and money theft, the court finds you guilty. Willard Grimes, the court sentences you to ten years in the West Virginia State Penitentiary. Bailiff, remove the prisoner."

I was taken to the county jail to await my transfer to the state pen. Later in my cell, Jonesy came to see me.

"Ten years isn't bad. It would have been far worse if things had gone further with the girl. You do have the possibility of early parole with good behavior," Jonesy said.

"Make sure you tell my folks that."

I wondered what had really gone down in Judge Wilks' chambers before court but Jonesy wasn't talkin'."

Willard

Several days went by before two deputies came for me puttin' me in handcuffs, with chains around my waist. They put leg irons on my ankles. Flanked by the deputies, I shuffled my way to the backseat of the patrol car for my ride to prison to the West Virginia State penitentiary in Moundsville.

It was June 25, 1947, a day of low-hangin' and gloomy clouds, when I began the first day of my sentence. Inmates were workin' in a garden with guards lookin' on and things didn't look so bad. Then I saw the gray walls of the gray castle prison and I was spooked. I had never expected to end up here. I was hoping to be sent back to Virginia.

Gettin' out of the backseat of the car I began a slow walk to the prison entrance. The guards didn't rush me. They knew a man wanted to take in all that was on the outside before he was inside for good.

"In our sleep pain that cannot forget falls drop by drop"
Aeschylus

Willard

Sometimes at night, I heard the walls talk about what was taken away from a man when he entered the pen. My mind got to wonderin' about who else lay awake in this very cell. Most of the old cons were probably dead and sometimes I had a feelin' some of their ghosts were hangin' in the shadows.

My bunk mate, Elton, was a man with a chiseled chin and steely eyes. He used to be a textile worker. But now, he was known as the cell house lawyer, spendin' all the time he could in the library. He told me once if he hadn't been prone to a life of crime he would have been a real lawyer. Elton spent hours readin' law books and writin' appeals. Elton got his trial transcript and managed to get mine. He picked them apart lookin' for mistakes that could prove the basis for somethin' called a writ of habeas corpus that could get us new trials. Elton was servin' twenty years for counterfeitin' and paper hangin'. If I had to have a cell mate, Elton would do.

Once a week, I got a letter from home. I wrote too, but it was hard to come by things to say. I didn't want my folks worryin' about me so I put a sugar coatin' on everythin' I wrote. I had been here a year when I got a package from Pa. He had sent me a Bible. I put it under my mattress. I didn't want the other prisoners thinkin' I was weak by havin' one. It felt good to know I had it as a reminder of Pa. Maybe someday I would open it and read some scriptures, when there wasn't no one around to see me do it. It wasn't long after I got the Bible, Ma wrote a letter that got me to thinkin.'

Dear Willard,

You have always been different from the rest of my children. Maybe it is because you were my first born and I doted on you more. I didn't spoil the others like I did you. You have always been a wild one, forever looking for a quicker way to do something. The war changed you as did Rhodessa dying. Perhaps if she and the baby had lived everything would have turned out different for you. There is no telling. With the help of the Lord, that can change if you just let Him into your life.

Your father says that you can have good fruit trees but when the fruit is ripe, some is just gonna fall from the limb, roll where it shouldn't and bruise or rot. Where it lands is not up to us, and there is nothing can be done for it. Some things are just not meant to be understood while we are here on earth, such as Rhodessa and your son being taken from us. Maybe when we all get to the other side, we will know why.

Stay strong in Christ and come home to us.

Ma

Willard

Boxin' was a big deal in prison. In the spring it was softball. I had not joined any of the prison sports. I saw no use in it. I wanted to keep my nose clean. I heard stories about fights breakin' out and men gettin' sent to the hole and given more time for any number of reasons. I'd seen enough fightin' in the war and I wanted no part of it.

It was just before Christmas when a screw came to me sayin' Warden Mullens wanted to see me.

Warden Mullens was sittin' in a big leather armchair behind his desk. Another man I hadn't seen before was sittin' across from him. "How are things going for you, son?" Warden Mullens asked me.

"As well as can be expected seein' where I am," I replied.

"I want you to meet a personal friend of mine, Referee Williams."

Referee Williams was a tall, slim, but muscled man. He got out of his chair and extended his hand to me, somethin' that hadn't happened since I had been there. We shook hands. Still, I wasn't offered a chair but continued to stand.

"Willard, I've been thinking about you being here, a war hero and all. You can't spend so much of your time in the prison kitchen and in your cell. It's not healthy for you. I have insured the prison has a good regime of physical fitness and recreation activities, particularly boxing. You aren't one of those library hounds are you, Willard?" the Warden asked me.

"No sir, I reckon not." I said.

"The prisoners look forward to boxing. Violence and aggression have decreased, and the convicts are a lot calmer when they box. It allows inmates having a problem with each other to settle it in the ring. Prison fighting is reduced, and that makes me happy. Referee Williams is willing to teach you how to box on his own time as a favor to me. How about it, son?" Warden Mullens asked.

"Thank you for being concerned, Warden. But I want no part of it. I'll keep goin' to the exercise yard and stay to myself as best I can."

“That’s no life for you. Being in the boxing program, you can make and keep a bit of money to spend in the commissary. Things could be a lot better for you than they are now. Think long and hard about it, Willard.” The look in Warden Mullen’s eyes had changed. I was no longer a son, but a lower than dirt prisoner. I was dismissed and told to return to my cell.

That night there was a lockdown. My cell was searched. The screws turned everythin’ upside down. They said a shiv was missin’ from the kitchen, and they aimed to find it. The Warden was teachin’ me a lesson.

My walk to solitary was one of increasin’ darkness, down to the basement, with danglin’ light bulbs and water drippin’ off the pipes. I had a mattress in the night but the screws took it away durin’ the day leavin’ me with nothin’ but an old army surplus blanket. I could hear rats, but worse than that were those metal doors openin’ and clangin’ shut, scrapin’ at my soul like nails on a chalkboard.

I did not mind the meager rations and water so much as the endless days and nights, I could not tell which. I stayed huddled in one place on the floor not speakin’, pullin’ myself into a cocoon. I did not speak to the screws when they shoved food through the slot in the door. Where I went in my thoughts no one could go. They could not enter my mind, and that made me laugh.

Men had been left down here for years, for insultin’ the screws or breakin’ some kind of rule. Some died or blew their tops, throwin’ food, spittin’ and cursin’ hopin’ to show the cons on the outside that they were tough. Others broke down and never recovered, returnin’ to their cells old men. How long would I be there? I was filthy and cold. I wished I had the Bible Pa sent me. I would read the scriptures now.

I got one of my headaches. I felt it comin’ on. My head was full of light but at the same time I was blind. The pain shot through my head like arrows from a bow. When they came for me, I was laughin’ so hard I couldn’t talk. The screws looked at me with narrowed eyes.

When I awoke I was in the infirmary. I heard the doc talkin'. "Might be a migraine, a seizure or even cancer in his brain."

After a few days, I was returned to my cell. It was good to see Elton. Things got back to regular, and I was allowed to go outside. Cons were playin' checkers and dominos but I wanted no part of their mindless games. I heard birds in the prison yard, yet I could not see one. I wanted to see one, but they were not in plain sight. I could think of little else than wantin' to find one of them singin' birds. That, and the sore place in my mouth where I had bit my tongue. The doctor determined I had somethin' called a grand mal seizure in solitary. After a while, I gave up tryin' to find a singin' bird and my mind got to thinkin' about Ma's words about makin' myself useful. There wasn't nothin' I could do here but push a mop, peel potatoes and box.

Willard

I had a visitor. An unkempt slob with slick greased hair sat on the other side of the glass window. He didn't tell me his name. "Big Jim doesn't like your attitude, Grimes. Warden Mullens did you a favor by giving you time in the hole to come to the right conclusion. They want you to train with Referee Williams before you get in the ring. Not everyone gets to train with Williams. He knows his stuff although he's not allowed to referee professionally anymore. Williams has been in a little trouble of his own," the goon laughed. Big Jim had all kinds of men workin' for him and this one didn't look right in the head.

"And if I don't go along with this?"

"Big Jim and the Warden control boxing, and they control you. Big Jim figures you can make him money. If you do what he says you can pay off your debt to him and come out of here alive. You don't want to turn down this opportunity. You won't be getting another." The goon opened his jacket, showing me the six-inch shiv he carried.

The metal bars keepin' me from freedom clanged behind him as he left. In my mind, I unloaded my revolver into the back of his head.

Daylight came creepin' into my cell. I had not slept but lay in a cold sweat. Big Jim had come for me. Interest was mounting on the money I owed him. I was goin' to have to meet with Referee Williams, it could not be avoided.

Willard

I got to be a regular at the ring. I was allowed to spend as much time there as I wanted so I went every day. It broke up the monotony. Williams met with me several times a week. I ran laps around the gym until Williams said I could quit. Then there was shadow boxin' till I built up a good sweat by sparin' and jabbin' with the heavy bag, followed with thirty minutes of jumpin' rope. I kept with the routine even on days Williams wasn't there.

Williams staged practice fights in the afternoons with other cons. I learned a lot then.

"Willard, I'm impressed with how quick you are catching on. You got a good chin and seem to roll with the punches. It must be that strong farm-boy neck of yours," Williams laughed.

Maybe Williams was right. I seemed to be able to take the blows better than the other cons. I was gettin' a reputation as being tough and unrelentin', always tryin' to stay in punchin' range of my opponent.

When Williams wasn't around I listened to the screws who seemed to know everythin' there was about boxin'. They were always talkin' about the matches they had seen on television while drinkin' at bars, particularly the ones that featured Sugar Ray Robinson and all his knockouts. I wondered if the other cons were payin' attention to the special favors I was gettin'. I had been classified as bondable, which meant I was able to work outside the walls. My request to work in the prison garden was granted. I no longer had to work in the prison kitchen. New issues of *The Ring Magazine* showed up in my cell. Warden Mullens was lettin' me see how a good boy could be rewarded in his prison.

I was well into the second year of my sentence, and I continued to box. I had a knack for it and learned fast. I didn't hear much from Big Jim and rarely saw him although I could spot his goons at the matches, so I knew he was keepin' tabs on me. Big Jim was waitin' to see what kind of boxer I was becomin' so he left me alone while I developed my new talent. The Warden had given me a new name. I was now "Warlock." He thought it was a good name considering my war record. My reputation as a boxer was spreadin'.

Willard

It was January and colder inside my cell than outside. I was in the gym warmin' up when Williams came in. "Get ready for your first big match, Grimes. Your opponent is Benny, 'The Hammer.' Benny was a rail yard worker who had beat up hobos. A watchman tried to stop him, but Benny beat the watchman to death with a hammer. He's in for life."

"It doesn't matter to me who I fight."

"Let's get to practicing then. There is no time to lose."

Saturday came around. I was anxious though I didn't let on. I entered the ring. The Hammer was a mongrel hound, part black, part somethin' else. He was grindin' his teeth, the ones he had left anyway. Benny was about my weight but wiry. He looked older than me but it was hard to tell a man's age in prison.

We began with a fast and furious barrage of fists. At one point I was backed against the ropes gettin' pounded hard. Benny caught me with a good body punch, and I went down. I rolled over on my back and struggled to my knees. Mad, real mad, I was back up to the count of seven. The prisoners and screws were cheerin'. I felt a sudden confidence and cockiness too. I knew Benny's weakness; he had trouble with his bowels. Referee Williams had told me before the match.

I went in for the kill, poundin' his belly over and over. Right, left, right, left. The prisoners and screws were laughin'. The Hammer had shit in his pants. People were screaming my name – "War-lock, War-lock." I was declared the winner. I looked into the crowd and saw a familiar face. Big Jim. I had won my first big match.

Willard

Five years had passed. I had won thirty-two of forty-five fights by knock outs. Not too bad, if you ask me, and I was only gettin' better. The screws were bettin' money on the matches. They liked to tell me how much money I had made them or were a little sore when a match went the other way. Gamblin' was where the money was. Big Jim was a highly diversified criminal. I just learned that word "diversified." I liked to use it. It rolled off my tongue. One day I would be diversified, when I made it out of there.

The warden wanted to see me. I wasn't surprised.

"Big Jim is coming to the prison to watch you fight this weekend. There will be a lot riding on this fight." Warden Mullens stared at me hard.

"I don't plan on losin', this match or any other."

The warden looked at me a little funny.

It was Saturday night and eight o'clock came around. The crowd was bigger than usual. The prison had been buzzin' about the upcomin' fight. There was an excitement about this match I hadn't sensed before.

I unbuttoned my prison shirt, as I walked through the gym to cheers of "Warlock, Warlock." I shook my fist triumphantly. The natives were restless. This crowd was looking for blood.

My opponent was Louie, "The Preacher," a country man with a passel of children I was told. He had gotten himself in trouble embezzlin' from the church and not payin' his fair share of taxes. We were matched in weight, give or take a few pounds. I wondered what got a church goin' man into boxin'. It didn't seem a natural thing for this kind of man to do. Before I knew what hit me, a rabbit punch was delivered to the back of my neck, and I went down. A woman screamed. I was so close to her I could smell her perfume, I got up. I don't know how I did it, maybe it was pure anger.

Preacher could have killed me right off, and Referee Williams, a real shit, didn't do nothin' about it. Rabbit punches were banned in boxin' as the blows to the neck or base of the skull could end a man's life, but Williams didn't care. This wasn't the jurisdiction of the World Boxin' Association. This was prison boxin'. Anything went.

Preacher and I continued poundin' away at each other, round after round. The crowd cheered loudly. There was blood everywhere. I lost concentration, and Preacher hit me with an overhand right followed by a left jab. I fell and Williams started his ten count. I was out.

All I could think of was a rematch. Neither Preacher nor I were goin' anywhere for a long time.

Willard

Workin' the prison garden got me through the days. I thought about Rhodessa while I worked, rememberin, our courtin' times when all was sweet with us on Cahas Mountian. I had read some scriptures in the Bible Pa sent me. I was taken back by the letter I found tucked inside. I read it so many times it was about worn out. I couldn't believe my good luck in what Pa had done, buyin' me and Rhodessa a small farm back when she was sick. It was like Pa to put the letter in the Bible, a good joke really as Pa couldn't have been guaranteed I would find it. I was grateful to my old man. I never saw this comin'.

Pa would be proud to see me sowin' seeds down the long rows of the prison garden. He taught me well. I could space the seeds evenly and make a double row when I was furrowin' the soil. Squash did well when sown on a little hill of soil, and I could do this faster and better than anybody. Many a day, I spent hoein' or on my hands and knees hand weedin'. I dug, sowed, planted and harvested, feelin' satisfaction in my work. It was good to be outside. The screws didn't watch me as there were other cons lookin' like they had rabbit fever and could make a run for it. Me, I was gonna serve my time and get out of here. After readin' Pa's letter I had big plans for my future.

Willard

When my next visitor came, I was surprised to see it was Myrtle. It had been a long time since her last visit. Ever since Myrtle was a little girl she threw her arms around me whenever she saw me. But that was before prison. Myrtle hung back when she saw me come into the room. She looked tired and was little more than skin and bones. As she walked towards me I could see she had been cryin'. "Willard, there is no good way to tell you this, but Pa is dead. I wanted to tell you myself. I couldn't imagine you readin' it in a letter."

"What happened Myrtle?"

"Pa must have known he was sick. He had lost a lot of weight and was looking poorly. Several times I asked Ma if she and Pa were alright and she would just smile that little smile of hers saying everything was fine."

"It was just two weeks ago I was sitting with Ma in the kitchen talking. Hours passed and Pa didn't come home. I could tell Ma was worried. There was a chill in the air, and Pa had not taken his sweater. It was about seven when Pa came into the house. He said he had down at the creek the whole time talkin' to Jesus. Ma made coffee, and we all sat and talked."

"What did he say Myrtle? Did he talk about me?"

"Pa said he knew in his heart you would come home and fly right. Then he teased me about settling down. I told him I would if I could ever find a man just like him. He thought that was funny. That night Pa went to bed and never woke up. The doctor said his heart just stopped. Jonah and Michael built his coffin and did a fine job. Pa taught them well. At the funeral people had fine things to say and are still bringing food over. Ma is so sad; I expect she will be for a long time. I might as well tell you this now. The homeplace is being sold. Ma can't keep it up, and Jonah and Michael have their own lives now. Ma will move in with Jonah and his wife. They have a nice house in Vinton. Their home is close to Aunt Nancy and Uncle Henry, so Ma will have family around her. I live close by with a couple of girls I work with at the plant."

I was stunned. I couldn't believe the farm would be no more. I could find no words. I felt bad I had not gotten word to Pa that I had found his letter and thanked him for what he had done for me and Rhodessa, had she lived. Now I would never get the chance.

"I am going home now, Willard, and I don't know when I'll be back. I'll write when I can. Take care of yourself," Myrtle said and then she was gone.

Willard

I was back in solitary. The smell of piss was my constant, but silent, companion. Maybe it was Pa's passin' that made me mouth off at the Warden. I went into a blind rage when he started talkin' to me like I was a nobody after I had won so many matches. I knew I had made him lots of money. The screws let me out for an hour a day for exercise, and then it was back to solitary. The exercise yard was supervised so I couldn't speak to nobody, not that I wanted to, but I needed to do somethin' to keep me sane. I concentrated on squirrels when I was in the yard, even though I rarely saw one. There were no trees. Every so often, there was a squirrel on top of the stone wall that surrounded the exercise yard. I pretended I was back on the farm with a shotgun shootin' real and imaginary squirrels. I got to thinkin' about the good times Pa and I had rabbit huntin' at Coopers Cove when I was a boy. I missed Pa's voice and even his lecturin' ways. I opened the Bible he sent and read scriptures thinkin' of him. I re-read his letter. If only I had a chance to go huntin' with him again, to laugh with him, and let him know I could be a better man. I wanted to be out in the prison garden. I felt closer to Pa there, close to the land.

The first week of solitary was the hardest. I did pushups and sit-ups by the hundreds. Sometimes hate piled up in me. I tried to think about walking up Cahas Mountain, holding Rhodessa's hand to keep from goin' crazy. The time drew out. I thought they would let me out soon, wantin' me to fight and make them money.

Unlike most of the cons, I refused to make lines on the walls markin' off how long I had been here. As best I could, I ignored the time. I did not feed the past 'cause it would grow hungrier and eat on what was left of me. I had seen a lot of men come in since I had been here. I had watched many of them become dim-eyed or worse. More and more when it rained my joints hurt. I did not like the rain.

Willard

I had been here seven years and seven months. Sometimes it felt like ten. I had been a good boy, makin' the warden and Big Jim lots of money. I had my own cell, a real privilege I was told. Ma would be proud. I had made myself useful.

My headaches came more often now. I saw a funny light before one of them came and I had my fits. I tried to find someplace dark and alone. If the prison doc knew how bad my head was, they would make me stop fightin'. I would not be able to pay off Big Jim. I would not leave here except in a box.

My hands were makin' money in the ring. I had a radio in my cell. The Warden and screws turned a blind eye to the bottle of 'shine I paid off the guards for. I drank after the lights were out.

Havin' a private cell, away from so many prying eyes, I was able to live in a more civilized fashion. In 1951, I listened to Joe Louis as he tried to make a comeback by puttin' away Rocky Marciano, a fight which went the other way. Every Sunday afternoon, I lay in my cell and listened to *The Hour of Champions* and wondered why Pa, Rhodessa and my baby son had to die.

Willard

There was nothin' but time. I watched the seasons go by. In spring, there were sacks of seed for plantin' in the prison garden followed by weedin' and pickin' in the summer. I had long corridors of floors to mop which kept me in the pipeline of information. I had asked for the added duty as I liked hearin' things, things I might find useful to know. I had an occasional visit from Jonesy. There was never good news. Myrtle came a time or two but seemed to lose all faith in me after Pa died.

I was Big Jim's star attraction in the ring if the truth be known. He came around the prison more often now havin' a big time with Warden Mullens. Big Jim acted like a damn promoter and had gotten the Warden into charging big bucks for seats.

Every match was different with the rules changin', but I was gettin' to my pot of gold at the end of the rainbow. My debt was almost paid off.

Willard

Time went by slowly. I listened while Archie Moore was knockin' Marciano down in a furious battle in Yankee stadium in 1955. Marciano was an unknown in 1947 the year I entered prison. Rocky Marciano retired in 1955 as world champion, undefeated in his career of forty-nine bouts with forty-three knockouts.

Marciano had fought his last fight, and tonight would be mine. I was havin' my rematch with Preacher. Marciano had retired and so would I.

I kept my breakfast down on the day of the fight, but I don't know how. My stomach went bad whenever I thought about throwin' this fight. I had been eatin' crackers like a pregnant woman to stop the cramps in my belly.

Every seat in the house was full. I knew where Big Jim would be sittin', up front, ringside, smokin' his cigar. His apes were all around him. He was expectin' me to throw this fight but he would be surprised tonight. I was gonna beat Preacher to a pulp and win this fight. I was tired of bein' one of Big Jim's monkeys.

The openin' bell rang and the boxin' started. The first four rounds were tight. I stayed close to Preacher, not giving him the chance to pull another of his rabbit punches on me. The bastard was a dirty fighter, a known fact among us cons. I stalked Preacher around the ring, sacrificin' myself by takin' punches in order to land my own blows.

In the fifth round, Preacher's speed had begun to slow down, so I was surprised by the sucker punch I took to my kidneys. Preacher didn't stop there but continued with a head-butt, openin' a cut above my eye. Referee Williams sent Preacher to his corner and waited for me to get up off the floor. I wasn't goin' to lay down. Hell, no! I needed to hurt this man. The crowd was in a frenzy. Big Jim must have been pissin' in his pants.

In the seventh round, I threw a left hook to Preacher's jaw. Preacher dropped to his knees, with his hands pressed to his face, but he managed to get up before the bell rang.

In round eight, I landed a right to Preacher's head and a left to his body sendin' him into the ropes. He was a little dazed but not for long comin' at me with punches landin' below my belt.

Referee Williams warned Preacher several times he would disqualify him if he continued. It was round nine. I was mad as hell after gettin' hit in the balls. I went into a blind rage and couldn't nothin' hold me back. I came at Preacher, attackin' him as viciously as I ever had anyone. The crowd went wild. They were all on their feet yellin', "Kill Preacher." They knew a dirty fighter when they saw one and didn't like it.

I landed a left on the side of Preacher's head and then a right to his chin, sendin' him down face-first. Who would have thought Preacher had a glass jaw? He didn't get up.

Later, the medical examiner said my head punches caused a hemorrhage in Preacher's brain. I had killed him. The crowd got what they wanted.

The newspaper headline read: **"SHOULD FELONS BE ALLOWED TO BOX?"**

It made us sound like ruthless criminals boxin' to our deaths. The truth was we were cons bein' used to make a dollar by organized crime.

The Federal Bureau of Prisons had never mattered to Warden Mullens until now. He ran his prison the way he saw fit. Now the bureau was on to the warden and takin' a real hard look at how he had been runnin' things. Warden Mullen's good time had gone horribly wrong.

Willard

Big Jim Amos was dead. Shot down in cold blood. The excitement of the news traveled up and down the cell blocks. The screws couldn't stop talkin' about it. Big Jim had been killed by a local racketeer who wanted to be the next kingpin. That's what the rumors were anyway. One of the screws snuck me a real newspaper although I had to pay him plenty for it.

PROMINENT WEST VIRGINIA MAN, JAMES AMOS, SHOT DEAD AFTER GRANDSON'S CHRISTENING

"Dead at 66, James Amos, from Wheeling, West Virginia was shot down in cold blood after attending his infant grandson's christening at The Church of The Holy Virgin. James Amos was known to be a humorous and generous man helping many a downtrodden soul.

It was February seventh when gunfire rang out. Mr. Amos was shot as family members watched in horror. A scene of hysteria took place as a lone vehicle sped off. No one else was shot. No one got a good look at the vehicle. The priest from The Church of the Holy Virgin ran to assist Mr. Amos only to find his vestments soon covered in blood. James Amos was declared dead on the scene.

At this time, there are neither suspects nor motives in this vicious attack. Mr. Amos leaves behind his loving wife and daughter, son-in-law, sister, and infant grandson, James Amos II. Anyone with information is asked to contact the Wheeling police department."

Big Jim had taken the lives of many men. It was likely there were hundreds of men that had crossed Big Jim's path that didn't live to talk about it. I was one of the lucky ones. Big Jim, who had had me in his web, was gone.

Willard

I got paroled eight months early. I guess the warden saw fit to let me out seein' I wasn't useful to him anymore and in fact could be a major liability. Warden Mullens didn't want me in his prison, especially if the prison commission started askin' questions. I had done nine out of my ten years. Good behavior was what Warden Mullens called it at my parole hearing. Referee Williams gave his blessin' as did Jonesy, who spoke in my behalf at the hearing. The new young Catholic priest at the prison told how I had found God.

Now it was over and I was a free man. I would miss no one except Elton who had gotten accustomed to life in prison. The idea of livin' on the outside was too much for him. He told me he was an old man now and planned on spendin' the rest of his life reviewin' other inmates' cases. Elton wasn't but forty-five.

Willard

I was wishin' I had a warm jacket when they let me out on March 17, 1957 nine years and four months later. I had to wear the same clothes out of prison I had worn in. They didn't fit so good anymore, but I didn't care. They were my clothes and not that damn prison uniform. I put on my watch and set it to the prison clock, which said ten o'clock. I took Pa's letter and put it in my jacket pocket. I left the Bible for Elton to remember me by. I could always get another one. I looked in my wallet. There was twenty-two dollars and a picture of Rhodessa in it. I had forgotten I had that picture, and there she was lookin' back at me, a young, pretty girl. I had a key ring with keys that would not open any doors anymore and two sticks of gum.

Walkin' out of the pen, I felt a chill. I was leavin' behind the ghost of my sealed off life and walkin' out a free man. I was more than surprised to see Belle sittin' behind the wheel of a 1955 black Cadillac. She looked like her old self, but different. She motioned for me to come over and get in the car. When I got in, I saw she was wearing a dress, one that could be worn to church even. She looked a little older and her red hair was smoothed down and in a bun. The first thing she did was light two cigarettes, handin' me one. I drew on it slow, holdin' my breath. Belle started the car and drove several miles before she started to talk.

"I've been keeping tabs on you, Willard. I wanted to know the exact date you'd be getting out so I could be here waiting when you walked out those doors."

"You are about the last person I expected to see. I figured you were done with me and good riddance."

"I was angry for a long time. When I came here three years ago to testify against you at your parole hearing I brought a plate of cookies for Warden Mullens. I was hoping to butter him up and flirt with him to make sure he saw things my way. That's when I saw a tired looking woman get out of an old green Ford. She had a red haired boy in overalls with her. They both looked so sad. I handed the boy my plate of cookies. You would have thought I had given him a thousand dollars. Something in me changed when I gave the boy the cookies. I knew I had to forgive you. Not all of this was your fault; some of it was mine."

"I don't get it, Belle. I did wrong."

"Bobby Jo told me the whole story or at least her side of it. She's a grown woman and feels bad for what happened to you. She's married now and has two kids of her own."

"I'm real glad to hear she's doin' good and doesn't hold nothin' against me," I said meaning every word of it.

"I've done some serious thinking since that night about what could have happened to my niece. What was I thinking letting her pretend to be one of my girls? Bobby Jo didn't have any idea of what my real business was. My own sister didn't know and she trusted Bobby Jo to be with me. My family thought I ran a secretarial service. That's why I had all those desks and typewriters downstairs. But I have changed all that now. I have gotten myself out of the business and become an almost-respectable member of the Wheeling community. I had to. It got to where I was greasing palms every day to keep from being arrested. So I called in my markers. I reminded the city fathers of my excellent bookkeeping skills and my up-to-date client list," Belle chuckled.

"If anyone could get all that straightened out, it would be you," I said laughin' a little.

"I've always been a good business woman. After all I ran the most profitable brothel in Wheeling. One of my biggest johns was the President of the Wheeling Bank. For years, I had a private lock box where I kept my ledgers and weekly deposits of cash. I always made sure my girls smelled like beautiful flowers. Everybody knew which lockbox was mine cause of the whiffs of perfume that came out of it when I opened that box. It served as a reminder to the bank president about what I had on him," Belle laughed.

"What's happened to your girls now?"

"They will always be loyal to me and keep my secrets. I helped many a girl who otherwise might have starved to death. My girls weren't shiny when I got a hold of them. I fed them good, taught them how to dress and treated them right. I always closed the establishment on Sunday so my customers would stay home with their wives and children and go to the church. I even had a prayer meeting with my girls at three p.m. It was mandatory for every girl to attend. I sure as hell didn't want to get on the bad side of our good Lord Jesus. I made my girls into sophisticated women who knew how to treat a man. Every bordello in Wheeling that tried to cut into my business shut down. Nobody could compete with Belle Adler!"

"What are you doin' now? You got to eat."

"I've been buying up real estate for years, and I have a nice nest egg. My name is on the list of about every charity drive list in Wheeling. Now I walk my little Maltese, Honeybunch, up and down the sidewalks myself. Did you know how I used to let my clients know I had a new girl? I would have her walk my dog. Now, it's just a little joke and my old johns get a chuckle when they see me walking Honeybunch. My house of ill repute is now my private residence, complete with brass room keys and abundance of naughty nighties and silk hose," Belle chuckled.

"I got something to ask you I have always wanted to know. How was it that a good woman like you was so close to Big Jim?"

"I understood him. Times were hard during the depression. He wasn't but twelve, when his parents took off. They thought their children would be better off in the orphanage. Jim wasn't gonna have nothing to do with that. He took to selling newspapers and fighting other kids to entertain the adults who would throw coins at them. Cards came after that. Pretty soon Jim got to selling bootleg whiskey and stealing anything that wasn't nailed down. Then he graduated to betting on the horses. Jim lived by his wits and didn't anyone dare mess with him. He was what you call a born leader."

"How do you know all this, did Big Jim tell you?"

"Hell no, I'm Big Jim's little sister. I thought you knew that! Come on home with me now, and let me take care of you for a few days. You need to eat some good food and sleep in a real bed."

Willard

It was good to be in a house with a real bed and clean sheets. I took several long, hot showers just because I could. It was a good feelin' to take a shit with no one watchin'.

Even though Belle was out of the business, she still had a few tricks up her sleeve. "I have a charity event this evening, Willard. I didn't want you to be alone on your first night home. I invited a friend of mine to come over and spend some time with you. I didn't think you would mind. I'd feel better knowing you had some company while I'm out."

It was eight in the evening when the doorbell rang. My companion for the evenin' arrived compliments of Belle. Standin' in the door was a small pretty girl with long dark hair and big brown eyes.

"You look mighty young to be a whore," I said without thinkin'.

"Old enough. I'm eighteen," the girl said.

"You sure about that?"

"Belle don't have friends that are under eighteen."

"Come on in then."

The girl did as I said. Takin' off her coat, she girl walked across the room and hung it in the parlor closet. The girl knew her way around Belle's place. I liked the clickin' of her high-heeled shoes and the smell of her perfume. The low cut pink dress she was wearin' caressed her curves, just like I would soon be doin'. I hadn't been with a woman in a long time. She walked over and kissed me on the mouth. I was instantly hard. I went to kiss her again, but she laughed at me and pushed me away. "Down Tiger, let's have a cocktail first," she proposed. The girl turned on the radio and went about makin' us drinks. She knew what she was doin'.

"I thought Belle was out of the business," I asked the girl.

"She is. I'm just doing her a special favor. You must be somethin' special to Belle. She wants to make sure you have a real good time."

We stood by Belle's fireplace and downed our drinks. The girl showed me her empty glass and grinned at me.

"Fix us a couple more drinks and take them upstairs," I told her. "I'll be up directly."

I watched her as she climbed the wooden stairs. She looked back at me once and blew a kiss.

"You know, I could give you this for free. You're kinda cute," the girl giggled.

"If you are lookin' for money, I haven't got any. Just my good looks."

"Like I said before. This is on Belle."

I did not go to her right away but fixed a drink and then another as I sat on Belle's sofa lookin' in the fire. Starin' at the flames I recalled things I had long put out of my mind. My thoughts went to my beautiful, now dead wife Rhodessa. When Belle's clock chimed eleven p.m., I remembered the girl upstairs waitin' for me and I climbed the stairs. I went to call her name but didn't know it. "Are you awake," I asked walkin' into the bedroom.

"Yea," she replied throwin' back the covers. "Come, get in bed with me."

I took off my clothes lettin' them fall on the floor. I got into bed and grabbed onto the girl. My snake, who was so eager and willin' earlier in the evenin', wouldn't wake up.

Later, as I struggled for sleep, my mind kept wonderin'. What was I doin'? Nothin' felt right. I could taste Belle's liquor in the back of my throat. The sour stuff came up and I swallowed it down again. I got up before sunrise and took a long hot shower tryin' to wash the memories of the penitentiary down the drain.

Willard

I was surprised to see Belle up so early. I could smell coffee brewin'.

"Would you like a fried egg?" Belle asked me as I walked in the kitchen.

"Two if it would be alright and plenty of strong coffee, if you don't mind."

Belle handed me a cup, and I took short sips smilin' as I drank it down. I couldn't believe I was sittin' in a kitchen being served breakfast by Belle rememberin' where I had been just twenty-four hours earlier.

Belle handed me a plate of eggs, bacon and toast, then fixed her own and joined me. We didn't say much while we were eatin', both of us seemed to have a lot to ponder. Finally I broke the silence. "You sure have been good to me, Belle, but it is time I get goin'."

"So what are your plans, Willard?"

"I haven't got it all figured out yet but I'll be headin' back home."

Belle took a small roll of money from her housecoat pocket and handed it to me. "Here's enough to get you on the bus and a little extra. You're welcome to stay here for a while if you want too."

"Thanks Belle," I said, pocketin' the money.

I walked upstairs to get a few things together. I counted the money Belle gave me. All totaled it was one hundred dollars in fives and tens. I went into the bedroom where the girl was still sleepin'. I put five dollars in the candy dish by the bed. It wasn't her fault my snake didn't wake up.

Willard

It was early, not quite eight when I wandered into town and found the bus station. There was a bus leavin' for Roanoke at noon. I had time on my hands. I found a place to buy cigarettes and food to eat on the bus. It would be a long ride. I hoped Belle wouldn't miss the bottle of bourbon I took from her cabinet. It was half full and good stuff. I suspect she would have given it to me if I asked her but I didn't want to. She had done so much for me I couldn't think of askin' her for anythin' else. I found a bench and sat down to read Pa's letter again:

Dear Son,

I purchased a small farm for you and Rhodessa while you were overseas. I never imagined Rhodessa would not be alive when you came back from the war. The farm was old man Tate's. I bought it at a fair price as Tate's son didn't want to keep it. The place is forty acres, mostly timber.

The old house is far gone now and should probably be torn down. We can build another in its place with runnin' water and a bathroom, you and I. Rhodessa used to talk about wanting a garden for flowers like her mother. Perhaps you can plant a garden in Rhodessa's memory? Put the foolishness of youth behind you and don't look back. The Tate place is yours now. The deed is in your name. You have a place to come to when you have served your time. Once you are on your feet, you can start paying me and your mother back over time.

Your mother and I await your safe return,

Pa

I took a swig from Belle's bottle. I had a few more while I waited for the bus. Half of my life was still ahead of me. I had done bad things in my life, things I regretted but couldn't dwell on. My bus arrived. It was time to go.

I had been ridin' a couple of hours when a white pain, like a bolt of lightnin' flashed in my head. Luckily the bus had to make a stop at a service station. I didn't have any of Belle's booze left so I had to settle for buyin' some Blue Ribbon Beer and a pack of Camels. I went to piss in the station's toilet. My head told me I'd been on a bender but there was somethin' else behind it comin' at me like a silent evil screamin' in the wind. I vomited everythin' that was in me all over that bathroom floor. I climbed back on the bus. Somethin' was comin' for me or I was comin' to it. There was no way to be sure.

"The weakest kind of fruit drops earliest to the ground."
William Shakespeare

Willard

Almost ten years gone and I was finally lookin' at the rundown farm Pa bought me not five miles from where I grew up. The old house was set far back in the woods and down a long dirt road. It was all overgrown with briars and thickets everywhere. I had wanted a place with fields and dales where the revenuers could not find my stills, and this place wasn't bad. There was a creek ran through it and lots of deep crevices in the hills. Without knowin' it, Pa bought me a fine place to get my 'shine establishment goin' again. Workin' my stills and plyin' my trade by night – wouldn't nobody know what I'd be doin' except those that I wanted to have the knowin'.

Ma and Myrtle had been in the house and left me stuff in the kitchen. I had written Myrtle from prison lettin' her know when I would be gettin' out. I made it clear I didn't want nobody waitin' for me when I arrived. I needed time to adjust.

.There was a wood stove for heatin' and cookin'. The electricity had been cut on but there was no runnin' water, just a pump on the front porch and a spring house not far away. Ma left a percolator, coffee and other canned goods. She also left a Bible. A note was stickin' out of it askin' me to see her as soon as I could and fifty dollars that I knew came from her egg money. It would have taken Ma a long time to save up that much. The note beseeched me to meet her at church so I could start my new life in Christ. Mama was always beseeching. Mama used that word a lot.

The house didn't have much but I didn't need much. Pa was right about this place not bein' fit for Rhodessa. It would do for me, no problem. There was an old bed, dresser, a kitchen table, rockin' chair, a few dishes and an iron skillet. I didn't remember any of this stuff from home so they must have been old man Tate's. Ma and Myrtle must have put in some long hours gettin' this place to a tolerable condition. That's what the two of them were though, hard working do-gooders.

After a couple of days of gettin' my bearings, I hitched a ride to Beard's store. I played it low-key not wantin' just anybody to know I was back. I knew who would be useful to me and me to them, if they were still around. I bought yeast, sugar and malt with the money Ma left. By the end of the week I made my connections. I had a rifle and a used truck. I was back in business.

PART THREE

LILY

"THEY HATCH COCKATRICE EGGS,
AND WEAVE THE SPIDER'S WEB;
HE THAT EATETH OF THEIR EGGS DIETH
AND THAT WHICH IS CRUSHED
BREAKETH OUT INTO A VIPER."
ISAIAH 59:5

LILY

I just done things as they come to me. I just done 'em. When you start out in an orphanage that's how it is. Nobody ever come for me. I was just dropped off at the Baptist Orphanage like some stray pup not even off the tit. Never knew who my ma was, just that she was young and pretty. I've been told my pa was a honey man. It seemed he went from flower to flower with warm hands and a mouth full of sweetness. When I turned eighteen, the door slammed. "Get out," they told me. So I did. You can't stay on at a state orphanage after you be of age.

I got a job at the Vinton Weaving Mill. That's where I met Myrtle. She showed me how to do my job and then she and I went on to be friends. One Friday night, she asked me if I wanted to go to town. I had just turned nineteen. Myrtle told me we needed to celebrate with pie and coffee at the Vinton Diner. Myrtle was in her thirties and it seemed to me like she had been around. She had a brother, Willard who would be out with a couple of buddies. Wouldn't it be good for us to unwind after working all week? It was something to do rather than go back to my rented room, wash my hair, and wait until Monday.

So me and my new friend Myrtle went into Vinton and there Willard was with two others in the back parking lot of the diner. They were all laughing and spitting a little Red Man juice. Willard had one foot up in the bed of his pickup, and a bottle of something in a brown bag. He wasn't a good looking man, kinda hard-faced and silent. The others ribbed him about not having a job like they did. Willard didn't talk like his sister Myrtle. In fact, Willard didn't seem to say or be much of nothing. I had seen the other two from the plant but hadn't been formally introduced until now. They was the kind of men took to girls like dogs take to coons and they kinda scared me with all their boasting about getting or kicking ass. Willard kept quiet, but raised his arm offering me a drink from a mason jar. It was my first taste of 'shine. It was clear-looking like water so I didn't figure it could hurt me none. But Lord, it was nasty tasting and burned like hell fire, but after a few more swigs, I felt good. Willard asked me if I wanted to take a drive, so we left the others behind. He took me up the crookedest mountain I had ever been, then turned off to a place called Cooper's Cove, heavy with trees, vines and briars, with a path leading to where mountain streams gathered. Willard and I got out of the car and walked the path to the edge of the water. It was really pretty seeing the stars overhead and being so close to the water I could put my toes in. Willard gave me more to drink from his mason jar. Then he kissed me. I began to feel things stirring inside myself, I ain't never felt before, like all was right with the world and I weren't scared or lonely no more.

I woke up as the sun was barely peeking through the torn shade in the window. My head was pounding hard and what was that awful snoring sound? I was naked in Willard's bed! Oh sweet Jesus what had I done? I pulled his arm off of me and got out of bed without Willard budging a bit. I knew we had intercourse 'cause I was so sore in my woman parts, and I could make out fresh blood on the mattress. Willard didn't have no sheets. I couldn't remember doing it and this was my first time. I felt real sad about that and ashamed as well. I knew it wasn't right.

I needed some place to clean up and something to put on. I found Willard's shirt, with my foot, as it was still mostly dark in the room. Willard's bedroom, if you could call it that, opened right out onto the porch, with its rotten boards and broken steps. I staggered out into the yard and threw up.

I wondered if Willard had a bathroom or a water pump somewhere. Looking at the old house I could tell it hadn't been painted in years. It was all blistered and full of shadows. There were rusty looking car parts, and mangy dogs lying on the porch. It knew it was hunting season'cause deer entrails were in the yard that the dogs had finished with. Willard was bragging the night before how he and his buddies had just killed several deer. I found a water pump on the porch along with a dirty towel. The Johnny house was about a hundred feet from the house, all covered in briars. I did my business and cleaned myself up the best I could.

I stood in that yard like a piece of unreadable stone and watched the swelling pumpkin sun rise, not wanting to be bothered by another living soul. Willard had taken off somewhere, and I was glad although I had no way to leave. I stood there all day not wanting food nor drink, just lost in thought until the sun set over Windy Gap Mountain and Willard came home and once again physically claimed me as his own. I did not know then there would be countless days to follow. That was all there was to it. Things just came to me, the orphanage, the drink and then Willard. If I haven't told you yet, people call me Lily Grimes, like Willard had ownership over me. We weren't married, not in a legal sense. Didn't much matter though. Never did.

Willard

I needed someone to cook for me, and Lily needed someplace to live. She never did go back to the Weaving Mill. Lily gardened, cooked, and learned how to handle the hog killin.' She did about everythin' that needed doin' at least whilst she was strong enough. She didn't fight hard anymore when I wanted her to spread her legs. I'd got her broken in.

I didn't have to use charm on Lily to get her to do what I wanted her to do. If I wanted somethin' cooked she did it. If there were chores needed to be done, she did that too. Times weren't like they were back in the time when I had money, a good suit, and the swagger of a man who had the world by the tail. I didn't waste time havin' conversations with Lily neither. Didn't need to. She knew her place.

After a year or so, Lily got herself pregnant. Hell, I didn't want no child and I especially didn't want to be nobody's Pa. I'd been drinkin,' at home until then, not feelin' such a strong pull to be off somewhere, and the headaches didn't seem so bad with enough 'shine. I told Lily I knew somebody could get rid of it, but she claimed to be too far along. I suspect she wanted it. I suspect it was her lying ways.

I started goin' to Coopers Cove with my 'shine after that. The place had always brought me a measure of comfort. I tried to forget about my time in the pen, Lily's swellin' body and the child mockin' me as it grew.

Willard

Somethin' had changed, I knew not what it was. Dread washed over me and the odor of dead soldiers filled my nostrils. It was a hot afternoon and the blue sky had greyed. Thunder was coming. I got in the my car and drove to Coopers Cove. I knew I had to get away from any livin' thing.

The afternoon passed slowly in intense heat and a deathly quiet. A fly made endless circles about my head, the only sound that was. My thoughts were wretched. Then HE came over me, causin' my body to jerk and my head to turn from side to side. I heard HIM laughin' as he played with me, makin' me a rag doll for his own pleasure.

The voices in my head caused sounds from my mouth to fall from my lips. I spewed HIS vomit, makin' unholy ground. Then it was over. Afterward, I lay spent in my own waste, in a place full of haunting, knowin' bodies without heads, arms without hands and eyes without sockets, would come for me again.

LILY

It seemed natural enough to name the baby after him: Willow Grimes. I thought Willard might go easier on me and the baby if she had his name. But it didn't make any difference to him. He did not care for Willow.

"If you were gonna have a child, it could at least been a boy, not an ugly red-faced screamin' girl, keepin' me up at night," Willard said when Willow was a month old. Willow was a colicky baby. Many the night, I had to rock her until the wee hours of the morning. The rocking chair's endless clunking caused by uneven floor boards, night after night, was more than Willard could take. More often than not he would take off sometimes for a day or more. I didn't know where he went but was glad he was gone. It was easier with him away.

On the mornings Willard was there, I poured him buttermilk and fixed him a plate of something I knew he liked to eat. Most days, I started cooking early. Willard always wanted food cooked to offer to people who dropped by to purchase 'shine. Being hospitable was good for business and you never knew who might want to sit down and play a game of cards. I did what he told me not wanting to rile him none. He'd gotten where he put his hands on the back of my neck pushing me, steering me where he wanted me to go like I was some farm animal.

I cooked beans and potatoes, fried okra and boiled eggs. Sometimes there was cornbread and chicken. I made do with whatever I had. I kept the food under a cloth on the kitchen table. But never once did we sit down and eat a meal together.

Willard got a new automobile. He was real proud. The car smelled like leather, 'shine and tobacco. He was in a good mood for a while after he got it. One day, he sat out in the yard with me and Willow, eating cherries and spitting out the seeds. He was making three-year-old Willow laugh and laugh. He actually let Willow crawl into his lap. I thought maybe things were getting better. How foolish I was. Willard started getting a hold of me again, putting a paper bag over my head, and doing his man business into my fighting body. It was no use. He got his way.

"O what a tangled web we weave,
When at first we practice to deceive!"
Sir Walter Scott

Willard

As long as I didn't have a bad spell, I could get things done. I never knew when it would happen or how bad it would be when HE came for me. Sometimes weeks passed between his visits. It didn't seem to make no difference to HIM if I was drinkin' hard or not.

I was gettin' regular 'shine customers. Sometimes people didn't have money, so I traded for stuff like chickens, a rabbit dog, a rifle, even some old bathtubs once. I always know a good deal when I saw it. I could recognize a sucker from a mile off.

The place was lookin' like a farm and a regular place of operation. I killed deer, rabbits and squirrels when I felt like huntin'. I had a hen house, a few goats and pigs. Lily took care of the garden. We had fresh eggs every mornin' and plenty to sell for whoever came by. My place looked good to me, not as good as Pa's though, he never had a bunch of whiny dogs or bottles in the yard. I didn't bother with the house though; it was good enough.

Now that Pa was gone, I didn't see the need to be payin' Ma any money for this place. Hell, she got good money when the home place was sold. Ma had Myrtle, Jonah and Michael lookin' after her. What did she need with my money? Ma never asked me for it, not directly. It was always Myrtle. She was like a dog with a bone sayin' Ma needed the money in her bank account for her old age. It took money to make money and I had to make up for my time spent in the pen. Most people would understand that but not Myrtle!

I got the notion to go to the stockyard in Roanoke and buy a couple calves. I was thinkin' I could raise a few head, butcher em' and have me some fine steaks and sell the rest of the meat. Maybe I would invite some of the fellas over for a barbecue and have a swell time. It would be good for business. Hell, I'd even take Lily and the kid with me to the stockyard. I would look like a family man!

When we got to the stockyard, I ran into a couple of the boys and we started passin' the good stuff around. I sent Lily and the kid back to the truck while I went with the fellas to look at heifers. When we got there, my head started hurtin' bad. I went back to the truck.

"What are you doin' in my truck?" I demanded of the woman unable to recognize it was Lily.

"You brought me here you fool, don't you remember?" the woman hissed.

I got in the truck with nothin' else said. Anger was in my head and HIS voice was startin' to talk. The woman sat wordlessly holdin' onto the kid who was sleepin'. I was drivin' up the mountain when HE came into me pushin' the accelerator. My hands were twitchin' but they no longer belonged to me. White knuckles gripped the wheel. It wasn't me doing the driving - it was HIM. I could hear HIS mockin' laughter and the woman screamin' as the tires screeched at every turn. The truck accelerated from fifty to sixty to seventy. A truck came towards us flashing its lights. I didn't know what HE wanted but for us to die. The woman screamed as the approachin' pickup swerved past us all chrome and blastin' horn.

I bore down on the brake as I jerked the wheel hard takin' a sharp right on a dirt road. I turned off the headlights. The truck came to a stop. My teeth were grindin' hard; my mind stripped bare. The child was screamin'. The woman sat motionless and mute. I pushed the woman from the truck and pulled her into the woods. She fought hard yellin' about the child and not to hurt it. I knew what HE were yearning for, 'cause HE told me. I took what was mine and HIS.

The next mornin' there wasn't no buttermilk. Lily looked at me with her black midnight eyes as if she was starin' me right to hell. I could have killed her and the child and we both knew it. Nine years in the pen was a long time and I didn't plan on goin' back.

I stopped messin' with Lily then. Better to do my drinkin' at Cooper's Cove. If I had an urge for a woman, I knew where to find one. Hell, I could trade anythin' even to a whore woman. Besides I didn't want the kid I did have, much less another one. Things were startin' to improve around here, and I wasn't about to ruin it.

LILY

As Willow got older I wanted to put her in pretty dresses and take her places. I wanted Willow to have a pair of store bought shoes that fit her right instead of somebody else's hand-me-downs. I thought about writing romance books as a way of getting Willow and me out of here. Not that I knew anything about romance, but I could imagine and there wasn't nothing Willard can do about that. There were correspondence schools that taught writing in the back of the ladies' magazines Myrtle gave me. I could get a job selling Christmas cards to pay for the course, if Willard would let me. I'd call on people who didn't live far away as I would have to walk.

Willard tried to stop my dreams by working me hard but I kept those magazines under the mattress. If Willard caught me, I knew he would slap me hard and take my magazines away thinking he's some white trash God over me.

This wasn't much of a life for Willow but I didn't have much say in the matter. Maybe living like this was better than growing up in the orphanage the way I did or maybe not.

Times were hard in the orphanage but I had learned household chores and how to work with 2,000 leghorn chickens so having twenty or so don't seem like nothing. Willow liked chasing the chickens and was learning to care for them herself. I told her all the time what a good job she was doing. I wanted her to feel pride in herself, something I never had.

The boys at the orphanage did full-scale farming: repairing fencing; bringing in the corn, hay, wheat; and running the dairy operation. The girls took care of the cooking, gardening, canning and the washing, which was plentiful. I got a case of varioloid fever with I was fifteen. At least it wasn't full scale smallpox. I was lucky I didn't get such a bad case like some other people did. I had a few bad scars but they faded over time. I worried I wouldn't get a boyfriend 'cause of the scars. We girls picked daisies and pulled off the petals thinking they foretold who our husbands would be. We looked after each other at the orphanage.

I don't see much of Myrtle or Mrs. Grimes. They tried to come once a month to play with Willow. Myrtle brought hand-me-down clothes from friends of hers whose children had outgrown them. I shouldn't be resentful but sometimes I was. Myrtle had a good job. Couldn't she once bring Willow something store bought?

"When are you gonna get a boyfriend Myrtle?" I asked the last time I saw her.

"I don't tell all my business," Myrtle laughed.

"I overheard Willard talking about Lester Boyton being found after all this time. I won't say nothing else about it if you don't want me to."

"It's alright, I don't mind. Lester's body has been indentified and he's being sent home. He will be buried in Arlington Cemetery with full military honors. Lester was in the 1st Marine Division when the Japanese overran his defense position on Guadalcanal. I didn't have much hope he was still alive but I still held out. His high school ring was still with him. It had his initials in it; that's what helped identify him. Lester's folks said they want me to have it. It sure means a lot."

"Maybe you can get on with your life now."

"If I known the last time I was proposed to, was going to be the last time I was going to be proposed to, I would have said 'yes'. That would have been Lester. Besides marrying isn't what it's all cracked up to be. I like working at the Weaving Mill and making my own money. I'm not so old I can't still play the field even if it seems more like a cow pasture these days." Myrtle smiled at me.

"I got something for you." Myrtle pulled three romance novels from her purse. "I didn't dare give them to you when Willard was here. Willard told me not to bring you books, saying it puts foolish notions in your head. I say to hell with Willard." Myrtle handed me the books.

I was laughing so hard I almost peed on myself.

"Ma wants you to know she's praying for you and for Willow. She wasn't up to coming today but she sent these Hershey bars for Willow. Have my brothers been by to see you lately?"

“It’s been a few weeks since their last visit. Willard takes off as soon as they get here. He’s doesn’t like what they say about him getting out of the ‘shine business and marrying me legal like for Willow’s sake.”

“They must think Willard will change his ways having a child.”

“I could have saved them the trip. There ain’t no changing that man. He’s as mean as a rattlesnake.”

“Lily, I’ll come by here Sunday and pick you and Willow up, and take you to church. Would you like that?”

“I sure would, but there would be hell to pay for it. I know Jesus understands it’s better for us to stay right here than face the wrath of Willard Grimes.”

“Next time I come, I’m bringing you a Bible. Keep it in a safe place to read when you’re alone. Read it to Willow when you can. It will be a comfort.”

“I would like that Myrtle,” was all I could think to say.

After Myrtle left I got to thinking how every Sunday Willard’s family went to church. Jonah had taken up preaching. One whole pew was filled with Willard’s family. I knew that made Mrs. Grimes proud. What I wouldn’t have given to take my daughter to church on Sundays.

LILY

My arthritis had gotten so bad over the last few years that I couldn't do much gardening or canning. I couldn't hold a pencil, much less write a story. For the most part I sat in my rocking chair in the kitchen covered in an old, dirty quilt, looking like there wasn't enough beneath my blanket big enough to be bones. It looked like Willow had sucked the fat off of me and put it on her own self.

Some mornings I was able to fix my coffee myself; other days, Willow got the percolator going. All day long, I drank coffee well after it was stone cold. Sipped coffee, rocked in my chair, read a little romance, read a little Jesus until the sun went down or Willard came home whichever comes first.

Time had moved on and Willow had expanded to what you might call a robust girl, a woman really as she got her curse at thirteen. She was strong and able to do the garden and take care of the critters as well as the cooking. The more I had to put down, the more Willow picked up. Willow didn't have much better chance of getting off Willard's farm than I did.

Willow went to school. It was the law. She caught the school bus at the top of the road. Willard knew if Willow missed much school somebody would come down here checking to see why. Willow liked school but got picked on 'cause of the clothes she wore. She hated those boxes of used clothes the churches collected for poor children that were given to her at school. She had a tough hide though and didn't want to burden me with her worries. I could see it in her eyes, how she'd like to be like the other kids. If Willard had his way she wouldn't go to school at all but would stay home and do chores.

Sometimes Willow took off walking in the woods for hours. Willard was downright mean to her when she came back and sometimes took his belt to her. It didn't seem to matter as my Willow kept on walking.

I didn't know exactly when Willow started meeting the colored boy down by the creek but I expect it was when she was fourteen. That's when I saw a change come over her, and she stopped listening to me like she always had. When Willow was fifteen, the man on the next farm came over to tell me what he had seen with his own eyes. He wanted me to put a stop to it before somebody got hurt, knowing Willard had a mean streak. I told him I appreciated him letting me know and I did.

I tried talking to Willow but it was no use. The girl was in heat and there wasn't no way around it. She had the itch and was going to scratch it. No matter how I tried Willow wouldn't tell me who the boy was.

It was a good thing her Pa was usually gone. Willard would tie them both behind his truck and drag them until you couldn't tell them apart colored or white. Willard had his own kind of justice and was known in these parts 'cause of it. All Willow wanted was love.

Willow

Ma sat in her rocking chair by the fire with nothing but her bones talking to keep her company. I knew her days sure were long. I couldn't be with her much with school and chores. Pa took off, sometimes days at a time, going who knew where and doing no good, I am sure.

I taught myself to drive the truck as nobody was around to teach me. I couldn't ask Pa 'cause he surely would have traded it away knowing I would have a way off this place. I watched everything Pa did and then practiced driving in the field behind the house. I had only driven as far as our dirt road to the main one and back, but I figured I could make it to the store. Pa had traded a bunch of Guinea hens for the truck, the best trading he ever did.

"Ma, you and I are going to the store!" I announced.

"But how are we going, your Pa's not here?" Ma looked up from her romance magazine.

"I got the keys to the truck. I hid them before Pa left. I can drive now, so let's go."

This was the day Ma met Clover, a middle-aged Negro woman, who just started working at the general store a couple of miles from the house. Clover was behind the counter sewing. She seemed timid, not looking at us directly but I could tell she was listening and taking everything in. Clover helped ladies with fabrics, patterns and quilting. She also stocked the shelves and kept the store clean.

Ma and I took our time looking around at everything. When you were with Pa you had to hurry and get things quick: coffee, flour, sugar and such. Ma and I looked at the fabrics, the hoop cheese and the knick-knacks like we had never seen them before. The front of the store had the stuff women bought like patterns, buttons, soaps and such.

I could tell Clover was putting two and two together and figuring out Ma was Willard's woman and my mother. Pa was a regular at the store. Everybody knew Willard Grimes. I had heard people joke and tease that Willard Grimes was the mayor of these parts.

There was a potbellied stove in the back where the men hung out playing checkers and telling lies. I knew they would have plenty to talk about with me and Ma being in the store without Pa. I wanted to buy a transistor radio that day with money I stole from Pa when he was passed out. Counting out the money at the counter, I didn't have enough. The way Clover looked at Ma and the way Ma looked back at Clover it seemed they understood each other without saying words. It could have been 'cause they both had bruises showing inside and out.

Clover opened up her little beaded change purse and counted out nickels and dimes until there was enough change for me to buy Ma the radio.

"Thank you Ma'am, thank you ever so much," I said. Clover gave me a knowing smile.

"I'm glad to help you and your Ma if I can," Clover said just loud enough that Ma heard.

"Ma, this radio is for you. You need something to listen to while I am at school or doing chores," I said giving it to her.

Ma looked at me with tears in her eyes. I just nodded my head to say *yes, take the radio. It is alright.*

Mama and I left the store and got in the truck. Ma looked at me with a puzzled expression while holding on to the transistor radio.

"That was sure nice of that woman to do. You would think she knew us," Ma said. I didn't say a word.

LILY

Clover came to see me whenever she could. She walked through the woods mostly, preferring not to be a colored woman walking alone on the roads. She said she didn't live far away as the crow flied. Often she brought me her spiced peaches in pretty blue mason jars. They were a special treat and I always gobbled them down fast saving the last few for Willow. I talked to Clover about my dreams for Willow, about how I wanted her off this farm, to travel and see places I have only read about in my romance novels. Clover listened real good and sometimes held my hand. Clover was the color of pine cones and always smelled like the forest. She had the sweetest giggle and could always make me laugh, even though she covered her mouth to hide the fact so many teeth were missing. Clover made me a quilt to put over my legs since I often felt cold to the bone. She said it was a dreaming quilt full of soft meadow colors of yellow, green and pink.

Clover held onto my arm and helped me walk into the woods where we lay down on the dreaming quilt together. Clover touched my face so gentle. It was the nicest thing anybody ever did, touching me that way. Clover and I seemed to understand each other without saying a word. My Clover had talking eyes. I have never said this to Clover, but I wonder sometimes if it was better to not have dreams at all than to see them die. Maybe it was better if dreams not be born.

I wanted to see Clover more often, but she was busy working at the store cutting and sewing pretty things for rich ladies or spending time in the forest collecting special things she kept in her blue jars. Clover saved time for me though and I had nothing but time on my hands.

LILY

It was November and all the signs said the cold was here to stay. The fur on the rabbits' feet was thicker than usual and the carrots Willow planted had grown deeper than ever. When Willow was a little girl sometimes, her Pa and I would take the hogs to the stockyard to sell. When the moon was growing, the hogs weighed more, and when the moon was shrinking, the meat would too. I thought about how my heart was like a moon that never grew. With Willard it only shrank and shriveled over the years, with no kindness, with no nothing at all.

It was hard on Willow seeing me suffer, sitting in my rocker with little to say. I spent my days worrying about Willow though I didn't let on. One day just followed another as I rocked in my chair listening to the radio. Willow's only comfort seemed to be eating them cakes and pies that come from the Piggly Wiggly Store. Her Pa knew she drives the truck some. He left but a little gas in it and no money for getting more.

When Clover came to see me she brought a big wicker basket and I gave her eggs that she sold for me at the store. The money Clover gave me I gave to Willow.

The only chores that got done were what Willow did and her Papa knew it. When Willow wasn't doing chores she was meeting a fella in the woods. I knew 'cause I could sniff the man smell on her. I prayed for sweet Jesus to care for Willow and not let her get caught or get in a family way. If only I was stronger. But I was getting thinner and thinner. Willow was becoming a mountain while I was becoming the wind.

Clover hadn't been to see me for the longest time and I felt so alone. Usually she came every couple weeks but I hadn't seen her and deer season had come and gone. Willow and I took Pa's truck the first chance we got and went to the store to see if Clover was alright.

As soon as I walked in, I recognized a woman Clover did sewing for. I asked her if Clover was sick. The woman put a finger to her lips for me to shush and indicated for me to follow her outside. "I'm not going to say anything the men might overhear. They can be worse gossips than women and start more trouble," the woman whispered.

"Do you know where Clover is?" I asked.

"I just know what I've heard but I have no knowledge directly." The woman was looking around to be sure no one was near.

"Please, just tell me what you know."

"Well, you know how colored people are, all suspicious and everything, so you probably shouldn't believe a word of this. The owner of the store called the sheriff to see if a deputy could check on Clover, seeing she missed a week's work and that wasn't like her. One of Clover's neighbors saw the deputy's car go down Clover's road and followed him. Listening through the window, the neighbor heard the deputy talking to Clover's husband. He claimed he didn't know where Clover was and acted real spooked. He said on the night Clover went missing, he pulled back the blankets to go to bed when a coiled up rattler struck him, and he's been real sick since. There isn't no accounting for how the snake got there," the woman said.

"Is anyone looking for Clover? Are they searching the woods?"

"I'm sure the deputy put it all in his report. But what can he do? Colored people are getting in trouble all the time. If you ask me her low-count husband killed her. He only does odd jobs, drinks mostly. I suspect he slapped her around some. I'm sure if anyone looks hard enough they'll find her buried behind the house. You know how these people are. Poor Clover, I'm sure she's six foot under by now, and I need to find somebody else to do my sewing."

"The spider taketh hold with her hands,
and is in kings' palaces."
Proverbs: 30:28

LILY

Time crawled after the news of Clover's disappearance. It didn't look like anyone was going to look for her, being she was a colored woman, and that made me sad. One day whilst I was sitting and pondering, I thought about an old cardboard box I had put away years ago that had papers in it. I knowed where it was, down in the root cellar. It took me the better part of a day to scoot my fanny across the floor and down them dirty steps and back up again. I had hid the box good. There were spider webs all down the stairs and spiders and their eggs in the cardboard box. I didn't mind though. They were living creatures. That's what I wanted the box for, to see that I was a living creature before Willard. There weren't much in the box, a paper where I had been baptized at the Holy Rock Baptist Church near the orphanage when I was twelve and a small Bible that I had pressed wild flowers in. There was a card with the Ten Commandments on it. I had been right with the Lord then.

In the box was a pale pink ribbon. It had been in my hair when I was a baby and left at the orphanage. It must have been my Ma. She had to have loved me once to have put that ribbon in my hair. I spent hours looking in that box and feeling that ribbon against my cheek. My Ma had touched that ribbon, maybe against her own cheek, and now, I was touching it too.

I watched the spiders that lived in my heart box with my baby ribbon. They were pretty little things with what looked like a fiddles on their backs. They danced as they moved. Perhaps they were making music only they could hear. I said the first prayer I had said in many a day: "please Jesus, if I listen hard enough will you let me hear the music the spiders play in my heart box too."

“With spiders I have friendship made,
and watched them in their sullen trade.”
Byron

LILY

I don’t rightly know when it was that Willow left. I found her note under the kitchen table where it musta fallen off. Willow had gotten herself in a family way and run off with the baby’s daddy. That’s what the note said anyway. It must have been that colored boy she’d been meeting down by the creek ‘cause as far as I knew there hadn’t been no other.

I never thought my Willow would run off and leave me this way. I’m glad she did. Maybe now she had a chance as long as her Pa didn’t find her, but he didn’t care enough to look. Willard wasn’t around much. He didn’t care about this place anymore. It was all falling to ruin. Willow said in her note she’d come back for me and not to worry. No more weeping, Willow.

My spiders kept me busy, and I didn’t have time for nothing else. They were forever weaving webs in different places, and I would have to find them least they get into trouble and not be safe. We were forever playing hide-and-seek. Mostly I slept all day and stayed up all night with my spiders. This was what they liked best. It got where there wasn’t no food in the house except in the cellar, but I didn’t mind ‘cause I wasn’t eating much. When I had to, I scooted my fanny down the cellar steps and got some beans or peach preserves. Willow must have planned her leaving ‘cause I didn’t remember so many canned goods. She knew I’d find them in the cellar and I’d have enough to eat.

Going to the cellar was hard on me, and I didn’t go much in the beginning. But more times than not, I’d find me a new fiddler friend to add to our family, and that made the trip worth going. I always asked the new spiders if they wanted to come upstairs with me, but sometimes a fiddler was busy spinning new clothes or in the middle of a courtship so I’d leave them be. More often than not, they wanted to come live a new life and have an adventure.

I took my new fiddler and introduced him to his new family. I’d gotten where I can tell if they were male or female. Mostly the females were bigger. Sometimes the female ate the male. I watched it happen.

In the beginning, I was unsure of who was who as spiders are just as different as people are. After awhile, each one of them approached me cautiously and told me who they were and what they needed from me.

LILY

I played games with my spiders for their amusement and mine. They liked *Itsy Bitsy Spider*, climbing all over me, like I was their water spout. They knew I'm not no Miss Muffet to be frightened away. Not once did they bite me. I gave them names: Elizabeth, Timothy, Vaughn, Jane, Marie, Peggy, Charles, Noelle and Evelena.These were the names of children at the orphanage.

How my fiddlers liked to leave their webs at night to hunt! I put sheets on Willard's bed and let my fiddlers sleep there. Willard was gone most nights, drinking and carousing and when he did come home, he liked to lay on the floor in front of the wood stove to sleep. Clover had bought me the sheets at a church yard sale. I never had sheets before. I saved the sheets for something special and thought my fiddlers needed to be comfortable after being up all night. My fiddlers didn't mind sharing a bed with Willard, especially with them sleeping all day while Willard slept at night when he came home.

Clover had showed me how spiders liked to play in tree bark. I liked peeling bark from trees to see what treasures might lay underneath. Pulling tree bark started me tearing away moles and scabs from my own skin, making little scars that would stay on my body forever, helping me remember I was alive.

Each morning I made sure there was a piece of tree bark in Willard's bed. It was my special kiss to my babies for a good day's sleep. My fiddlers slept on soft sheets. Those sheets weren't for me, no sir! I slept in my chair with my baby ribbon pressed against my cheek. I wanted to wake quick in case one of my fiddlers needed me. One, two, three, four, five, six, seven, eight, nine. I make sure they were all accounted for. I cared for my fiddlers and they cared for me.

"For death is come up into our windows,
and has entered into our palaces."
Jeremiah 9:21

Willard

I felt no pain although there were dark spots and blisters on my face and legs. The next day, the spots on my legs were darker and there were open sores. I was hurtin' bad and itchin' on my back and down in my male parts. Somethin' must have bitten me whilst I was sittin' on the privy or while I was sleepin'. Every part of me needed scratchin'. I was tired, real tired. My joints hurt, hell, everythin' hurt. One minute I was hot with fever, then I was cold. I tried to lay down but couldn't. I had to keep movin', couldn't give in to it. Being still made it worse. Drive. I would drive. I had to get my mind off the pain. Rhodessa. I wanted to see Rhodessa. But she was dead, wasn't she? Back to Cahas Mountain that's where I would drive.

The thoughts wouldn't stop comin' but the head poundin' stayed away. I had not driven to Cahas Mountain in years. I hadn't wanted to go back there, but somethin' was telling me to go. I climbed into the truck, barely makin' it 'cause of the pain. Should I drive to Cahas Mountain? Why not? Why not go? What was there to find or not to find? I started the truck and drove. Memories came floodin' back as I took the once familiar roads to Rhodessa's home place.

"Rhodessa, here's the road where we had our picnic, where I first kissed you. You remember don't you honey?"

I turned to look at her. She wasn't there. My mind was playin' tricks on me. Had she been there? Did it really happen? *Rhodessa is dead*, I told myself again. *She had your baby. He is dead too.* Over and over, my head swirled with pieces of thoughts that wouldn't stop movin'. No thought would stand still long enough for me to see it clearly and know what it was. There was no way to take a good aim at the thought and kill it if it needed to be killed.

I parked the car at the old house. Deserted it was with broken boards and the front door open. I could tell hunters had laid claim to it durin' huntin' season. There was a dirty mattress somebody had drug in. Discarded bottles and empty cans of potted meat were on the floor. Mice were livin' here now. Torn piles of papers and mattress stuffin' were everywhere. I walked upstairs to the bedroom I shared with Rhodessa. All that was left was a torn shade and mouse droppings.

I could almost make out Ruby and Hattie's whiny voices callin' out, but then my mind came clear and told me it was the wind. I walked the mountain path, to the cemetery like I had done with Rhodessa but now I walked alone. "Gone but Not Forgotten" was written on her tombstone. But try as best I could I could not conjure up Rhodessa's face. I had been hopin' to remember by comin' here but it was gone. The ground was hard and cold where she lay. There was nothin' left of her but bones in a box. I turned and walked away.

I must have passed out on that old mattress in the house. When I came to, I was feelin' real bad. I had to get to Dr. Riddle. I made it to my vehicle and got behind the wheel. I pert near couldn't drive for the pain. Places on my body were open runnin' sores and pieces of my skin were turnin' black like I was being eatin' alive; even my piss had turned black. Somehow I made it to Rocky Mount. When I walked in the waitin' room people stared at me then looked away. I could smell my rotten flesh. A nurse rushed me into an examinin' room to get me away from other people. I didn't wait but a minute before Dr. Riddle came in. He stared at me not saying a word while he put on his plastic gloves and started examinin' me. "Willard, it looks like you have been bitten all over by spiders. By the looks of the ulcerations and decaying flesh I suspect it's the brown recluse. You may know it as the fiddle-back. They are common enough in this area but I usually see people with only a single bite maybe two. Not like this. I don't know how it is possible that you have been bitten so many times but you have. We need to get you to the hospital right now. I am not equipped to help you here at the office."

"I don't cotton to no hospital. Ain't there something you can do?"

"You've got more than twenty bites, Willard. What you are seeing is only the beginning of what's to come. How you managed to drive here yourself I don't know. Let me call an ambulance for you. You can't drive like this."

“Hell no, I don’t want no ambulance or no hospital either.”

“If I was you Willard, I would get my affairs in order. There’s not much any one can do for you now other than clean you up and bandage you. You need something strong for the pain. Call someone in your family to come get you and take you home. I’ll talk to them when they get here. Let your family tend to you.”

“Family,” I laughed. “That’s a good one. I ain’t got no family except for an old woman who is crazy as a loon and a no-account daughter who has run off with a colored boy. I ain’t got no place to go die.”

“Here’s some pills for the pain. I’ll write you a prescription for more. You are going to need them. Get someone to fill it for you and get to a hospital. I don’t like you leaving my office like this.”

My mind was whirling. None of this could be real. I got the truck to start and drove off as fast as I could. What was happenin’ to me? Nothin’ made sense. I made it to Cooper’s Cove and almost drove into the water, not being able to stop the truck until I hit a tree.

I took an old blanket and a jar of ‘shine from the truck. The pain was like hell fire, I guzzled my ‘shine, and took all the pills Doc Riddle gave me hopin’ to pass out and not wakeup.

Everythin’ went black and I heard HIS voice comin’ for me. I had to get away! Feelin’ my way, I went from tree to tree not knowin’ where I was. I stumbled along until I was in deep snow, hearin’ tormented screamin’ behind me. I was freezin’ cold. When I could walk no further I took to crawlin’. The buzzin’ of bees came towards me, but I slunk away like a beaten dog. The sounds grew louder and louder in my head. I was so hot, so thirsty, burnin’! What kind of hell was this? And then I knew - it was the stingin’ torment of my own wormwood life. I was alive in my own damnation!

“Please Jesus, if you are real, take me from this awful place!” I cried out.

Then it was over. The pain stopped. I was in my own Virginia Mountains and could see again. Laurel was bloomin’, and there were deer in the fields. I walked with my bolt-action twenty-two, but I did not shoot. I did not want to maim or kill in this place. I walked through scrub cedars, cow pastures, and cornfields. My dark soul felt camouflaged here. Then I saw them: Rhodessa Rose and her sisters, walking arm and arm. They walked past me and didn't see me at all.

"Rhodessa Rose, it's me Willard, I'm back from the war!"

She did not turn her head to look at me but kept walkin'. There was a boy. He stood by a lake skippin' stones with my Pa beside him! Pa had his hand on this boy's shoulder, my boy's shoulder!

I hollered "Pa!" but he did not answer.

The smell of cooked food was carried by a light breeze. It had to be Ma cookin'. I hoped she had baked my favorite pies, lemon meringue and cherry. I wanted to eat her homemade bread and beef roast hot from the oven.

"Ma, it's me Willard!" I cried out to her.

Where was she?

"Ma, it's me Willard," I tried again. No answer.

Pa, my boy, Rhodessa, Hattie and Ruby were laughin' as they walked into the kitchen. Everyone sat down and Pa said grace. Everybody was drinkin' buttermilk. Ma was nowhere around. I called again. No one could hear me or see me!

I couldn't stand it any longer. I walked past my old bedroom. My catcher's mitt and croquet set were still there. I left the house sobbin'.

I walked through briars and underbrush tryin' to make sense of things. Was this a queer joke? Had I gone mad with fever? I saw wild turkey and quail. Still I did not shoot. I was in an apple orchard with dogwood trees nearby and rollin' hills of green. I walked until I came to a creek full of flowin' water with white quartz rocks all around. There was soft moss on the ground and a truck nearby. I saw a man lyin' on a blanket, an empty Mason jar beside him. I recognized the man. It was me, and I was dead.

"I will restore to you the years that the locust hath eaten."
Joel 2:25

LILY

I was sitting in my rocking chair letting my babies crawl over me when Lawyer Simpson came calling. The rain had been pouring, and the man was soaked to the bone. Lawyer Simpson looked a bit taken back by my spiders and kept staring but what did he expect when my babies were just waking up?

"Have a seat, and tell me what you came for," I said.

"Willard's been deceased just a short while, and I am sorry to intrude on your grief but there are some papers I need to go over with your daughter. You don't have a phone and I didn't want to send these papers by mail without some personal explanation."

"Willow's not here. I reckon you can tell me what this is all about."

"As you probably know, Willard was married to Rhodessa Rose Hartman Grimes from Cahas Mountain. Rhodessa died many years ago. There was a will and being that Rhodessa was the last living daughter, her home place on Cahas Mountain was left to her. At Rhodessa's death, it went to Willard. I know these things can be complicated, Lily, but I hope I can help clarify the situation for you. Now with Willard's passing, what was his is now Willow's, being her father's only child.

When Willard came back from prison I sent word he needed to see me. Rhodessa's homeplace would have been lost due to back taxes if I hadn't paid them while Willard was in prison. I took care of everything for him. Willard and I always had our special arrangements. I probably shouldn't say this, but I am partial to a nip now and then and Willard always had the finest 'shine in three states. I entertain a lot in my kind of business. Willard kept me well supplied. I figured when he got out of the pen our arrangement would continue.

Both Willard and I knew he couldn't live on Cahas Mountain. He had made to many enemies, particularly the Sheriff and the Perdue boys. There were others as well. It was a godsend his Pa bought him this place, Lily. Willard and I went back to our usual business arrangement and I paid the taxes on Rhodessa's home place so Willard didn't have to be bothered with it. Now, with Willard's death the estate passes on to Willow. So I am here to fulfill the terms of the will and to offer you my condolences."

"I don't rightly know what to tell you other than I'll keep the legal papers for Willow until she comes home."

"Lily, perhaps you had better let me keep the papers in case you become sick from a spider bite perhaps? Is there someone I can call to look after you since Willow isn't here?"

"No need in worrying about me. I will make sure Willow gets her papers. You came and said your piece, so now you can be on your way."

Lawyer Simpson tipped his hat and left.

Willow

"Ma, it's me. I'm home," I hollered walking into the old house.

I knew I would find Ma in her rocking chair just like I left her. It took me aback seeing spiders on her face. She wasn't acting like anything was wrong so I didn't say anything, not wanting to cause Ma to move and the spiders to bite her. "I'm sorry I left you for so long, but I am back now, and I have so much to tell you."

Ma seemed stunned and couldn't speak for a full minute. "Willow, where have you been girl? You've filled out woman like! What a sight you are!"

I could barely talk to Ma, seeing the tears in her eyes as she looked first to me then to my daughter whom I was carrying in my arms. The lump in my throat was bigger than a potato. I hugged Ma long and hard, in spite of the spiders, making sure the baby was kept a distance from Ma's face. We had to stop hugging afraid we might squish the baby. Ma and I got to laughing hard; finally I was able to speak again.

"She's eight months old. I was shelling a pot of beans when my labor started that's why I named her Shelly Bean. I would have come home before but I wasn't about to bring Bean around Pa. I would have killed him if he was mean to her. I got more to tell you Ma. If you will put the spiders away, I'll let you hold Bean while I get my other two surprises."

Ma gently placed her spiders in a heart shaped box and I placed Bean in Ma's arms. I left for just a minute and came back with my next surprise.

"Ma, this here is Jeremy. He's my husband and Bean's daddy."

"Are you the young colored man Willow was meeting down by the creek?"

"Yes Ma'am," came the voice of a tall young man with skin the color of maple syrup.

"Well I'm glad to finally meet you. Have you been good to my daughter and granddaughter?"

"I try my best ma'am. I love them both. I work hard and would never hurt a hair on their heads," Jeremy answered.

“That’s all I can ask then,” Mama said satisfied with his answers.

“Ma, I have one more surprise for you. It’s a big one so get ready”.

Clover walked slowly into the cabin taking her time to reach Ma as not to startle her more than she already was. Clover stood silently looking at Ma while I did all the talking.

“Ma, Clover is Jeremy’s mother. When Jeremy told her I was going to have a baby, Clover came up with a plan to disappear. She got a job in Roanoke, where she has family and made a home for me and Jeremy to come to. She didn’t tell anybody where she was until she was ready for us to come. She was afraid Jeremy’s father would find her and bring her home. Clover wanted us all to be safe. That is the only reason I went off and left you here. Jeremy was able to get a job driving a delivery truck while I waited for the baby to come.”

“Clover, I thought you were dead, and now you are alive and come back to me, sweet Jesus!” Ma said.

“It wasn’t going to be easy for our children, but easier than it would have been if their daddies knew. It grieved me to leave you alone. My plan wouldn’t have worked if you and I both disappeared at the same time. Now that Willard is dead and my husband has taken up with another woman, we are finally free and back to stay!” Clover said with a grin that covered her whole face.

“No you are not,” Ma said. “Not one of you is staying!”

I looked at Ma with my mouth hanging open. I thought she would want us back. But she didn’t. I never dreamed this would happen!

“Nobody is staying. Not even me. We are moving to Cahas Mountain!”

The next morning, Willow and I went to see Lawyer Simpson. All of us wanted to move to Cahas Mountain as soon as we could, but it would take money to make it happen and none of us had any.

"Willow, the home of Willard's first wife is now yours free and clear. I have the paperwork for you to sign. Once you do, I will record the deed at the Franklin County Courthouse," Lawyer Simpson said.

"What about Willard's place? Doesn't that belong to me now?" I asked.

"Virginia law does not recognize common law marriage. I know it's not right for all the hard years you spent with Willard, but that goes to Willow as well," Lawyer Simpson said.

"I never expected anything different."

Willow and Lawyer Simpson started talking all legal like. I couldn't make sense of it so I went and sat in the front office and drank coffee the nice secretary brought me.

It didn't seem like no time before a public auction was set up to get rid of Willard's farm. The house didn't bring nothing but the land it was sitting on did. A Franklin County real estate developer bought the land, saying he was going to tear it down and build a race track on it. He called it a speedway. Can you imagine that?

Lawyer Simpson contacted Willow when he had papers for her to sign. When Willow and Jeremy returned from Rocky Mount, Willow handed me a check. "Ma, this is for you."

I took the envelope from her outstretched hand. "I will open this on the drive to Cahas Mountain. We are making new memories and I don't want to read it standing in Willard's house."

We gathered the few things we were taking with us. There wasn't much. It all fit in the delivery truck Jeremy borrowed from work.

"Ma, what should we do with this house? I don't ever want to see this place again. There ain't nothing but bad memories of Pa. I don't want nobody else to feel what went on here."

"We will burn it to the ground."

Willow and Jeremy poured what was left of Willard's shine all over the floors in the kitchen, bedroom and porch. "Ma, here's the matches. It's you that needs to start the fire."

The house lit up like the Fourth of July. Clover held my hand as we stood at the top of the road and watched the house burn down. For us there was no looking back.

All of us squeezed into the front seat of the truck with Clover holding the baby. Jeremy started our drive to Cahas Mountain. None of us could speak having watched the past burn away to nothing but smoke.

After we had driven several miles Willow reminded me of the letter. There it was, a check made out to me, Lillith McKay, the name that was on my birth certificate. I hadn't seen my last name written down or spoken in many a year. I knew right off what I was going to do with the money. Our new home would have pretty kitchen curtains. There were going to be sheets on all the beds and all the walls would have fresh paint. I would have a porch swing where I would rock my grandbaby. Dreams for Willow and my sweet granddaughter would come true. Clover and I would giggle and have coffee at the kitchen table. My mind was swimming with the possibilities of our new life.

"For I will set mine eyes upon them for good,
and I will bring them again to this land
and I will build them, and not pull them down;
and I will plant them, and not pluck them up.
And I will give them a heart to know me,
that I am the LORD:and they shall be my people,
and I will be their God: for they shall return unto me
with their whole heart."
Jeremiah 24:6-7

LILY

Lawyer Simpson had given us directions to the farm and a survey map of the land so we had no trouble coming up on it. When we got to the edge of the property, I told Jeremy to stop the truck.

"We need to feel our new home. We need not come upon it all at once but to introduce ourselves gently to this place that is new to us and us to it. I do not want to startle what lives or lives no longer and awaken what need not be awaked, at least not yet. Leave the truck where it is and we will walk the dirt road to our new home which now lays claim to us and us to it," I said.

"I'll take Bean and Mom to the store for food and camping supplies and leave you and Willow to walk the place. We will be back before dusk," said Jeremy.

Willow and I were taken back by Cahas Mountain. We stood there gazing upon her. A mountain this beautiful must be female with her shapely curves and gentle slopes. I looked forward to talking to her and getting to know her better. I knew she had stories and I had the rest of my life for Cahas Mountain to whisper in my ear. At first, Willow and I could not see the old house for it was all but smothered in nature's wild growth claiming the house for its own. Blackberry brambles and pokeweed, uninhibited and unruly, hindered our walking as if to say "take heed of us. We were here first, and we are watching you."

Slowly we tread, not talking but listening to what might be told to us by years past and by quiet watching. A weathered picket fence showed itself in places, but hid otherwise under living vines bearing it over, low to the ground with the weight of grief gone by.

Pulling open as far as possible, the warped and creaking door, Willow and I stepped into the house, watching for rotten boards. The once white farmhouse allowed us to enter and to examine her. The house knew we meant no harm. Still the house held secrets, as she should, until she knew us better.

Over the kitchen sink was a window with broken glass, from which a slight wind blew, moving shreds of curtains which still hung on. Old wooden cabinets held true, with doors barely hanging from worn-out hinges. Field mice had built comfortable homes and I could not blame them for it for inside the cabinets it was warm and dry.

The parlor's wallpaper still told a faint story of pale green leaves and pink roses. Someone had chosen this pattern, Rhodessa's mother, most likely. It was a lovely choice, one I would have picked myself had it been me. Perhaps we could find the same wallpaper. The house would like that, to know and remember what it had been and could be again.

The steps to the bedrooms were solid, although the railing was loose. Wasps had built their home in the front bedroom. This room would be for Willow and Jeremy. There was a small bedroom for Bean and another for Clover and me to share. How I liked the thought of Clover and me talking into the night and being close to one another again.

Willow and I walked the path to the family cemetery to show our respects. Sweet smelling honeysuckle covered the fence that surrounded the souls who belonged to this place. Untangling the bewildered vines and briars, which guarded the gate, admission was granted for us to enter. Willow and I spoke to all the graves calling each one by the names on their markers, including the child Willard Grimes, whose name appeared with his mother's. A marble statue of an angel with a small child stood over them.

Clover, Jeremy and Bean came back with sleeping bags, brooms, tools, canned goods, charcoal, a grill and all kinds of things. We stayed at our new home the very first night feasting on sardines and crackers by candle light. The next day, we all went to the bank. I gave Willow the first check from my brand new checking account, the first I had ever written. I signed my name to the check but left the amount empty. Then we all went and waited for Willow as she got her driver's license. That afternoon, Willow was driving a new pickup truck, her very own!

By winter, the house had new windows, wiring, paint on the inside and running water. We had a permit for a bathroom to be built as soon as we could. Until then, we had the Johnny house. We had our worries about the house meeting inspection but Jeremy was handy and knew what had to be done and who to call to help him. Come spring there would be a bathtub and flush commode. Clover and I had gone to town and picked out wallpaper. I had found the same paper that was on the walls before, pale green with pink flowers. I knew I would.

Just before Christmas, I made an announcement: "Tomorrow morning all of us are going to downtown Roanoke and buy new clothes. There will be no hand-me downs in this house again. Throw everything away except what you are going to wear tomorrow. We are going shopping."

We had great fun picking out clothes, trying them on together, making big piles on the floor which we hung back up. The sales ladies looked at us real funny especially when I pulled out a roll of cash to pay for everything and told the salesgirls to throw away the clothes we came in wearing. Afterwards we went to lunch in a fancy restaurant. Oh, you never saw the likes of us!

Life was good now. I found three new fiddlers in our new house and introduced them to the others. My arthritis still hurt but not so much as before probably 'cause Clover kept me in her remedies and Bean was old enough to fetch me things. Mostly it was because I was happy.

Whilst working on the house Jeremy uncovered some hidden mason jars which I knew must have been Willard's. Willow and Bean came across an old still out in the woods while they were playing. Jeremy got it going and it wasn't long before he was making a little apple 'shine. Apples were plentiful as there was an apple packing plant only a stone's throw from our place. Jeremy and Willow were like little kids climbing apple trees in the early evenings, always spotting the most beautiful apple on the highest limb. It made me laugh seeing them so happy, grabbing on to a piece of childhood they never had.

Jeremy started his own business helping people move and picked up some delivery jobs in Roanoke. He carried a little 'shine for a few special customers. Willow had a job at the apple packing plant working in the office. She answered the phone and did filing. Willow was good at it and liked dressing nice and being with people. She came home every day for lunch. Clover and I always had it waiting on her. Us grannies took care of Shelly Bean.

There is nothing like the smell of newly turned earth especially when it's your own place. Clover was forever planting gardens with vegetables, flowers and her own healing herbs. To my old eyes there weren't no better times than these.

Preacher Shiflett

I was surprised by the letter I received from Mrs. Grimes saying it was imperative we meet. She asked if it was possible for me to come to her as she had no means of transportation without having to disclose the nature of her business. Mrs. Grimes and I met at her son Jonah's house. She chose a day her son would be at work and his family was busy with other activities.

"Thank you for coming. What I want to discuss with you is of a highly personal nature. I do not want to share the details, for no one needs to know other than the recipient of the letters." Her voice was soft, not much above a whisper, even though no one was home to overhear. Each word she spoke was measured and weighed with exactness of speech. Mrs. Grimes was determined things go exactly as she planned.

"I have kept this letter in the bottom of my keepsake trunk. I placed it there after Rhodessa's death for safe keeping. After all this time, it slipped my mind. At my age I am getting forgetful. I was getting something out of the trunk recently when I came upon it. I should not have opened it. It was not mine to open. I am ashamed that I did. Now that I have, I have to do what is right even if it pains me. I have another letter written by me. Please deliver them both to Jethro Greer."

I gave her my word and asked no questions.

Jethro came over the same night I called. We had a fine talk on the front porch before we got to the business at hand.

"I'm in a new line of work now. I got my CDL license and am driving long haul trucks. I like the travel and the job gives me plenty of time to think while I am on the road," Jethro said.

"Speaking of change; I want you to know I don't touch the bottle now. No more getting the Spirit except through the good book. I quit a few years back. I used to think I had to drink with the 'shiners so they would trust me, in order to save their souls, but it didn't necessarily work out that way. Over the years, I saw what 'shine did to families. It's just me and Jesus now and not a drop of alcohol. But you didn't come to jaw with me all night, son. Let's go on in the house so I can get the letters."

I stopped talking. Being an old preacher, I could go on for hours. I was lonely with the wife passing, but the good Lord whispered in my ear to quit my blabbering and let the boy have his envelopes and be on his way. I hoped it was good news. Good news from a long time ago.

Jethro Greer

Preacher Shiflett had shrunk right much since I had seen him last. But he still had those piercing blue eyes that could see right through you and a firm handshake. I always liked the old man even when I was sheriff and knew he was running interference with the law.

I took the letters from Preacher Shiflett's outstretched hand. The image of Rhodessa walked thru my mind. *Rhodessa, is this about you? What is this all about?* I hurried home to read them where there would be no chance of disruption. I walked in my front door and locked it behind me then I took the phone off the hook. I fixed myself a bourbon and branch. I didn't normally drink, but this was an exception.

LILY

I had visitors. A man named Jethro Greer came to the door with a young woman named Rachel Rose. She had long dark hair, high cheekbones and brown eyes. She was a beauty.

Mr. Greer said he knew the family that lived here before us and with my permission could he and the young woman visit the cemetery? Of course, I said yes. I could tell something weighed heavily upon them.

I didn't ask no questions, but I watched them walk up the path to the cemetery from the porch swing. They had a pretty day for a walk with the rhododendron blooming.

I saw Jethro Greer give the girl something to read, not a book exactly, more like a paper. For the longest time the girl didn't move. Next thing I knew they was gone. I must have fallen asleep in the swing. That happened a lot lately.

I was feeling older than my years and thinking my time on earth would end sooner rather than later and my skeleton would soon be all there was of me. I wondered when I would be called to the other side. Most days I sat on the front porch with one of Clover's quilts over my legs looking at the mountain. Every day, I noticed how something had changed. Sometimes it was the simplest thing like a new bird's nest or a color of pink I had never seen in the sky before.

It was one of those days that I saw a new spider web. I had Clover get me an empty matchbox from the kitchen. She gently picked the three spiders from the web and placed them in the box. The spiders kept me company as I watched the mountain relax in a contented familiarity of colors, changing from green to bluish green to the color of ripe plums while the cicadas talked among themselves about the many things they had seen.

Mrs. Grimes

My Dear Rachel Rose,

As the years have passed, it has been my pleasure to witness you turn into a beautiful young woman. As I write this letter to you, I have my doubts I am doing right by you. This is my decision and no one else's and it weighs heavily upon my heart. I want you to know the truth about your birth and the facts as they are. I am your grandmother and Mr. G., as you always called him, your grandfather. Now you understand why we doted on you at church and always remembered your birthdays.

How surprised I was when you made your appearance into this world. Taking a pair of sewing scissors, I cut the cord that bound you to your mother, who died during childbirth as did your twin brother. I wrapped you in a shawl and placed you in a willow basket. As fast and as safely as we could your grandfather and I walked through the woods to the home of our dear friends, Mavis and Dalton Pollard praying every step of the way that you would live.

Taking one look at you, so tiny and frail, Mavis knew what we were there for. Mavis, having just lost her babe days before, took you from the basket, suckled you, and made you her daughter that very minute. Dalton, the only father you have ever known, claimed you as his own.

When this letter comes to you, it will be time to ask your parents any questions you may have. They are no longer bound to promises made a long time ago. Preacher Shiflett and Sheriff Jethro Greer, both of Cahas Mountain, knew your real mother, Rhodessa Rose Hartman. She was married to my son Willard. Within Preacher Shiflett and Sheriff Greer lie answers about your people. I will never understand the path my son took in life. Willard had a troubled soul and it was Rhodessa's wish he never knew of you, a request we honored.

I want you to hear of the loveliness and sweet temperament of your mother for these are the same qualities you possess, as well as her likeness in physical appearance. The same goodness I saw in your mother, I see in you.

I pray that you have no ill will for me for it is better to know the Truth and be set free to cast your lot in life.

Your grandmother,

Ida Grimes

"A new heart I will give you and a new spirit I will put within you;
I will take out of your flesh the heart of stone
and give you a heart of flesh."
Ezekiel 36:26

RACHEL ROSE

Most times when the moon is full, I take a trip to Cahas Mountain to visit the grave of my birth mother. It feels a fitting time for me to go with the moon glow soft and gentle like a mother's love. My mother's spirit is strong, and I feel her presence with me. Sometimes I call Jethro. I still can't call him father as the Pollards are my real parents to me. I like Jethro more all the time. I know I can trust him, and I know he loves me. He tells me often how like my mother I am and how much I favor her. Each time I see him he tells me more about her. Tears came to his eyes when he told me of how he gave my mother the opal ring I wear. Whenever I ask him if he wants to join me on Cahas Mountain, he always says yes unless he is having to take off on one of his long runs. My beau, Elbert, reminds me of Jethro. He is a fireman in Roanoke. Hopefully after we are married a few years we will have a daughter. We have talked about naming her Rhodessa Rose.

At full darkness, when the moon is at its highest, Jeremy brings out a bottle of 'shine and his mandolin and we gather on the porch. "It is time for the mountain goddesses to take their places," Jeremy says laughing.

Then our ritual begins. We each take a swig from the Mason jar, which is passed around.

Jeremy plays wild and crazy mountain music on his mandolin and we twirl and spin while we howl at the moon. If Jethro is with us, he dances with me like he is a gypsy king.

As the night goes on, Lily will lift her old withered arm to make a toast. It is the same toast and never changes. "On nights like this my moon heart grows larger than the night sky!"

Lily never drinks though. She is too weak for something strong as 'shine.

Instead, Lily holds up her Diamond Matchbook box which holds her spider family: Mary, Joseph and Jesus.

Willow

When Shelly Bean started school, Jeremy and I got out of the ‘shine business. We didn’t want our girl growing up seeing her parents doing stuff that was against the law. Bean has never had a hand laid on her, and there has been no name calling either. It seems an evil spell has been put to rest with loving kindness. Jeremy has done well for all of us. He has been able to get several trucks and drivers and expanded his delivery business.

Every week we go to Sunday school and church and listen to Preacher Shiflett. Between all of us we fill a pew! People come from all around to hear him preach, and the church is busting at the seams. He must be close to eighty years old! Every night we take turns reading scripture, and we say prayers at all of our meals.

Often a neighbor or wayfaring traveler stops at our white rock well and takes a cool sip of water from our dipper. We are happy to oblige for our lives have been truly blessed on Cahas Mountain.

I never have visited Pa’s grave. He was buried near his family at Evergreen Cemetery where his father and grandparents lay. The story is there’s a ghost of a man that wanders up and down Cooper’s Cove. Sometimes, I have caught a glimpse of Pa here on Cahas Mountain. More often than not he has a mason jar in his hand.

THE FOLLOWING POEMS WERE FOUND
WITH RHODESSA ROSE'S BELONGINGS
AFTER SHE WAS FORCED TO LEAVE
THE SANATORIUM AGAINST HER WILL.

"TO THE VIRGINS"

Robert Herrick

Gather ye rose-buds while ye may
Old Time is still a-flying;
And this flower that smiles to-day,
To-morrow will be dying.

The glorious Lamp of Heaven, the Sun,
The higher he's a-getting
The sooner will his race be run
And nearer he's to setting.

That age is best which is the first,
When youth and blood are warmer;
But being spent, the worse, and worst
Times still succeed the former.

Then be not coy, but use your time;
And while ye may, go marry:
For having lost but once your prime,
You may for ever tarry.

“RUE”

English Folk Song

Come all you fair and tender girls,
That flourish in your prime,
Beware, beware make your garden fair
Let no man steal your thyme.
Let no man steal your thyme.

And when your thyme is past and gone,
He’ll care no more for you
And every day that your garden is waste
Will spread all over with rue.
Let no man steal your thyme
Let no man steal your thyme.

A woman is a branched tree
And man a singing wind.
And from her branches carelessly
He’ll take what he can find.
Let no man steal your thyme
Let no man steal your thyme.

"ELEGY"

William Blake

O Rose, thou art sick!
The Invisible worm,
That flies in the night
In the howling storm,
Has found out thy bed
Of crimson joy:
And his dark secret love
Does thy life destroy!

"I HAVE NO LIFE BUT THIS"

Emily Dickinson

I have no life but this,
To lead it here;
Nor any death, but lest
Dispelled from there;

Nor tie to earths to come,
Nor action new,
Except through this extent,
The realm of you.

“WILD NIGHTS! WILD NIGHTS!”

Emily Dickinson

Wild nights! Wild nights!
Were I with thee
Wild night should be
Our luxury!

Futile the winds
To a heart in port
Done with the compass,
Done with the chart.

Rowing in Eden!
Ah! The sea!
Might I but moor
To-night in thee!

"THE DAFFODILS"

Robert Herrick

Fair daffodils, we weep to see
You haste away so soon;
As yet the early-rising sun
Has not attain'd his noon.
Stay, stay,
Until the hasting day
Has run
But to the evensong;
And, having prayed together, we
Will go with you along.
We have short time to stay, as you,
We have as short a spring;
As quick a growth to meet decay,
As you, or anything.
We die,
As your hours do, and dry
Away,
Like to the summer's rain:
Or as the pearls of morning's dew,
Ne'er to be found again.

"COMPENSATION"

By Edgar A. Guest

I'd like to think when life is done
That I had filled a needed post
That here and there I'd paid my fare
With more than idle talk and boast;
That I had taken gifts divine.
The life of breath and manhood fine,
And tried to use them now and then
In service for my fellow men.
I'd hate to think when life is through
That I had lived my round of years
A useless kind, that leaves behind
No record in this vale of tears;
That I had wasted all my days
By treading only selfish ways,
And this world would be the same
If it had never known my name.
I'd like to think that here and there,
When I am gone, there shall remain
A happier spot that might have not
Existed had I toiled for gain;
That someone's cheery voice and smile
Shall prove that I had been worthwhile;
That I had paid with something fine
My debt to God for life divine.

"The Path to Home." 1919